LAND OF ENCHANTAS

Corey L. Bissonni

Corey M. LaBissoniere

Martin Sisters Publishing

Published by

Martin Sisters Publishing, LLC

www. martinsisterspublishing. com

Copyright © 2013 Corey LaBissoniere

Martin Sisters Publishing, LLC, Kentucky.
ISBN: 978-1-62553-016-5
Young Adult/Fantasy
Printed in the United States of America
Martin Sisters Publishing, LLC

DEDICATION

I'd like to dedicate this book to my mother, Tammy LaBissoniere. Her encouragement, wisdom, and love have inspired me to never quit and believe that all my dreams are possible. Thank you mom! You have always been there for me and I will always love you!

ACKNOWLEDGEMENTS

I would like to thank Cyndi Perkins for all of her encouragement and help with writing this book. Also, thanks to all of my friends and family who believed in me, read my drafts and gave me ideas. Without you, this book would not be possible. Thanks again!

PRELUDE

It was a cold winter day in Enchantas. The valley trees were bare and lifeless, but the rainbow-colored snowflakes gently floated down covering the ground and presenting a magnificent sight. The green sky was cloudless, and the bright white sun beamed down on the blanket of snow, causing it to glimmer and sparkle. The air smelled like a candy shop, tantalizing the senses with sweet cotton candy and peppermint. The weather may have caused most animals to hibernate during this season, but it did not hinder the valley's young rabbits at play.

Unexpectedly, a yellow-furred rabbit hopped out from behind a yellow-needled spruce tree. He wore a long, purple cotton jacket and a bright red winter hat. His orange and blue striped scarf dangled behind him as the wind swept through the valley. The rabbit glanced around the valley, moving his head to the right and then to the left as if he were hiding from someone or something. His long, fuzzy back paws crunched in the snow as he tried to hop quietly toward another spruce. He stopped at a rock, bent over, and peeked out from behind. Not too far in the distance stood another furry rabbit. This one was light blue and plump, wearing a red jacket, yellow hat, and matching striped scarf. He crept quietly around a bush, on the hunt for something.

The yellow rabbit quickly ducked down, giggling to himself. As he sat slowly, his fuzzy white tail snapped a fallen branch, making a loud, crisp sound that echoed through the valley.

"Trixie!" the blue rabbit hopped up. "I see you!"

"You will not be able to catch me, Mumbles!" Trixie jumped up and hopped away as fast as he could.

"Trixie!" Mumbles panted, as he was not as fast as Trixie. "Wait up!"

"Mumbles." Trixie started to hop backward taunting his friend. He reached the top of a small hill, kicking a large, blue glass bottle into a snow bank. "That is the name of the game. Kick the bottle!"

"I know and I always lose." Mumbles pouted.

"Hey, Buttons," Trixie cried. "You can come out now!"

Another rabbit jumped out of a red pine tree and hopped up the hill. His fur was bright red, and he wore a blue cotton coat and cap. He pulled his purple and green striped scarf from his buck-toothed mouth and moaned, "Is it over already? I had the perfect hiding spot."

"Let's play again!" Trixie exclaimed with excitement.

"Fabulous." Buttons smiled. "I have an even better hiding spot this time."

"Do we have to?" Mumbles huffed. "I am getting really tired of this game."

"Don't be a poor sport, Mumbles," said Trixie.

"Yeah." Buttons started toward a small group of trees. "Just count to ten tacks, and we will go hide."

"Fine. Hurry up, though." Mumbles covered his eyes with his long, fluffy ears.

The other two rabbits scuttled away from Mumbles with a renewed sense of urgency, racing to the closest and best hiding spots they could find.

"One Enchantian, two Enchantian, three Enchantian . . ." Mumbles counted until he reached ten, and then shouted, "Ready or not, here I come!"

As his ears lifted from his eyes, he saw a flash of orange, and a large creature pounced on him just like a cat would on a ball of yarn.

"Hena, look what I got here." A fox held Mumbles to the cold snowy ground using all of his weight. "A little far from home, are you not?"

"Get off of me!" Mumbles cried.

The fox had orange fur and was dressed in a dark blue trench coat. His yellow eyes gleamed with hatred as he glared at the small rabbit.

"What now, Bax?" another fox said with a lisp as he hurried up a hill. He was wearing a dark green trench coat and was a little chubbier than his friend. "Another rabbit? Come on, there are better things to do than to hassle these pathetic creatures."

"Let me go!" Mumbles cried again.

"What's going on?" Trixie hopped up to the three. "Leave him alone."

"Oh," Bax taunted. "A brave rabbit?" He pushed off of Mumbles and marched over to Trixie. "So you think you're pretty tough huh?"

"Shut up and go back to your ghastly stench-ridden village," Trixie laughed.

"Yeah, Bax." Hena was frustrated. "Let's not even bother. They're no match for us anyway."

"What's going on here?" Buttons also hopped up. "I thought we were play – oh great. Foxes."

"Nice, there's three of them!" Bax snarled showing his razor-sharp jagged teeth. "This should be fun!"

Suddenly the sky turned dark, and pale blue lights came from behind a cluster of bare trees. The lights bounced around the darkened valley, flickering and shimmering like a beautiful ballet. It looked just like the lights from an indoor pool reflecting off the walls and ceiling. As they watched this unpredictable, illuminated pattern move toward them, the five Enchantians stared in wonder and fear as the lights became brighter and brighter.

"What magic is this?" Bax's eyes widened with fear. "Let's get out of here, Hena!"

The two foxes scurried away quickly, leaving the three rabbits staring in bewilderment at the blue lights.

"Let's go check it out!" Trixie was excited and hopped closer to it.

Buttons remained silent as he slowly followed.

"No," Mumbles disagreed but tagged along reluctantly.

As they crept closer, the lights became more radiant and formed a silhouette of a medallion six feet in diameter and about two feet thick. The blue lights within the large medallion seemed to liquefy before their eyes as it settled against the side of a small hill. The liquid twirled in streams of blue and silver, projecting a glorious sparkling beam of light around them.

Buttons shivered. "What do you think it is?"

Suddenly the light vanished and the sunlight emerged in the sky once again. A dark cave with an entrance of wood and stone appeared where the mysterious six-foot medallion had been.

"It's a cave!" Mumbles exclaimed. "Where did it come from?"

"That is not just any cave." Buttons trembled in fear. "That is the Forbidden Cave."

"No, it's not." Trixie laughed nervously. "Is it?"

"Yeah, it is." Buttons walked closer. "My father is on the Knights' council, and I saw a painting of it in one of his books."

"Oh wow!" Trixie hopped and bounced with excitement. "This is going to be so much fun. Let's go inside!"

"No!" Buttons yelled. "No way!"

"Why not?" Trixie asked. "What is the worst that could happen?"

"I've heard stories from the Knights themselves of what happens to Enchantians when they enter this cave. I dare not repeat it."

"Those are grown-ups fibs," Trixie argued. "They always tell us lies just to discourage us from doing fun things! You know how they are. They'll say anything to stop us kids from doing things they don't want us to do." He looked at Mumbles. "Remember when we went to explore the tunnel of slides?"

"Yeah, that was fun."

"Exactly." He looked back at Buttons. "They ended up closing it because they were afraid we would hurt ourselves."

"Mumbles did hurt himself," Buttons replied. "He broke a toe."

"Oh, that was nothing. Mumbles is just clumsy." Trixie chuckled. "So what do you say? It sure beats kick the bottle."

"Sounds like fun, Trixie, but I agree with Buttons. Let's go back." Mumbles rubbed his flabby belly. "Besides, I'm pretty hungry."

"No." Trixie smiled. "Not yet. One of us should at least check it out."

"Again," Buttons sighed. "That is not a good idea."

"Mumbles," said Trixie with a smirk. "I dare you to go in there."

"No, Mumbles. It is too dangerous."

"Fine. I double-fox dare you to go in there."

Mumbles bit his lip for a tack. Normally he would never think of attempting such a dangerous exploit, but this was a double-fox dare.

"Mumbles," Buttons continued. "Please don't."

"But Trixie double-fox dared me!"

"Yeah, Buttons, don't be a poor sport."

"Whatever. Do what you want." Buttons flopped down in the rainbow-colored snow, crossing his paws against his chest. "Remember that I warned you."

Mumbles slowly made his way to the cave. The cave was eerily dark and smelled stale and musty the closer he got. He turned back, hesitantly questioning his decision. Trixie rubbed his paws with excitement as Buttons stiffened in fear for his friend.

"Hurry up, Mumbles!" Trixie waved him on. "Tell us what it's like."

As he stepped into the cave, the light from Enchantas became dimmer with each passing moment. Suddenly Mumbles' fur began to change from blue to white and gray.

"What the carrot?" He looked at his paws in shock as they began to shrink right before his eyes. "What is going on here?"

His entire body shrank until he became a small white and gray furred rabbit. He was suddenly unable to speak, and as he turned around to hop out, the entrance to the cave closed and vanished, leaving him inside.

From the outside his friends watched in shock as the cave disappeared.

"Mumbles! Mumbles!" Buttons screamed, hurrying to where the cave entrance had been. "Where did he go?"

"I—I don't know!" Trixie said frantically.

"You see?" Buttons cried. "I told you daring him was not a good idea!"

"What do we do?" Trixie screeched.

"Come. We must inform my father." Buttons grabbed Trixie and pulled him away. "He will consult with the Knights."

They hopped as fast as they could through the cold valley in search of Buttons' father. Little did they know: Mumbles would be lost forever.

Chapter I
The Morning

The sun was rising, and the glare reflecting from the mirror blinded her. She moved slightly and stared at herself, wondering what the day had in store. She was a pretty girl, but she hid that fact in the way she wore her hair and her style of dress. Her glasses covered her beautiful blue eyes, and her straggly hair was a dull light brown. She was unaware of her hidden beauty. On her dresser was the only grooming item she owned, a brush. She wore faded blue jeans and a brown sweater her grandmother had knit. Saddened and discouraged by her appearance, she turned away and picked up her books from the bed. She walked slowly toward the door of her bedroom, stopped, and glanced back for a few minutes. The room was bare, with only a bookshelf full of romance novels, a bed, and the dresser with the giant mirror. An inexplicable, uneasy feeling came over her, and she wondered if she would ever see it again.

She had been troubled for a few years now. Since the night her parents had died, in fact. Since their bodies had never been found, she had always hoped for their return, but it was only in dreams that she'd seen them. A tear flowed down her cheek, and she quickly wiped it away before anyone could see she was crying. She had always been afraid to cry in front of others.

"First day at school," she moaned to herself. "Why do I have to go?"

"Sally, dear!" A southern voice floated up from downstairs. "Yar bus will be here soon and I fixed ya up some breakfast. Hurry it up now, honey. It's gettin' cold and ya don't wanna be late!"

Without a word Sally darted down the stairs to the kitchen and sat at the small table. "Thanks, Grandma. I love pancakes!" she said with a wide grin.

"Well, ya know I like to spoil my favorite granddaughter."

"I'm your only granddaughter." Sally chuckled.

"Well yeah, but yer still my favorite," the old lady said as she turned back to the kitchen sink to clean a glass dish.

Her grandmother had moved from Alabama to take care of Sally after her parents' funeral. She was a short, plump, happy old woman who always found a way to cheer Sally up. The day her grandmother moved in, she threw a birthday party for Sally to lift her spirits. Ever since that day four years ago, Sally and her grandmother had formed an unbreakable bond. But she was fourteen now and growing up, maturing into a beautiful woman as her grandmother would say. Growing up and maturing is never easy for anyone, but it had been especially tough for Sally. She was sure her loneliness exceeded that of any other person in her school by far. She had always thought of running away. That would solve all of her problems at school. It could end the loneliness, and it would definitely end the continuous teasing and taunting she received at school. With no friends but her grandmother, Sally was a very lonely girl. Then again, if she did run away, her grandmother would be alone. Running away was out of the question; they needed each other.

"Sweetie, I know what y'all are thinkin'. Now don't ya worry. I don't think you'll be treated the same as ya were in that gawd-awful middle school. The kids are maturin' now, just like you. This is Willington High School! A whole different ball game, ya know? It may be a small town, but there are enough kids in that school to make at least one friend."

Sally sat at the table, silently looking at her plate.

"Just give'em a chance. Make friends! Not for me, but for yourself. Ya need 'em. Ya know I'm not going to be here forev—" She stopped, suddenly realizing that what she was about to say might bring up some bad memories. "I just wantchya to be happy. And now, since it's your first day, ya can start over." She winked at Sally.

Sally blushed and put her head down, pretending to be interested in her pancakes,

"Now, ya listen to me." Her grandmother tilted Sally's face toward her, "You are a beautiful young lady, a gorgeous southern belle! Don't ya let anyone else tell ya otherwise. Anyone would be lucky to have ya as a friend. If they don't think so, then that's their loss! Now don't ya forget that!"

"I know, I know. It's just that I can't relate to anyone there. They only care about themselves and their 'special' little cliques. I feel like a loner, and I hate school."

Out of nowhere, a horn sounded. Sally's grandmother looked out the window above the sink. "Honey, I think ya bus is here. Y'all better get going," she said, looking at the clock.

Sally gathered her things and hugged her grandmother goodbye.

"I love ya, Sally! Have a good day!" her grandmother yelled through the screened window.

"I love you too." She ran up the bus steps and grabbed the first seat behind the driver. The doors closed, and the bus drove away.

During the short ride, Sally sat quietly, listening to the other kids talking and goofing around. The motion of the bus sent Sally into a thoughtful state, and she began to daydream. She remembered years ago when the other children would tease her and throw her book bag around. The bus drivers had always helped her, but it never eased her troubled heart or stopped the tears from flowing. Since then, she felt safest sitting behind the driver. As the other children made friends and enemies on the bus, she remained alone with the driver. This driver was a short man with a scruffy beard, and he seemed to be smiling all the time—or maybe that was the shape of his mustache.

The bus came to a complete halt and the doors opened. All of the other kids in the back of the bus rushed forward before Sally had a chance to get up.

When the bus finally emptied, she grabbed her book bag and stepped off the bus. Sally stood for a moment, gazing at the school and the dozens of kids running toward it. Four stories high and a small block in length, the school accommodated hundreds of teens, much more than the middle school. She wondered for a moment where all these students had come from, especially since the town of Willington seemed so small; but how would she know? She never seemed to leave her own house.

Afraid of the unknown, her heart started to race. She was mostly anxious about the other teenagers and how they would treat her. Her extreme bashfulness was her own worst enemy. She walked slowly with her head down, mostly so she didn't have to meet anyone's eyes, because then—God forbid— she might have to talk to them. As she walked toward the school, dreading this first day, no one paid attention to her—not even the boy on the bike.

***

In a dark room somewhere else, an alarm buzzed and its annoying sound rode up the walls, getting louder and louder. The smell of cigar smoke surrounded a boy's head as he lay on his pillow. His hair was jet black and hung to the bottom of his earlobes. He awoke slowly and turned his head toward the ceiling trying to snap out of the deep sleep he was in. He fought to open his bloodshot green eyes, blinking, trying to focus. He rubbed them hard and blinked again only to find a tall, older man leaning over his bedside in just an undershirt and grubby boxer shorts. The man had long, dark, greasy hair that reached well down his back, and he was dirty with an unshaven face. His body odor stung the boy's nostrils. He held a beer in one hand and a cigar in the other.

"Wake up!" the man yelled as he kicked the boy. "And turn that damn alarm off! What the heck did you do last night? Get drunk again? You better not have. GET UP, I SAID!"

The boy struggled to sit up as he hit the alarm with his fists.

"Don't you get cocky with me, Johnny! I'll kick your butt right now." The old man backhanded John in the face. "Yeah, try to be a big shot now."

"Dad!" the boy yelled. "Stop!"

"Well, boy, you got school today and it's twenty to eight. School starts at eight o'clock, doesn't it?"

"Figures you wouldn't know. You're usually passed out on the couch by the time I get up for school," he said sarcastically and got out of bed, still wearing the same dirty jeans and old gray shirt he had worn the night before.

"Yeah, right. When was that? You're not going to skip this year like you did last year, are you?" He laughed. "What are you going to tell everyone when you meet them? Hi, my name is Johnny and I'm a sixteen-year-old freshman."

"Shut up, you frickin' drunk." John whipped his hair away from the front of his face.

His father grabbed him abruptly by the arms and said, "Listen to me, boy! You better learn some respect for your old man. I put food on the table for you and your sister and put a roof over your heads."

His father reeked of alcohol, cigar smoke, and sweat. John almost gagged from the awful odor.

"Take your hands off me, you smelly old fart." He twisted his body away from his father. John wanted to make him feel as bad as he did, but he knew any harmful words from him wouldn't affect his father.

A small laugh came from the other room. "I better not hear a peep out of you, Becky Sue!" his father yelled as he let go of the grasp he had on his son. "And I want both of you home after school to get your chores done, is that clear?"

His father finally left the room. John hated mornings like these. He rubbed his eyes, trying to forget what had just happened. He tried to ignore his throbbing headache and turning stomach, consequences from the partying he had done the night before. He turned on his black light, which lit up the few rock band posters hanging from his walls. The posters covered fist holes and old faded wallpaper that was peeling away from the sheetrock. A lava lamp sat on the dresser he never used. Instead, his clothes were scattered all over the floor of his bedroom along with empty cigarette cartons.

He was not ready for the first day of school, but he knew his father was right about one thing; he needed an education. He couldn't repeat another year of ninth grade.

John took a few moments trying to pick the cleanest clothes from his floor but realized he was already wearing them. Not really caring what others might think of him, he grabbed two full packs of cigarettes, threw on his black leather jacket, and tucked a cigarette behind his ear. He threw on a pair of socks and shoes and stepped outside his room.

John was glad that he had friends he could talk to and hang out with daily, though they were more acquaintances than true friends. Besides, who needs a father when you have friends who care more about you? The stale smell of liquor and smoke became stronger as he staggered past his father, who was now passed out on the couch in the living room of the small, rundown trailer.

John despised his father and blamed him for their mother leaving them. He believed she'd left because of his father's drinking, but the real problems started after she left. Like many typical parents, they fought a lot while they were together. It was nothing out of the ordinary; only the usual *do the dishes* and *stop nagging*. One Saturday morning when John was eleven, he woke up and ran to the kitchen for the routine breakfast his mother made him, but he found that she was gone. He waited for hours, but she never returned. She left no note and took no belongings. Thinking about it now, John knew she must have been very angry to not take her clothes, makeup, or purse. Months later their father started to drink more heavily, unable to cope with his wife's desertion. That was close to five years ago. Only John and his younger sister were left.

His sister had just turned fourteen a month ago, and sadly, their father had forgotten. She was devastated, which broke John's heart, too. They were only two years apart in age, and they depended on each other for everything. John thought a lot about running away and leaving his father, but his sister would never go with him. She loved her school and her friends, even though staying meant she had to continue living with her father. So John stayed in this lousy good-for-nothing life just for her.

"Hey there, sis. Good morning," he said, trying to sound cheerful.

"Yeah, sure sounds like it," she said with her classic sarcasm. Becky Sue also had jet-black hair, but it fell gracefully down to her shoulders. She wore makeup and glossy red lipstick to make herself feel older and more mature.

"You better watch yourself, sis," he said softly, referring to her laughing at their father earlier. "I can protect myself from him better than you can, and I might not always be here, you know."

"Oh, don't worry, bro. Little do you know, I know how to fight." she said proudly.

"Hold on." He looked directly into her light blue eyes, deeply concerned. "Don't follow in my footsteps. I'm a screw-up. I can admit that, but I don't ever want to see my little sister turn out like her big brother."

"What?" She laughed. "Be a drunk like dad?"

"Hey, I'm different than him, all right?"

"Okay, John. We got to go. The bus is here. Are you coming?" she asked, looking out the window.

"No, I'm riding my bike."

"Well, you better get going, or you'll be late." She stepped out the side door.

"Yeah, yeah, I don't care," he mumbled softly, knowing she wouldn't hear him. He grabbed the buttered toast she'd made for him and ran outside. He jumped on his bike and shoved the bread into his mouth, chewing as he rode.

A few blocks away from his house John finished his toast and lit up a cigarette. He had been craving one ever since he'd gotten out of bed. The school was about a cigarette length away—for him at least.

The wind was at his back, which made going up the hills easier. As he rode, he thought about school and what he could do differently to make sure he passed this time around. That, of course, was if his father didn't make him stay home to help with chores around the house or give him rides to local pubs because he was too drunk to drive himself.

He looked at his cigarette and noticed he only had a few drags left, which was good because the school was only a block away. He turned the corner toward the school and pedaled as fast as he could, weaving through the kids who were walking to class. Skimming shirts and backpacks from side to side, he was on a roll until he looked up and saw a straggly brown-haired girl in his path. The sudden awful noise of a bicycle hitting a girl was heard around the schoolyard. Everyone turned to see what had happened.

"What is your problem?" John yelled as he lay on the ground tangled in his bike. "Don't you have enough sense to watch where you're going?"

"I'm—I'm—I'm sorry," she stuttered in fear. "I didn't see anyone."

"That's because you should look up when you walk. I was on a roll, dodging every—"

"What the heck is going on here? What's your problem?" a voice came from the crowd.

***

The door opened slowly, and steam poured out of the bathroom. A silhouette of a boy could be seen as he emerged from the doorway. He was built for his age. Stretching his arms above his head and wearing only a towel, he sauntered down the hallway toward his bedroom. He had an air of confidence about him—the kind of person most people admired and envied.

When he reached his bedroom, he shut the door and put on his boxer shorts, then started his daily stretches with jumping jacks, concentrating hard on his counts. He looked at the clock and it read 7:40 a.m. "I've got time," he mumbled to himself. He walked to the mirror and combed his short blonde hair. His eyes were blue like the sky and sparkled when he smiled. He almost winked at himself as he looked in the mirror, but stopped short and began his morning exercises.

He was not conceited, only sure of himself. He knew who he was and what he wanted from life. His room was filled with football and basketball posters, and there was a bookshelf full of trophies and medals for each of his accomplishments over the years. He loved athletics and participated in all the sports his school could offer. Football was starting, and he was excited to start his first season. Freshman football wasn't as big a deal as varsity, but he was proud to play and be a Willington Panther.

He took school much more seriously than most of his friends. They didn't care too much about getting good grades, but Ryan was the type of person who studied and did his homework. He finished every assignment and never got less than a B-plus. After school he would do fun things like play football, lacrosse, basketball, run track, go out on dates or just hang out with friends. He wasn't much into the partying scene like some of his friends, but he did go once in a while. His older brother would always throw parties at their house whenever their parents went on trips, a frequent occurrence in the past few months.

He finished his exercises, grabbed his backpack from the floor and put it on. He started toward the door when suddenly he remembered he only had his boxers on. He slapped his forehead, chuckling to himself. He opened the closet picking his favorite white and blue football jersey and a pair of jeans. He put them on with his usual slow manner and slipped on socks and shoes. As he walked down the stairs, he noticed a light and a noise coming from the kitchen. Curious, he turned the corner and found his older brother making lunch.

"Hey, Ryan. Good morning," his brother said with a smile as he cut a sandwich in half. He too was blonde and well built, wearing a buttoned-up blue shirt and khaki pants. He was a star football player who had broken almost every record at Willington High. It made Ryan want to try that much harder so he could beat his brother's records.

"Morning, Ben." He leaned on the breakfast bar in the middle of the kitchen. "Hey, do you think you could give me a ride to school today? I mean . . . now that we go to the same school and all."

"Not a problem. When's the last time I said no to my little bro?" he said as he shoved some chips into a bag. Ryan had always looked up to his brother; they had always been best friends. They had to be—they only had each other. "I made lunch for you too. Would you like an apple?"

"No thanks. Do you know where mom and dad are?"

"Phhh, where do you think?"

"Work?"

"No, they're on another trip."

"What? Where this time?" Ryan shook his head. They had already been on three long trips this year. "They just came back a few days ago."

"Florida Keys, I think. I can't believe they trust us after what happened last time."

"Well, they deserved it. They're always gone. They never have time for us anymore or even think about asking us if we'd like to go."

"I doubt they'd want us to miss our first day back at school, Ryan."

"I guess." He sighed. "Whatever, I don't care."

"So yeah, I'm having some people over tonight so -"

"Like who?"

"Sarah and Tonya." He smiled. "Just don't come home till later, okay?"

"All right." Ryan stretched his arms. "I have practice after school anyway."

"Oh shoot, it's 7:55, we're gonna be late!"

They picked up their stuff and ran to the car.

Ben pulled the blue, two-door convertible Corvette out of the driveway, the tires squealed as they sped off down the road.

Ryan thought hard about what it would be like to run away, if only to spite his parents. He had many friends in school and he loved football, so there was no real reason to leave. He only wanted his parents to see that they were neglecting him. He chuckled to himself knowing that it wouldn't matter if he did run away, because they wouldn't know he was gone anyway.

Moments later they arrived at the school, a large, four-story brick building with a few strategically scattered maple trees in front. He looked up to the top of the building and read the large engraved letters right below the balcony of the principal's office: WILLINGTON HIGH SCHOOL. The Corvette stopped and Ryan got out. He turned to say thanks for the ride, but Ben had already driven off to find a parking spot. As he scoped the schoolyard, Ryan heard a boy yelling and someone crying. He looked to see where the noise was coming from and noticed a crowd of people gathering in front of the school. He ran over and saw a boy, a bike and a girl lying on the ground. As the boy yelled at her, Ryan's eyes narrowed in anger.

"What the heck is going on here? What's your problem?" Ryan asked loudly enough for the boy to hear. He moved toward the center of the circle, pushing others aside. The boy stood up, and they met with their faces only inches apart. They were evenly matched in height and build, but there was quite a contrast in the way they were dressed. Ryan had a white and blue jersey on, and the other boy wore a black leather jacket.

"What do you mean 'what's my problem here?'" John said with a cocky attitude. "What's yours? And why are you sticking your nose in my business?"

"Look, I'm not stupid," he replied with a similar arrogant attitude. "You hit her with your bike, and you're blaming her. You're the jerk that should slow down."

John grabbed Ryan by his collar and pulled him closer. "Look, you son of a—" He stopped and looked deep into Ryan's eyes. "No one calls me a jerk. I should kick your butt right now!"

The crowd began to chant, "Fight, fight, fight!" The sound of the screaming crowd reminded Ryan of a basketball game. Ryan knocked John's hands away and pushed him to the ground. John got up quickly and swung at Ryan, who ducked and tackled John to the ground.

The two wrestled for a few seconds until the bell rang in the schoolyard. All the kids ran into the building, leaving only the two guys and the girl. *Not a good way to start the school year*, Ryan thought as he pushed away from John.

"This isn't over, jockstrap!" John picked his bike up from the ground and walked angrily up stairs. As he pushed his bike along, he realized it had a flat tire. Muttering to himself, he tossed it furiously on the rack and walked into the school.

"Sorry about that," Ryan said to the girl. "He's just rude and obnoxious."

"It's okay. I'm used to it," she said, sounding very sad. "You know, not being noticed, or if I am, getting yelled at for it."

"I'm sorry to hear that," he said, grabbing her hand to help her up. "What class do you have first hour?"

"History I think." She smiled.

"I'll walk you in. How's that sound? What's your name?"

"Thanks. Sally."

"I'm Ryan."

As they walked, she looked at him, and it suddenly registered for the first time that he *was* Ryan—the boy she'd had a crush on for many years. Now he was her knight in shining armor. She smiled and blushed as they walked together through the doors of the school.

***

It was 7:50 a.m. and the light in the basement was still on from the night before. A tall, gangly boy sat in a chair leaning over a desk with one hand on each side of his forehead. He wore glasses and had brown, curly hair that was neatly cut. The glasses weren't prescription; he only wore them when he was reading or in deep thought. "One more ingredient," he mumbled in frustration. "I wish I could remember!"

His bedroom was a huge laboratory located in the basement of his house. The lab was filled with different components, concoctions, and beakers of the type found in science classrooms at school. That was where he got most of his stuff, after all, though if asked, he would claim that it was all 'borrowed'. Open chemistry, physics, and engineering books were scattered around his bed. All of his shelves were empty.

He wore a neatly ironed, buttoned-up blue flannel shirt and a pair of khakis. His mother bought his clothes, so he had no say in what he wore. His mother was lenient, which countered his step-father's very strict ways. He was a smart boy, but he hated school. Since it was his only escape from home, he thought school was all about having fun, like pulling pranks on the teachers and his peers. He was a joker, a trickster you might say. He never took things seriously, and he didn't have many friends, but he didn't mind. He was content being by himself with his hobbies and prank-pulling.

"Mel!" a voiced hollered from upstairs. "Are you still awake? Have you been up all night?"

"Yes, Ma! I'm awake and I've been up all night," he replied in annoyance. "I'm still working. Please don't bother me!"

"Well, I'm sorry, but school starts soon and I've got some breakfast for you," she said as she poked her head around the corner from the top of the stairs.

"Just a minute." Mel shivered at the thought of his mother's atrocious cooking. The random mixtures of ingredients she would use were awful. Just a few days ago she had made a *tuna fish and mustard meatloaf deluxe dinner* and a *peaches-and-peanut-butter pie for dessert*. She seemed to embrace her own laws of cooking and created her own variety of dishes.

"Oh, yeah!" he exclaimed suddenly, remembering his final ingredient, and quickly ran up the stairs to the kitchen. He threw open one of the cupboards and grabbed a bottle. His mother watched with a puzzled look on her face as he ran back downstairs to his lab. He took a small beaker of green liquid and poured the new ingredient into it, then shook the beaker for a few seconds and set it down so it would settle. He took the cap off the beaker and inhaled. "Whew! Wow, that's the smell I'm looking for. The smell of an old-fashioned outhouse!" He chuckled. "I'm going to call it Stinkoffs." He twisted the cap back on the beaker and waited a few more minutes. He made five more containers of the mixture, then stuffed them all safely into his book bag. "I can't wait!" Laughing, he picked up his bag and ran upstairs.

When he reached the top of the stairs, his stepfather was in the doorway preparing to yell. "Mel, hurry it up, you have—oh, there you are. Come on, you're going to be late. Your mother made you a bite to eat."

"Yeah, I know, I know," Mel grumbled as he slowly made his way past his stepfather and went into the kitchen. He sat on his favorite chair at the table and inspected his food, then turned to shoot his mom a disgusted look. "Umm, Mom, what's this?"

"Oh, don't worry. You'll like it. Just try it. It's my special sauerkraut pancakes." She smiled.

"Well, I'm going to be late for school, so could you put it in a bag for me? I'll eat it sometime later at school." He handed her the plate.

"Mel, I hope you don't get into trouble in this school like you did over the past few years," she said with a firm voice. "I know you love to joke around all the time, but this is high school, and it's time to get serious about your schoolwork."

"Yeah, I know, but I hate school so much. I'll go crazy if I don't find a way to have fun."

"Well at least bring your books home so your father thinks you're studying. He's very worried about you and wants you to go to college."

"Fred is not my father. Besides, he doesn't just want me to go to college; he wants me out of the house."

"That's not true."

"What if I don't want to go to college? Why can't I make my own choices?"

"Sorry," a deep voice said from the hallway. "You don't have a choice."

Mel's stepfather walked in from the other room wearing a dark suit. "If it was my choice, I'd get you out of this house as soon as possible," he laughed. "I'd send you off to military school. Besides, you are going to graduate from college! You're not going to be some low-life loser working at a fast food restaurant or a bowling alley for the rest of your life. I know you're smart. Why do you waste your talent?"

"What if I wanted to work at those places? Have you ever thought of that?"

His stepfather leaned toward Mel, getting closer and closer to his face. Putting his right index finger on Mel's chest, he said firmly, "Listen here, son. As long as you don't live here until you're thirty, you can do anything you want. But while you live under my roof, I'm going do everything possible to make sure you

28

amount to something in your life—whether you like it or not." He put his arm around his wife and continued, "Besides, I have a good job and a wonderful family, and that's what I want for you."

Fred left the room abruptly, going outside and making a lot of noise on the way. They heard the car start, and he drove off.

"Wow, I sure pissed him off." A feeling of satisfaction came over him. Mel always thought about running away. He had become tired and annoyed with the same routine, especially his mother's odd cooking and, of course, his stepfather's lecturing. He was always on Mel's back about something from chores, to homework, to becoming the next famous scientist who cured cancer. Then again, Mel's twisted humor got the best of him as he enjoyed the thought of living at home till a ripe old age just to irritate his stepfather. He got much pleasure from other people's misery, particularly his stepfather's.

"Well, you just need to understand that he only wants the best for you." Mel's mother put her hand on his shoulder. "He just wants to see you try as hard as he did and succeed in life."

"Yeah, right. I could never do that. The way he tries to motivate me makes me want to screw off even more. I don't want to be like him."

"Well I want you to be yourself, okay, Mel? Let's get going. I think you're late as it is."

They both got up and went outside to the car. As they drove off, Mel wondered about his stepfather and what had made him become a hard-core workaholic.

Mel glanced at the clock; it read 8:05.

"Here's a note for being late." His mother smiled as she handed him a piece of paper.

"Thanks," he said, and then asked, "Hey, Mom, did Fred ever have fun in high school, or was he a workaholic like he is now?"

"Well, don't tell him I said this, but your stepfather was a complete goof-off in high school," she said with a laugh. "But I think he wants you to succeed where he didn't. That's why he's so strict."

"Oh," he said, turning his head to stare out the window. Watching the buildings and trees go by, he thought about the times he and his stepfather had gone to the fair when he was younger. He remembered the fun they'd had and the rides they'd gone on. As he daydreamed, he saw a vision of his stepfather smiling; he couldn't remember the last time he had seen that. His stepfather always worked late now, and it seemed that his job had taken over his life. He sure didn't want to end up like his stepfather. It would be awful to lose the spirit inside you.

As they turned the corner he looked up. The schoolyard was empty. Everyone else was in class by now. His mom stopped in front of the entrance and he climbed out.

"Have a good day, I love you," she said, leaning over so she could see his face.

"Yeah, I will," he said while shutting the door behind him. Mel turned and looked up at all the windows of the school and thought about how large they were. Maybe he could try and get a desk by the window so he could daydream and ponder fun and exciting adventures while sitting in mundane classes. As he reached the door, he glanced back. His mother was still sitting in the car as it idled. *Waiting to make sure I don't skip school*, he thought. He turned back toward the school, took a deep breath and walked in.

The lockers in this school were a bit larger than the ones Mel was used to. Amazed at how much wider the hallways were, he walked down the corridor, glancing into each room to see if he recognized anyone. He pulled out his class schedule. As he turned a corner, a running girl collided with him, and books went everywhere as she tumbled to the floor. Feeling guilty, he looked down and saw a young brown-haired girl wearing an old brown sweater.

"I'm so sorry." He tried to help her up. "I guess I wasn't looking."

"It's okay, it's okay. It's not the first time this has happened to me today," she said in an irritated voice as she picked up her glasses.

"Someone bumped into you already?" He chuckled. "Not a great start to the first day of school."

"Not at all. I was hit by a bike!" She picked up her books. "Well at least you weren't a jerk about it like the other guy."

"What do you mean?" He bent over to help pick up her books.

"You know, I don't even remember, and I'm not having a good day as it is," she said, walking away abruptly. "So could you just leave me alone? I need to go to class."

"Hey, my name is Mel, and I'm really sorry!" Mel hollered after her.

Sally looked down at the ground while she walked. She thought about how her day was going, and was about ready to cry. Any other person would have talked back to that rude boy, but she wasn't that type of person. She was the type of person who was kind to everyone, even those who were not kind to her. But at this moment she was considering changing her values and principles just to protect herself. Her day was not going well at all, except of course when she'd spoken to the man of her dreams. She'd had a crush on Ryan since she was a little girl. He was a blond-haired, blue-eyed, handsome guy, whom she remembered watching on the playground during recess in fifth grade. She'd always been afraid to talk to him because he was so popular. But today she felt unbelievably comfortable doing just that. Maybe it was because Ryan was the only guy who'd ever stuck up for her. Maybe things would change for her this year like her grandmother said. She didn't want to get her hopes up too much, though.

As she finally stepped toward the classroom doorway, she paused and took a deep breath to relax. Her eyes began to water, and she wrinkled her nose as she smelled the worse stench ever. "Oh, gross! What is that?" She blocked her nose. The odor was beginning to make her feel queasy. She grabbed her sweater and took a whiff, discovering the culprit—a splattered green stain on her sweater. Mel had apparently accidentally spilled a small amount of his concoction on her during their collision.

"I thought my day couldn't get any worse." She shook her head, imagining everyone's faces and how disgusted they were going to be when she walked by them, but at that moment she didn't care anymore. Her day officially couldn't get any worse. Could it? At least she would be prepared for the looks of disgust when people caught a whiff of her.

The door opened then, and a brown-haired, slender woman asked in a kind voice, "Hello there. Are you here for Hist— Oh, what is that god-awful smell?" The stench permeated into the room, and all the kids covered their mouths and noses in disgust. "Is that you, dear?"

Sally looked up and watched the woman's face turn green with nauseated horror.

"It wasn't me. I don't know what it is!"

"Go home and shower!" a kid from the classroom exclaimed.

"Wow, that girl stinks!" another kid yelled.

With tears of embarrassment, Sally turned and ran down the hall toward the main doors. Once outside and in the front court-yard, she muttered to herself, "This is the worst day of my life! I need to go home." She began running down the street.

Chapter II
The Well

A classroom door flung open, and a boy with long black hair stormed into the hallway.

"Go to the principal's office right now!" a gray-haired man with a long beard yelled from the doorway as he pointed down the hall.

"Oh no, not the principal's office!" John mocked the teacher. He knew he was in trouble, but he didn't care. "I'm so scared now. What will I do?"

"You'd better be scared. I don't think Mr. Wilson will be as lenient with you this year as he was last year." The teacher's eyes burrowed into John.

"Yeah right Mr. Mill*nerd*!" he said with his usual cocky attitude.

"You will not make a mockery of my name, John." Mr. Miller clenched his teeth. "Or my class, for that matter."

"Phhh, like I care about either."

"I didn't think you did, since you're repeating the class," he replied, walking back to the front of the room. "I don't want the same thing that happened last year to happen this year, John. You have potential. Why don't you just try?"

"Because I think school is bull! And I think Mr. Wilson can kiss my—" John wasn't able to finish, because the teacher slammed the door in his face.

As John walked down the hall, he kicked the floor, rubbing the bottom of his shoe and swinging it up into the air. "Darn it!" he mumbled to himself. Every year he seemed to get into the same confrontations with teachers. He would always be the wisecracker and get into trouble. *Why do I do this to myself?* he thought. *Maybe I just hate rules. Maybe that's why I hate my dad so much. No, I hate him because he's an arrogant jerk.* John was always afraid he'd turn out just like him.

He skulked aimlessly down the hall, avoiding the principal's office, rubbing his fingers across the lockers and making a squeaky noise. The sound echoed down the hallway.

As he roamed the second floor, John put his hands in his front pockets and felt his pack of cigarettes, sparking an urge to smoke. He walked into the closest restroom and was hit with the most repulsive stench he had ever smelled in his life. He rubbed his eyes, which burned from the vapors. The restroom walls were painted white and a couple of windows were on the far wall. There was only one sink with a large mirror on the left; the toilet stalls were to the right. The smell that hung in the stale air of the room was really horrible.

Covering his nose, gagging from the pungent odor, John hurried over to one of the windows and yanked it open. A crisp fall breeze filled the space as he gazed out over the back courtyard of the school.

Leaning against the window screen, John took a few gasps of air. He looked back and said in a loud whisper, "Is there anyone else in here?" He listened for a few seconds, and unsurprisingly, no one answered. He couldn't imagine anyone wanting to stay in here for long. He sat on the window ledge and lit up a cigarette. The first drag coaxed a smile from him as a sense of calm ran through his body.

John was walking toward the toilets when one of the stall doors burst open. His heart skipped a beat as he expected to come face to face with a teacher. A tall, lanky boy with brown curly hair came out instead, stopping when he noticed John.

"Well, hey there," the boy said politely. "I'm surprised you can stand the smell."

"I can't, but I really needed a cigarette," John replied, puzzled. "So if you don't mind, I'd like to be left alone."

"I'll leave in a minute." The boy chuckled and went back into the stall. "I have to finish up first."

"Gross!" John cringed. "What the heck did you eat?"

"No, no, no." The boy giggled and flushed. He walked back out holding a green vial in his hand. "I invented my own stink bomb, and I'm putting it everywhere in the school. Bathrooms first."

"Nice!" John was impressed. "I wish I'd thought of that."

"Yeah, I'm pretty proud of it." The boy marched to another stall and dumped a few drops on the floor. "I'm hoping they'll call off classes once I've strategically sprinkled the school."

"Good idea. I hope it works." John took another drag from his cigarette. "I can't stand it here much longer today."

"Me neither, obviously," Mel said with mischievous grin.

"My name is John," he said as he tossed his cigarette into the toilet.

"I'm Mel." He put out his hand.

"Well, nice to meet you." John smiled. "I think it's brilliant of you to think of this."

The bell suddenly rang, and they both stepped out of the bathroom.

"Do you have a place to sit during lunch?" Mel asked.

"I wasn't really planning on going. Why?"

"I may need help with the rest of this stuff. You interested?"

John grabbed the bottle from Mel and said with a menacing smile, "I'm a step ahead of you."

"Great." Mel smiled. "I have to stop at a few places first." He was surprised; he'd had no idea that this prank would actually result in finding a new friend.

They both laughed and quickly parted ways.

***

Meanwhile, outside the school, Sally stepped out of a car and shut the door. She bent over, facing the car window as it rolled down.

"Grandma, I wish I could die," she lamented.

"Y'all know I don't want that, dear." She smiled.

"Well, I want something. I want a break from everyone. I hate school, I hate people, and I hate my life. I don't want to be here anymore."

"Oh, hon, ya don't want that. There might be troubled times in ya life, but remember there is always good in everything."

"Like what? What was good about today?"

"Well you're building moral fiber by not becoming like the people who hurt ya."

"But I don't do anything. Why is this happening to me? Do I really have that much bad luck?"

"Don't worry, child. Good things will happen. I can feel it."

"Yeah, right. I don't care; I just wish I could disappear."

"Hey, hey there. Ya know, I can already see you changing, Sally."

"How?"

"You're strong. Strong like your parents, dear."

36

"How's that?"

"Well, I don't know anyone else who would want to go back to school after an incident like you had today."

"I want to get ahead in my schoolwork."

"I'm sure you do. That's what makes you so special. Now off you go before you're late for your next class."

"It's lunchtime, Grandma. I won't be late."

"Well ya still don't want to be late for that." She chuckled.

"Okay, Grandma. I love you."

"I love you too, sweetie. Remember to watch your step." She drove away.

Sally smiled as she walked back to the school. Her memories of her parents were vague, but hearing good things about them always made her happy. The more she heard what great people they were, the more she tried to be a great person, too. With a confident stride, she walked directly to the lunchroom.

***

The cafeteria was packed with a long line for lunch. John and Mel stood for a few moments waiting for plates and then hurried over to the lunch line. They took turns discretely stepping out of the queue for brief moments to dabble drops of the liquid around the room. Minutes before, they'd finished placing the Stinkoffs around the rest of the building. Now there wasn't a stench-free spot to be found.

"All right," Mel whispered as he flashed an empty bottle. "That should do it."

"Awesome." John handed Mel a full plate. "Let's find a place to sit."

The room was full, and they hesitated for a few moments looking for the best place to view the coming mayhem. Most of the tables were lined up parallel the wall, with a few in the middle of the room.

As they walked toward an open table, they looked around anxiously for others to start smelling it. They giggled, hands over mouths, trying not to look conspicuous as everyone else sat at their tables, talking amongst themselves, oblivious to what was about to happen.

"Any minute now," Mel said, focusing on the crowd.

***

Sally walked into the lunchroom and grabbed a plate. As she stood in line, she noticed kids holding their noses and pointing at her. Confused, she took a part of her new sweater, lifted it to her nose, and inhaled. There was no awful stench. As the seconds went by, more and more students covered their noses and mouths. A lot of them were murmuring and pointing at Sally. She frantically sniffed her body but didn't smell a thing. She pushed her glasses up on her nose and held her head up, trying to maintain confidence.

She went and got her food and went to a table. The muttering of the students grew louder and louder until it began to sound like a sports arena. Now everyone was staring at her, and a lot of people dashed out of the cafeteria. She could not take this again, especially from the entire student body. All of her peers would call her names for the next four years of high school. This day was not getting any better. Tears flowed down her cheeks again as she restrained herself from racing out of the lunchroom. Suddenly, a foot came out of nowhere. Her plate flew straight up into the air, and green beans scattered across the floor. Sally put her hands out as she tumbled face first. She was on the floor when she turned around to see what she had tripped on, and the remainder of her meal was dumped on her head, covering her hair in potatoes and gravy. Stunned, she wiped some of the gravy off her glasses and noticed a tall boy with long, dark hair standing over her. Everyone in the lunchroom started to laugh, though most were in tears from the stink bomb. Sally sat in total disbelief.

"That's what you get for giving my bike a flat tire!" the boy yelled.

As she focused, she realized it was the guy from the morning who had hit her with his bike. She noticed that beside him sat the boy who'd bumped into her earlier that morning. "I'm sorry about your bike," she said in a trembling whisper.

"I don't care. All you had to do was watch where you were going," John said firmly. "I want five dollars for my tire you whiny little—"

All of a sudden John was pushed onto the floor. He slid a few feet, and his head slammed onto the wood surface with a thud.

"What in the heck is your problem?" asked the boy who now stood over John.

John shook his head and looked up as he sat trying to catch his breath and collect his wits. His blurred vision cleared, and he recognized the same kid from the morning confrontation. "You again!" he said, getting to his feet quickly. John marched up to the other boy and stood in front of him until they were chest to chest. "I should have kicked your butt earlier when I had the chance!"

"Yeah, right." Ryan chuckled. "You wish!"

While the two argued, everyone else piled out of the lunch-room. No one could stand the awful stench of Mel's Stinkoffs.

Suddenly a fire alarm blared and the principal's voice poured out of the public address system loudspeakers. "Students and faculty, due to a sewage leak, school will be cancelled for the rest of the day."

Sally had not moved from the floor. She was still crying. Ryan moved to help her up, but John shoved him aside. "We're not done yet, buddy!"

"What now?" Ryan shook his head. "Can't you see she's been through enough?"

"Why should I care?" John pushed him.

"Hey, why don't you all cool it?" Mel said firmly, separating them both by the length of his dangly arms.

"I don't think so, Mel," John said, but he walked away anyway. "This isn't over, jockstrap!"

Mel hurried after him and Ryan reached for Sally. "Looks like you could use a hand."

Sally smiled as she wiped her wet eyes and cheeks as she glanced around the empty lunchroom. The Stinkoff smell didn't faze them, at least for the moment. Ryan grabbed extra napkins to aid Sally's hasty cleaning job. Although she was sticky, she was able to mop off most of the food.

Sally's mind was whirling a mile a minute. *It's Ryan! What do I do?* she thought. *He is so cute and so popular. I'm so nervous. What am I saying? He has no interest in me. No one likes me... except my grandmother. But what am I going to do? Ask him over to watch movies with my grandma and me? No, that's ridiculous. Wait, Sally; calm down. He's a nice guy. You should know. He helped you out twice today. But that doesn't mean he likes me. He probably was just trying to impress someone else. It wouldn't take much for him to look good. He is so cute. He's got dreamy blue eyes. Am I saying that out loud? Oh, no. What if he hears me? He'll think I'm a goof. Okay, Sally, you've got to say something quick. You can't let him get away.* She inhaled deeply.

"Ryan, thank you so much for everything."

"No problem. That guy is a jerk anyway. Since school is cancelled, would you like me to walk you home?"

"I'd like that."

They chatted as they walked outside. The wind was blowing hard, and the air was a little colder than usual for September. The trees swayed back and forth; the leaves ruffled as they blew down the street, making a loud noise that sounded like a rattlesnake.

"Wow, it's pretty windy." Ryan said, looking up at the trees.

"Yeah, it reminds me of this one time I—"

"Hey, jockstrap!" a voice came from down the street, interrupting them. "Wanna finish this, or are you too much of a wimp?"

Ryan and Sally saw John and Mel making their way up the street.

"John, don't hit the girl this time," Mel said, stepping in front of John as they made their way toward the other two.

"Don't worry; it's between me and this guy right here." He pointed at Ryan.

"I don't want to fight you," Ryan said as he tried to turn away. "It's not worth it."

John pulled Ryan toward him. "Boo-hoo. Sounds like something a wimp would say."

"No." Ryan laughed. "Sounds like something someone with common sense would say. Unfortunately, you lost that during your fourth freshman year."

John punched Ryan in the face, and Ryan fell to the ground.

"Will you two stop it?" Sally cried.

"Yeah, she's right!" said Mel. "The street isn't safe for a fight. Let's go over there."

Ryan got up, and the four of them walked to the field Mel had pointed out, Sally protesting the whole way. Large pine trees surrounded the property, forming a natural fence. The grass was waist high, but they could see the road from where they were in the middle of the field. Cars zipped past, but no one noticed them.

"All right, this is perfect!" Mel crossed his arms.

Not too far away from the other three, Sally backed up and bumped her heel on something. Glancing behind her, she saw a large well. It was round, made of old stones. It wasn't very tall, only reaching her knees. She sat on the stone lip comfortably to watch the fight.

Ryan and John circled one another, opponents eyeing each other intently. For a couple of minutes they both seemed hesitant. Then John ran to Ryan, grabbing his head and trapping it in a headlock. He punched Ryan several times and hit him on the top of the head, trying to knock him out.

Ryan wiggled out of John's grip and twisted his arm up and over to grab John's chin. He pulled back with all of his might and John flew back to the ground. Then Ryan punched John in the face. John counteracted and punched Ryan when he wasn't expecting it. His fist landed on Ryan's neck and Ryan couldn't breathe for a few seconds.

Mel prowled around the two as they fought. Cheering them on and acting as their referee. "Wait, John. Let him breathe."

As the two boys wrestled, Mel was accidentally shoved to the ground. John and Ryan jumped on each other like two wild cats fighting for food. They rolled on the ground, simultaneously throwing punches at each other. Ryan was on top of John, banging his head against the ground. John took his right foot and kicked Ryan in the back of his head. John turned over on top of Ryan and started to punch him in the face. Ryan threw him off and gasped for breath.

John didn't mind because he was winded, too. "I have got to quit smoking," he panted.

"Just stop. This is so ridiculous!" Sally shouted from the edge of the well. "This is all my fault. Why me?"

Mel stood up and approached her slowly, "Hey, you won't understand this, but guys don't usually talk about things. I guess you can say we're more physical. So just sit back. It'll be done in a matter of minutes. I promise." He turned back to watch the fight.

Mel was blocking Sally's view. Frustrated, she stood up. As she peeked around Mel, she noticed a gray and white rabbit hopping a few feet in front of them.

"Hey, look! A bunny!" she shouted, happy to be distracted from the violence.

The rabbit sat down in front of Sally and Mel and curiously tilted its head with its floppy ears down.

"Well I'll be." Mel bent down closer to the rabbit.

The rabbit tilted its head the other way in wonder, seemingly unaware of the fisticuffs going on behind it.

At that moment Ryan stood up and ran at John. He grabbed him by his waist and picked him up as he had learned in football training and ran—with John in his arms—directly toward Mel and Sally when he tripped over the inquisitive rabbit.

Mel and Sally had no time to move out of the way. Ryan and John crashed into Mel, who fell on top of Sally. The foursome toppled like dominoes.

Sally screamed as she fell back, wrapping her arms around Mel's neck, and they plummeted into the well. Mel grabbed at John's upper body, gripping him firmly as a counterbalance, but momentum was not in his favor. He pulled John and Ryan into the void with him.

As the quartet descended, howling and hollering into the abyss of the well, the rabbit, shaken but unharmed from the encounter, slowly hopped away across the field, oblivious to the turmoil happening behind him.

Chapter III

Lost

Their bodies bounced like rubber balls off the rock walls, and the four teenagers screamed in terror as they tumbled down the dark hole. It seemed as though they had been falling forever when they finally splashed into a cylindrical pool of water.

As four dripping heads surfaced at the waterline, they gaped at each other in shock. The pool was cold and so deep; they could not touch the bottom.

"Is everyone all right?" Ryan hollered as they treaded water.

"Yeah," the other three replied simultaneously, unbelievingly.

John swam over to one of the walls and tried to climb it. He grabbed one of the rocks but could not find a handhold. "Darn it. The walls are too slippery."

"I don't think we'll be able to climb back up," Ryan told John.

"Well, DUH!" John replied. "It's your fault we're down here in the first place!"

"Shut up. I tripped over something. Besides, like I knew there was a well there."

"Can you both please be quiet? I don't know how much longer I can tread water!" Sally cried as she struggled to stay afloat.

They looked around the pool, but there was nothing but darkness. The only light came from the hole above them.

Mel groped around the perimeter of the walls. "Hey!" he said excitedly. "There's a tunnel over here!"

The others paddled over to Mel and saw the small opening a few feet away.

"What are we waiting for?" Ryan said as he started to swim.

The other three followed him. They could see a little better as their eyes adjusted to the darkness. The walls of the stale and musty cave were jagged and sharp. Small streams of water trickled down the walls and fell into the pool.

They continued swimming through the tunnel, searching for the end. The water began to flow faster and faster, and suddenly a rush of cold water carried them down a small underground river. They paddled as hard as they could as they were carried downstream, screaming and spluttering in the racing water.

"No!" Ryan shouted, looking to his right. The rushing water had turned to rapids, the current so strong it almost pulled Sally under. Ryan noticed Sally struggling and grabbed her by the arm, helping her stay above water.

Finally the flow ebbed, and in the diminished velocity they were able to catch a breath. It had a calming effect on them, and they assessed the far more peaceful setting.

By this time Mel was tiring and about to give up. He put his feet down and exclaimed with relief, "Yes! I can stand!"

Sally quickly put her feet on the bottom and let out a grateful gasp. "Oh, thank God. I didn't know how much more of that I could take."

"Shut up!" John said, extremely annoyed at this point. "Don't be a wimp."

"Don't talk to her like that!" Ryan exclaimed.

"Oh, don't even talk. If it weren't for you, we wouldn't be down here!"

"Will you both be quiet?" Mel stomped angrily past them, spraying water. "Let's find a way out of here."

They sloshed without speaking, making their way through the water and down another tunnel. The water became shallower as the cave widened. The air was cold, the tunnel hushed, except for the sound of water dripping down the walls of the cave.

"I am so cold." Sally crossed her arms, hugging herself in an attempt to get warm.

"I know. We all are." Ryan put a comforting hand on her shoulder.

Finally turning a corner, they found a small sandy shore and quickly sat down.

"Wow, I'm not used to a workout like that," John said as he gasped for breath.

Across from him, Ryan chuckled and shook his head.

"What are you trying to say?" John huffed. "Aren't you tired from getting your butt kicked earlier, or do you want more?"

"What's your problem? Do you *always* want to fight?"

"Yeah." John kicked him.

"Oh jeez, not again!" Patience waning, Mel stepped between the two combatants. "Can you both please put aside your differences and try to help us figure out how to get out of here?"

Sally sat a short distance from the other three, shivering. "Does anyone have a lighter?" She picked up a few sticks and some dried grass. "I think we can make a fire."

"I have a lighter." John laughed. "But I sure wouldn't give it to you. You owe me five bucks for my tire."

"Just let her use it!" Ryan argued.

"Shut up." John shook his head as he walked toward Sally. He rummaged through his pocket, pulled out two packs of cigarettes—one unopened—and his lighter. He squeezed the open pack and water gushed out. "Shoot, now I only have one pack of cigarettes left."

"Who cares about your cigarettes? Give me your lighter!" Sally trembled, teeth chattering.

With a nervous urgency, John ripped off the cellophane packaging from the other pack, extracting a cigarette and inspecting it. Dry. What a relief! He tried to light it. "What the hell? My lighter won't work."

"What do you expect?" Ryan said condescendingly. "You were just in water."

"Well, it was supposed to be waterproof." John threw the lighter at Sally.

"Hey!" Ryan stood up, angry. "Leave her alone!"

"Make me!"

"Shut up you two." Mel bent over to pick something up. "Check this out." He grabbed an old mining helmet and put it on his head. After he flipped a switch on the headlight above, he smiled. "Fantastic! It works. Now we can actually see."

"Great," John muttered. "Now I'll have to look at all your ugly faces."

"Oh, John?" Mel bent over again and picked up a shiny Zippo, tossing it toward the disgruntled teen. "Look what else I found."

"Yessss!" John flicked it open and quickly lit up. "Mel, you are a life saver."

"I'm cold and wet," Sally cried as she gathered little bits of wood and more dried grass. "I've had a horrible day, and now I just want to go home!"

"Gosh, you whine a lot." John threw her the lighter.

Sally tried to make a small fire but struggled with the lighter until Ryan came over to help. He had trouble lighting the fire;

everything was too wet. He glanced at Mel, who was sporting his newfound helmet. "Come on, guys. Forget the fire. Let's get out of here. Mel, you lead the way."

"I'm not going with you two losers." John sat back down. "Give me my lighter back."

"We're sticking together." Ryan tossed it back.

"I don't care what you think. I'm not getting out of here with you two!" John was referring to Ryan and Sally, and then turned toward Mel. "Let's go, Mel."

"Sorry, John. Really, this isn't a good time to be stubborn," Mel replied, giving John a serious look. "I'm going with them."

John hesitated for a minute; he didn't want to go alone, so he had no choice but to go with them. "Fine," he mumbled curses to himself, taking a drag of his cigarette.

They started down the tunnel, Sally walking between Ryan and Mel in tight formation so their body heat would warm them. John lagged behind, puffing on his cigarette.

The cave was still dark and gloomy, but the old musty smell wasn't as strong. The rock formations were jagged and sharp. Wooden braces were placed here and there, presumably holding up the walls. The cave did not seem safe. They all tried not to think about what would happen if the ceiling collapsed.

"I'm so hungry," Sally moaned.

"Why don't you eat some of the potatoes that are left in your hair?" John laughed behind them.

"Shut up, John." Ryan turned to sneer at him.

"I'm hungry too," Mel said. "Anybody know what time it is?"

Ryan stretched his arm and looked at his watch. "This isn't right. It says it's about 4:30. It must be waterlogged."

"What is wrong with you three? Is that all you do, whining?" John shook his head as he threw away his cigarette.

The four grew silent again and climbed down a little ridge.

"Doesn't it seem like we're going deeper into the cave?" John asked. "Shouldn't we be climbing up instead of down?"

"I'm sure there will be an exit somewhere," Ryan replied.

"Maybe this cave is that old mine that was dug decades ago," said Mel.

"Do you think so?" Ryan asked.

"Yeah, these old wooden braces are what the miners used," he replied as he leaned up against one. "Also, look at the way these rock walls are formed. It's as if someone chiseled and blasted their way through."

"They closed that place down way before we were born," said John. "My dad told me that a bunch of miners disappeared. My uncle was one of them. No one knew how or where they went, and no bodies were found. The owner closed it because no one wanted to come down here and work after that."

"What do you think happened to them?" Sally asked nervously. "Do you think they all died?"

"Stop it!" Ryan yelled.

"What?" John asked.

"Stop scaring her."

"Well, that's what I heard," John argued. "Anyway, does anyone else know about the cave at the end of town?"

"The one by the old sawmill with the huge gate in front of it?" Mel questioned.

"Yeah, that's the one. I think that could be this mine. Maybe that's where we'll end up."

"Then we'll know where we are when we get there," Sally said.

Everyone's stomach was growling, and they were getting tired. Sally noticed that the water wasn't dripping down the walls as much as it had been. She turned her head to look at Mel and suddenly tripped over a rock. She tumbled and fell to her knees, letting out a small scream.

"Watch out for that rock." John laughed.

"Hey, that's not funny!" Ryan grumbled as he helped Sally.

"Yes it was." John walked past them.

Sally sat down to examine her knees. Ryan looked at them too. "Does this hurt?" he asked, bending her knee straight.

"Ouch. Yeah, a little."

"Don't worry. It looks fine." Ryan got up. "Just a little scratch."

As she started to stand, weary from the day's many tumbles, Sally noticed a shiny object on the ground. Curious, she reached over and grabbed it. It was shiny and gold-plated, in the shape of a circle, with an engraving of a dragon on one side and strange hieroglyphic symbols circling the outer rim. Attached to a thin gold chain, the charm—or whatever it was—fit perfectly in the palm of her hand. As she examined it, she was amazed at what good condition it was in. She turned it over, and on the back was another engraving marked, *K.O.M.* She flipped it back over, and it opened automatically. Inside was an oddly marked compass. This dial twisted around rapidly, not stopping to give any direction.

"Oh, hey, look at this," she said, getting up quickly.

"What now?" John was aggravated.

"I think I found a compass." The guys peered at it; Mel's light offering a better view. "Oh, and it has an engraving that says" — she turned it around and read the writing— "*K.O.M.* What do you suppose that means?"

"Probably someone's initials," Mel suggested.

"What's it doing?" Sally asked.

"Huh?" They stared as the compass dial twisted rapidly.

"That's weird," Ryan said.

"Really odd," Sally agreed as she realized the points on the compass weren't normal. "Instead of North, East, South and West, it says, "This Way, Here Way, That Way, and There Way.""

"Yeah, yeah, really odd! Who cares?" John muttered. "Let's find a way out of here."

Sally put the compass around her neck, stepped over the rock she had previously tripped on, and followed the others. "We *are* lost, aren't we?" Sally moaned.

"Why don't you look at that stupid compass and tell us where we're supposed to go?" John shouted.

"It doesn't work."

Suddenly a small light appeared up ahead.

"What the—" John paused, "Is that a light?"

"I think so," Mel replied, taking the helmet off and dropping it to the ground.

The quartet walked briskly toward the light. At first it looked like a small candle, but the closer they got, the bigger and brighter the light became.

"What are we waiting for?" Ryan's eyes widened.

"Let's go home!" Sally screamed.

They stood there in silence for a few seconds and then, without a word, ran toward the light with excitement. Ryan was the fastest runner, passing John and Mel easily. Sally lagged behind, partly because of her scraped knee. However, she owned the biggest smile of them all.

They reached the clearing in seconds. As they exited the cave, they stumbled down a small, grassy hill, squinting in the extremely bright sunlight. When they finally came to a halt and fully opened their eyes, they couldn't believe what they saw.

"Oh boy!" Mel said with amazement.

"Where are we?" Ryan asked.

"I—I—I don't know," John stuttered, his mouth wide open in bewilderment.

"It's like something out of a dream!" Sally sat down.

They looked around, and there in front of them was the most unbelievably beautiful vision they had ever seen. Trees unlike any others were scattered unevenly over many hills and valleys; the leaves were red, indigo and blue. Behind them were a few colorful specimens overlooking a large sea, which was not the normal bluish-green of the sea they knew, but a bright shade of pink. The grass wasn't green either. Instead, it was different shades of blue, purple, violet, and lavender blended together. The sky appeared bright green, and the sun was lightning white. In the valley was a stream, the water appearing neon orange with sparkles glimmering where the sun played over its surface. A wall of mountains could be seen in the far distance, the aqua-colored snowcaps topping the gray mountains.

They heard birds whistling like an orchestra of flutes in the trees but could not see them.

The land smelled like a fresh spring day. The air was clean, and the entire valley was tranquil.

An orchard lay in the distance, and the four teens could see different types of animals frolicking on the hillside and into the forests.

They all felt a peace and serenity they had never felt before. The feeling of euphoria that consumed them was overwhelming, sending delighted shivers up their spines. For a few moments they all felt the same—they never wanted to leave this place.

"What is this?" Ryan asked, looking at the others in awe and confusion.

"I don't know, but let's check it out," Mel said, then started to walk slowly forward, anxious to explore this new and beautiful world.

"Heck no! I'm getting the hell out of here!" John quickly turned around toward the cave, but it had already disappeared. "Where's that cave?"

"What?" Sally whirled around.

"Whoa! Where did it go?" Mel asked frantically.

"I'm more worried about where we are," said Ryan.

"There's got to be another entrance to the cave." John ran up the hill toward a rock pile.

The three others scrambled up the small hill after John. Sally had a hard time with her sore leg, but made it fine with Ryan's assistance. Some of the rocks reminded Ryan of a mountain climbing class he and his brother had taken a few years ago.

As they caught up with John at the top of the hill, they stood silently, eyes wide in surprise. They found themselves at the edge of a cliff overlooking the pink sea and bright white sun. The waves rushed to the white sandy shore a few hundred feet below. They sat on the cliff, staring at the water and the long strip of bleached white sand. As the large waves hit the beach, the sand was covered in pink for a few seconds, reverting to white as the waves retreated.

"Oh, wow," Ryan said in amazement. "Where are we?"

"We're stuck here, aren't we?" Sally sighed.

Mel pointed toward the seemingly endless water. "That's what it looks like."

"No! I need to go home now!" Sally wailed.

"Sorry, Sally. We have to face the fact that we'll be stuck here for a while," Ryan said, a note of discomfort and uncertainty in his voice.

"If the cave is truly gone," Mel spat out bitterly, "which I really don't understand how that could happen, we will have to find another way home."

"This is really unbelievable." John shook his head. "I must have hit my head really hard falling down the well. We're all hallucinating."

"That could be true, but I refuse to believe we're stuck here," Mel said, starting down the hill. "I say we take a look around. I think I saw an orchard down the valley."

"I just want to get out of here." John lit up another cigarette and followed Mel. "What makes it worse is that we're stuck here with those two!"

Ryan sat for a while, trying to enjoy the spectacular scenery, but couldn't. He was too worried about how they would find their way back home.

"Ryan, Sally, are you coming?" Mel asked.

"Yeah, we're coming." Ryan slowly got to his feet.

"Where are we going?" Sally whimpered. "I want to go home!"

"Hurry up!" John shouted as he jumped from a ledge.

They scrambled back down to where John and Mel were waiting, and the four inadvertent explorers walked swiftly down to the valley.

Chapter IV
The Herald

They made their way curiously but cautiously into this strange, brand new world, staring around in awe and disbelief. They stayed close together, unsure of what was to come. They remained silent as they continued slowly down the hill toward the neon orange stream.

"This place is totally weird," said John. "I seriously want to get out of here."

"The only thing we can do is look around for another way home," said Mel.

"It feels as though we're on a movie set," Sally piped in. "I mean, this can't be real."

"I know. Are you sure we aren't dreaming?" Ryan added.

"How do we know if we are or not?" Mel asked. "For all we know, we could be dead! We did take a pretty good hit falling down the well."

"Whatever this place is, it sure is warming me up." Ryan lifted his hands toward the white sun.

"Everything here is odd," said Mel. "Look at the trees; they have blue leaves. The grass is purple. If you ask me, we aren't on Earth anymore. Probably another planet."

"That's a little far-fetched," said Ryan.

"Well," Mel huffed. "What's your theory?"

A moment of silence came over them as they came upon the orchard full of colorful trees. A gust of wind whipped through, ruffling their hair and the foliage. Sally focused on a single vivid leaf falling from one of the strange trees. The leaf twisted and turned and glided back and forth from side to side. It seemed to float aimlessly but somehow landed in the palm of her hand. She smiled, watching it in wonderment as its hue changed from blue to green to purple, cycling through all the different colors of the rainbow in the matter of seconds. She tilted her hand and let it waft to the ground. Farther into the orchard the trees began to get smaller, the colors of their leaves a mixture of blue, green, and red. The trees were aligned in four parallel rows. Each branch was loaded with dozens of pink cubes the size of an apple or an orange.

"Looks like these trees were planted here." Mel walked underneath one. "You see? They were planted in rows."

"So?" John kicked at a trunk in frustration. "Who cares?"

"It means," Mel said as he approached John, "that we at least know there is intelligent life here, and someone may be able to help us find a way back."

"Oh." John quickly shut up, feeling a little foolish.

"What are these pink things hanging on the trees?" Ryan plucked one and studied it.

"Don't eat that!" Mel put his hand over the fruit. "It might be poisonous."

It was as big as a baseball but light as a feather. The surface was bright and was covered in a layer of thin fuzz. The peculiar fruit smelled like sweet cherries.

"I'm hungry, aren't you?" Ryan looked at him. "If we're going to be stuck here, then we might as well eat."

"Well, I guess it can't be that bad." Mel mulled it over. "These trees *were* planted on purpose."

Ryan was still studying the fruit cube when an odd, squeaky voice called out, "Don't eat me!"

"What the heck? Where did that come from?" Ryan looked around, mystified. "You all heard that, right?"

"Yes!" they all replied, seeming as confused as he was.

"I says don't eat me!" the squeaky voice called out again.

"Where is that coming from?" Ryan asked, irritated.

"Uh, I think it's the pink cube in your hand," John said, pointing at the mysterious fruit.

Ryan dropped the pink cube. It hit the ground, bounced back up, and landed in Sally's hand.

"Whee! That was fun!"

"Oh boy, it won't leave us alone," she said, letting it fall to the ground again and taking a few steps back.

"Ahh! I'm falling again!" the fruit said as it hit the ground and broke open.

"Oh, no. I killed it!" Sally shrieked.

"You can't kill a fruit, Sally." Mel laughed.

"Let's get out of here," John mumbled. "This place was already weird enough, and now we have talking fruit."

They all stared at the pink cube lying broken on the ground. Suddenly the larger split piece started to wiggle and mumble.

"It's still alive!" Sally cried.

"Are you all nuts?" John exclaimed. "It doesn't have a frickin' mouth!"

"Shut up, John!" they all yelled.

John muttered curses to himself and sat down.

Ryan retrieved the cube, turning it around to examine. The juice from the fruit covered his hand in an odd sticky substance. He flipped it over and moved it to his other hand, discovering it wasn't the cube that had been talking. A small blue worm gazed up at Ryan with terror in its eyes, curling protectively into a ball.

"No! Don't eat me!" the worm cried as he wiggled his way out of the fruit and landed on the ground. The creature looked up at the foursome. "Whew, I thought you all was just gonna eat me," it said, wiping its forehead with its tail. The worm had big green eyes and was about as thick as a licorice stick.

"We wouldn't eat you," said Ryan.

"We only wanted to try the fruit," added Mel.

"Is that all?" He inched rapidly up the tree onto a low-hanging branch and used his body to disengage another pink cube from its stem. "Here you go. What kind of animals are you?"

"Animals?" Ryan laughed, picking up the cube. "We are humans."

"Humans!" the worm exclaimed, surprising them by slithering away as fast as lightning. A trail of dust floated into the air as the worm sped down the valley.

"What was that all about?" Mel asked, confused.

"Not sure, but that worm moves faster than anything I've ever seen before," Ryan replied.

"Well, hello there," a soft voice said behind them.

The kids turned around to find a short, stocky man with a long, curly mustache standing on top of a large rock. He wore a green and brown suit with brass buttons from top to bottom. His hat was long and pointy and stood straight up. He was about half their size, but the hat made him seem as tall as them.

"What the heck are you supposed to be?" John laughed. "A yard elf?"

"Yard elf? Why, no sir." His back stiffened as he stood proudly, obviously insulted. "I am a gnome. I come from a village in the forest." He pointed toward a set of trees in the distance.

"How did you get here?" Sally asked gently, feeling instantly comfortable with the gnome. His kind voice reminded her of her grandmother.

"Magic, my dear!" He jumped off the rock and strutted closer to them. "My name is Gitchy, and I am the honorary herald of this world! Enchantas, that is."

"Enchantas?" John looked at him with a corky smirk. "You're kidding me right?"

"Shut up, John." Ryan turned to the gnome. "Gitchy, is it? How did we get here? And better yet, how do we get home?"

"Yeah," Mel piped in. "We don't belong here."

"Of course not." Gitchy circled the group. "All of your questions will be answered in good time. You know, I have been waiting for the four of you for many, many Cycles!"

"Waiting for us?" Sally asked.

"Yes, it has been prophesied by our grand majestic Sage, the Great Owl, that Fate would send four saviors to bring peace to our world again. Our saviors were to be four young humans."

"Fate? Saviors?" John was getting annoyed. "Are you all seriously listening to this thing? So are you going to help us get home or not?"

Gitchy stared at John for a moment and then replied, moving his head to the left and then to the right. "No, I do not have the means to bring you home. However, our grand majestic Sage, the Great—"

"Okay, screw this," John cursed as he marched away in frustration. "I'm just going to find my own way home. This is bull!"

"John!" Mel shouted. "Where are you going?"

"Mel, just leave him be," said Ryan. "If he wants to be alone and get lost, let him. Now what were you saying Gitchy?"

"Yes, I was saying that I am the honorary Herald of Enchantas and was summoned by our grand majestic Sage, the Great Owl, to wait for four Humans to be delivered here. I have been waiting many, many Cycles for this day!"

"Sorry, I was actually referring to how we get home," Ryan interrupted.

"Oh, pardon me, young sir." Gitchy cleared his throat. "I personally have no means to bring you home. The Great Owl, however, may have the magic to bring you home. He has sent me here to bring the four of you to meet with him."

Suddenly the blue worm zipped back, slithering up to Gitchy's shoulders. "Ah, Slippy, there you are! Thank you so much for bringing the message of the Humans."

"You're welcomes," Slippy said anxiously. "Can I have payments now?"

"Payment?" Gitchy chuckled. "I believe we had an agreement that this was a good deed for all Enchantians, and you were doing it out of the kindness of your heart?"

"WHAT?" Slippy cried. "Not fair! I need payment!"

"I am truly sorry, my little friend. I have no payment for your deed."

"Ugh!" The worm snarled with frustration and slithered off again.

"Sorry about that." Gitchy turned back to the three kids. "Are you ready? The Great Owl is anxious to meet with you."

"What about John?" Mel asked.

"Good riddance, if you ask me," replied Sally.

"I'm sure we'll meet up with him sometime," Ryan replied and started to follow Gitchy. "We need to find a way home first."

As they made their way through the orchard, Gitchy gathered a few fruits and tossed them into his long, pointy hat. He threw each of the visitors one and said, "Here, try these Lixy Fruits. They are delicious!"

"Thank you." Sally smiled, moving closer to him. "I'm starving."

She was reminded of her grandmother's home cooking and was anxious to get home to find out what was for dinner. She took a small bite of a corner of the cube and squealed with amazement. "Wow! This tastes just like my grandma's chicken pot pies!"

Mel nibbled on his and shouted, "Mine tastes like pepperoni pizza!"

"Ah, yes. That is the magic of Lixy Fruit my friends." Gitchy chuckled. "They taste of whatever you crave."

"That is really cool," Ryan said as he took a large bite. "Oh my gosh, cheesecake!"

"So what is this place, Gitchy?" Sally asked, again surprised at how comfortable she felt around him. "How did it get here?"

"As I said, I am the Honorary Herald of Enchantas," he replied proudly, puffing out his chest. "My duties include the preservation of our history: past, present, and future. I have many stories about this place. However, it would take me many seasons to tell you them all."

"Could you tell us where this place came from?" Mel asked.

They had finally exited the orchard and entered another valley, where the grass was thick and came up to their ankles.

"I sure can," Gitchy continued. "Many, many, many ages ago, Enchantas was a young world. We creatures didn't know how to speak, play games, or have fun. We were wild and barbaric. Then one day, a magical door opened in the Cumberlake Valley, the same valley you all came from. It wasn't any old magical door, though; it has been said that it was Fate's doorway. You see, many of us Enchantians believe Fate is an essence that possesses all our destinies and plans our lives. It binds our world together and keeps it from chaos. Then again, there are some who do not believe this and argue or fight against these beliefs. That is why our world has been in turmoil."

"Turmoil?" Mel asked. "Not sure what you're talking about. It looks great here."

"Yes, it does; however, the deeper you travel into Enchantas and away from this valley"—he took a deep breath—"the worse it gets." A silence came over him for a moment, but he soon continued. "Anyway! So the door opened and legend has it, humans just like yourselves came through. They taught us Enchantians how to speak, read, cook, build, play games, and have fun. They became the protectors of the peace. They helped all of the creatures. They were called the Knights of Minerton." He pointed to the engravings on the compass around Sally's neck. "K.O.M."

"Hey, I found this in the cave!" Sally was excited. "It doesn't work, though."

"Of course it works." Gitchy twisted the compass toward him. "It says we must go *There Way*. This is Fate's compass. It will only show you where you need to go:

'This Way, Here Way,
That Way, and There Way.
Fate's Compass will forever
Guide you the Correct Way!'

"In short," said Gitchy, "it will show where Fate has destined you to go."

"What if we don't go that way?" asked Ryan.

"Then bad luck will come your way," Gitchy responded in a concerned voice. "Right now it is telling us to go this way because this is the way to The Great Owl."

Sally slipped the compass under her shirt as they continued to trek through the long purple-grassed valley.

"So what happened to the humans?" asked Ryan, concerned.

"The humans closed Fate's door so no one could go through the portal but them. Non-humans would enter it and never come back.

They would become lost forever. Hence, the name was changed to the Forbidden Cave; however, there have been a few times over the Ages that humans have come through."

"How many of us came to Enchantas?" asked Mel.

"The legend is that there were at least thirteen original Knights, but I don't know what happened to them. They all disappeared ages ago with no record in the historical documents as to where they had gone. Our grand Sage will tell you more, I am sure."

"I think I'm starting to put this together," Mel said. "You see, the miners that supposedly vanished from our world found this place and stayed here. In our world the owners closed the mine because they didn't know what happened."

"I wonder what happened to them?" Sally asked nervously. "What if we end up not finding a way back home?"

"Don't worry, Sally," Ryan comforted her. "We'll find a way back."

"Yeah," Mel added. "If these miners were able to close the doorway, cave, portal or whatever it is, then the reverse should be possible. There's got to be a way back into it."

Gitchy smiled. "Yes, that is true. But my belief is that Fate has brought you all here for a reason, and I am sure it will bring you all home safely."

Sally peeked at her compass again. A feeling of relief came over her now that they had a destination and purpose. It gave her hope, knowing that they weren't truly lost.

The wind picked up, prompting the group to pick up the pace. The grass got longer, but the thickness stayed the same, making each stride more difficult. They had to lift their legs higher at each step to avoid getting tangled.

"Gitchy." Mel tapped him on the shoulder. "How does your magic work? I mean, I used to do magic tricks in elementary school but nothing like I've seen here."

"There are many creatures in Enchantas able to produce magic," he noted. "For gnomes, our hats are the source of our magic. They are made from a special silk worm. Our hats, along with the wisdom and knowledge of our magic, are passed down to every generation in our family lines. The magic is used to protect us. There are other non-Mythics that do not have the natural means to produce magic, so they use Lixy Dust. Lixy Dust is mysterious powder that gives nonmagical beings and objects miraculous powers. However, it is very expensive. Only the rich can afford it."

"That's really cool. Can I learn magic?"

"But of course you can. Humans are very magical beings. I believe it comes naturally to them. You don't use magic back home?"

Mel laughed. "There are magicians but they do not use real magic like you. They usually use mirrors or other parlor tricks to deceive you. Like I said, I was into that type of stuff in elementary school. I got pretty good at it."

"Interesting, I am sure you could learn magic here." Gitchy took off his hat, wiped his forehead, and grabbed a Lixy Fruit. "Let us stop here and rest for a tick, and I will tell you a little about myself."

***

John continued to march in frustration. Unsure of where he was going, he tripped over a small bush.

"Darn it! This place sucks," he muttered to himself.

He continued to brood over how he'd gotten into this mess, how he got to Enchantas in the first place. He blamed Ryan and Sally for his present predicament; they were the troubled ones.

He crossed a small, yellow stream, noticing a forest not too far in the distance. The grass was thick, making it difficult for him to move quickly. After a few steps he noticed an orange fuzzy ball in the weeds. *What's this?* He wondered. It was as large as a basketball, fuzzy like a kitten, and squishy as a sponge.

After studying it for a moment, he decided to kick it. "Here goes nothing." He snickered and kicked it as hard as he could. The ball flew high into the air and landed yards away.

"Now that was fun!" he yelled out and ran toward it. Suddenly he noticed another one to his left, bright blue instead of orange. He kicked it high and far and spotted four more. After kicking them all he was out of breath. *Geez, I really should quit smoking,* he thought.

There was a sudden ruffling in the grass, and the sound of voices surrounded him.

"Hello?" he called out nervously.

"Let's play!" a soft, childish voice cried.

"Play with us!" A purple ball hurtled toward him, bouncing off his head before he had a chance to react.

"Ouch! What the hell?"

Another ball hit him in the back. "Come play!"

"What the—" Suddenly dozens of balls flew at him. It was like he was the last one left on a dodge ball team. "Holy crap!"

He ran from the flying balls as fast as he could toward the forest.

"Get away from me!" he bellowed, looking behind him only to find dozens more of the fuzzy dodge balls pursuing him.

As he reached the forest, he realized that it wasn't the smartest decision. The trees resembled chestnut trees, but the trunks and branches were twisted and woven together like a large, impenetrable cobweb. There was no way to get through. Looking up, with no other choice, he quickly decided to climb. Years of climbing trees as a child had prepared him; he easily reached the top. Looking down, he saw dozens of multicolored balls bouncing up and down.

"Come play! Come play!" they all cried.

"Get away from me!" He waved his hand frantically. "Shoo!"

"Ya havin' a wee little bit of trouble, I see," came a voice from one branch over.

John turned sharply to his right to find a short, chubby man wearing a green jacket and a top hat. He had large gold buckles on his belt and shoes and twirled a wooden cane as he sneered at John.

"What are you supposed to be?" John snorted. "Another gnome?"

"GNOME?" he cried. "Why, gosh no. You'd be insulting me, lad. I be a Leprechaun. Liddy's the name, and magic tricks are me game!"

"Well, I'm not in the mood for magic tricks, but it'd be nice if you'd help. What the heck are those things?"

"Ahh, those just be snuffballs," Liddy replied. "Annoying creatures if you ask me. No manners whatsoever. Always want to play, they do."

"So are you gonna help or not?"

"Ya know, I can help ye, me lad, if you'd like. For a price, of course. I really fancy that jacket you'd be wearin'!" He pointed with his cane. "Hmmm?"

"Oh, hell no!" John lit up a cigarette. "This is not for sale."

"Well how about I try one of those sticks that you'd be smoking." His eyes lit up. "Me pouch of Wimpleweed be empty."

"What, a cigarette? Sure." He handed one over. "As long as you get rid of those snuffballs or whatever the heck they are."

Liddy lit the cigarette with a match he produced from his waistcoat and raised his cane.

"Tricks and charms, quit your fun;
Shoo, you balls, this boy is done!"

A bright light came from the tip of the cane, and the snuffballs scurried away. "There ye go, me lad."

"Thank you," John said with relief and started to climb down.

68

"Wait there just a tick." Liddy stood up on the branch. "Where ye goin'?"

"I'm going home." He paused. "Or at least trying to find a way back."

"Now don't leave wit-out havin' a drink wit your new buddy Liddy." He started to climb down also. "Ya know, tis bad luck not to have a drink with a Leprechaun. Ya don't need any more bad luck now, ye hear?"

"Very true!" John looked up at the Leprechaun. "What kind of drink do you have?"

"Only the best in Enchantas." He pulled out a bottle. "Butchbark Whiskey."

"Never had it." John laughed as he jumped back to the ground. "But as long as its liquor, I'm sure I can handle it."

"Butchbark Whiskey is an ol' family recipe." He opened it and took a swig. "The only stuff I drink."

John took a drink from the bottle, and to his surprise it was the strongest liquor he had ever tasted. He didn't want to be rude, so he swallowed hard and inhaled deeply. "Ohhh, man!"

"Good ol' stuff, right?" Liddy took the bottle back. "The trick is to keep it under the rainbow for ten Seasons."

"Yeah, that was pretty strong."

"If you're not used to it, it'll put ye straight on your bottom."

"What were you doing on top of the tree?" John stuttered. He was already feeling the effects.

"I was hidin' me pot o'gold, but I believe luck has brought me two more," said Liddy with a mischievous grin.

"Huh?" John asked when suddenly he fell directly on his face.

"Hehe," Liddy laughed as he touched John with his cane. Suddenly, John began to float. His jacket came off and shrunk to the perfect size for the leprechaun.

"Thank ye much for the jacket, me lad. Now you'd be a great prize to barter with. Wonder what ye'd get me."

Liddy began to whistle his favorite tune as he twirled his cane and strolled through the forest. John lay silently, floating in the air while he followed Liddy. What was to come of John? Only Liddy knew.

Chapter V
The Sage

It felt as if it had been hours since they'd left the cave. The sun was still bright but seemed to be setting. The wind sent an uncomfortable chill over the land. Gitchy eagerly told his story as the three kids waited impatiently to continue their journey.

"And that is how I came to work with our grand majestic Sage, The Great Owl." Gitchy stretched.

"Nice story, Gitchy," Ryan stated kindly. "I think we should start moving along now."

"Oh, dear me," Gitchy jumped up. "What time is it? Our Sage is waiting for us."

"I'm not sure. My watch isn't working."

"Let's get going." Sally stood up.

"Yeah." Mel rubbed his stomach. "I'm getting hungry again."

They ambled down another hill and watched large birds circling the air in the horizon. "Those are Fluitenducks." Gitchy pointed up. "They are searching for worms, I suppose. Hope my little friend Slippy is all right."

The beautiful landscape was breathtaking. The wind had died and the weather was perfect—not too hot or too cold, not too dry or too humid.

Small hills covered with the blue, purple, and teal grass went on for miles. As the sun continued toward the horizon, the angled rays made the plant life sparkle. The shiny glimmers added to the group's astonishment at this new world they had stumbled upon. The colors of the clouds were orange, yellow and white and changed shapes rapidly, as if competing for the most attention by creating spectacular geometrical designs.

Ryan's eyes narrowed as he focused on what looked like a bunch of animals scurrying through the weeds and bushes ahead. Some were moving in rapid zigzag lines; others moved in small circles. As he watched the weeds flatten, forming bizarre patterns, he noticed a few of the things—whatever they were—jumping high into the air and landing back on the ground. He stared, marveling as the visitors and their guide moved closer.

"Gitchy, what's going on there?"

They were a few hundred feet away when the creatures began moving toward them; faint grunting noises grew louder as they drew closer. It reminded him of football, the players grunting and groaning, tapping every bit of their strength as they tried to conquer the opponent.

"I believe those are little snuffballs playing in the field."

"Are they dangerous?"

"Gosh, no." Gitchy laughed. "Although they have been known to be a little forceful when they play."

Suddenly, a small rumble came from a bush in front of him. Ryan froze. A small squeaky and childish voice came from the bushes, saying, "Would you like to play with us?"

Ryan stared in confusion as he walked slowly toward the bush. He bent over to see what was talking, and then another squeaky voice came from behind him and said, "Come on! It be fun!"

Ryan couldn't tell if it was the same voice he had heard before. Two purple snuffballs came from around the bush and rolled next to him.

"What do you mean? Play what?"

Sounds of laughter filled the air as Ryan spun around to see who was speaking to him. Mel and Sally watched silently as Ryan talked to the very unusual fuzzy balls. "Looks like they like you, Ryan," Sally said with a laugh.

Three dozen more fuzzy balls emerged from their hiding places.

"Oh, wow!" Ryan took a few steps back. At that moment they rolled around and surrounded him. "So what are you playing?"

"TAG!" The snuffballs all cheered and bounced up and down. "Do you want to play? Do you want to play?" they chanted.

A lavender snuffball pounced up and hit Ryan in the chest, "TAG! *You're it!*"

Ryan was startled for a second as they scurried into the field. His athletic instincts suddenly charged into overdrive as he sped after them.

"You can sure tell he's competitive," Mel observed.

Ryan was amazed at how fast they could roll. He noticed one of the snuffballs was a bit slower and decided to chase it. But as he entered a long grassy field he lost sight of all of them.

"Wow, this might be harder than I thought," he said to himself, calling out, "This isn't fair. I can't see you!" He was hoping to flush at least one out so he could chase it.

A few snuffballs finally bounced into the air, and Ryan ran through the long grass as fast as he could toward them. The snuffballs made little trails as they rolled through the weeds, but it was still hard for Ryan to catch them. They all went in separate directions. Ryan was rapidly overwhelmed, not knowing which way to go.

"This is more of a workout than football," Ryan mumbled to himself as he straightened up and moved his eyes back and forth, looking for an easy target. He heard movement behind him but pretended not to hear it. He thought that maybe one of the snuffballs would get close enough to tag.

His body grew tense as a bead of sweat trickled down his forehead. The pounding of his heart grew faster as he tightened his fists, waiting for the perfect moment to strike, all else forgotten in the thrill of the sport.

A voice behind called out, "Yoo-hoo, whatcha doing?" Before it finished, Ryan was already airborne and in tackle formation.

As he wrapped his arms around the furry figure, he noticed it wasn't a snuffball. By then it was too late; they hit the ground and rolled.

Ryan was holding a large green rabbit with long, floppy ears, a fluffy white tail, and large feet. It wore a long blue trench coat, a satchel around its shoulder, and held a rope lasso in one of its paws.

Ryan yelped. "Um, hello there."

"What did you do that for?" The rabbit asked.

"I'm sorry." Ryan released the creature. "I'm playing Tag with these umm... I forgot what they're called." He scratched his head. His eyes remained fixed on the field, still searching for a snuffball to tag.

"SNUFFBALLS!" The rabbit sounded excited. "I love playing Tag with them. They are so fun!"

"Too fast for me." Ryan mopped the sweat from his forehead.

"They are quick, but the best way to tag one is to wait for them to jump," the rabbit said as he gathered his belongings.

"Peaches!" Gitchy said as the three others emerged from behind Ryan. They shook hands as he continued. "How many Seasons has it been?"

"Gitchy, wow always a pleasure seeing you. How is the village treating you?"

"I have not been home in a while, busy keeping up with the historical journals, you know?" Gitchy smiled. "How about yourself? How is life down in Rabbit City?"

"Life is fine. The city is expanding."

"Rabbit City?" Mel was curious. "Where is that?"

"It is directly below us, surrounding most of Cumberlake Valley," Gitchy replied as he looked at the three kids. "Oh pardon me! Peaches, this here is Ryan, Sally, and Mel. These humans just arrived from the Forbidden Cave."

"The Forbidden Cave?" Peaches's eyes widened enthusiastically as he shook everyone's hands. "My great-great-great-great-GREAT grandpappy told tales of playing in the Valley many ages ago. He mentioned a boyhood friend named Mumbles disappearing in the Forbidden Cave."

"Ahh, yes, the case of young Mumbles the Rabbit." Gitchy nodded. "I remember this, I was but a young pupil interning with the Knights of Minerton during this council. This was the direct motivation to close the cave forever. It was right before the Witch and Warlock came to Enchantas?"

"Yes, that story is Legend in Rabbit City." Peaches smiled as he reminisced. "Grand Pappy tells us the story every snow season."

"The Witch and Warlock?" Mel questioned.

"Pardon." Gitchy straightened himself formally. "I may have said too much. I will let our grand Sage fill you in on that legend."

"Gitchy? How old are you?" Sally asked, curious. "You mentioned remembering something that happened when Peaches' great-great-great grandpappy was alive."

"I am very, very old, my dear." Gitchy smiled. "Mythics and Humans live for a very long time in Enchantas; however, animals and plants may only live for a few Ages. I am not referring to trees, of course. Some are older than the Great Owl."

"Ages?" asked Ryan.

"Our calendar works as so: there are one hundred days in a season and four seasons a cycle. One-hundred cycles an Age, and one hundred Ages in an Era. I believe we are only a few Ages away from beginning another Era." Gitchy took a deep breath and started to walk faster. "Now come along, everyone, we must not keep our Grand Sage, the Great Owl, awaiting!"

"So is that where y'all are headin'?" Peaches stiffened with excitement. "To see the Great Owl?"

"Why yes, Peaches. I was about to guide them to meet with our grand majestic Sage, The Great Owl."

"I have not seen that old fart in Seasons," Peaches smiled. "You know, he still owes me a bottle of Rittleroot Rum."

The three kids began to giggle.

"Mind if I tag along with y'all? I'm on a hunting trip but am always willing to go on any ol' adventure."

"I do not mind." Gitchy looked at his young charges. They all nodded their heads in assent. "Great! The more the merrier!"

Ryan was still on the hunt for the elusive snuffballs.

"They are gone." Gitchy patted Ryan on the back. "Let us move along. The Great Owl is waiting."

"So what is it like beyond the so-called *Forbidden Cave?*" Peaches asked in a mocking tone. He'd heard stories about that other world and was more skeptical than afraid. He was fascinated by the tales and not averse to being an adventurer and journeying through it. For the most part, he was fearless; only a pawful of things scared him.

"If you ask me," Sally replied, "it's a world of stuck-up selfish people. Only a handful of them are nice." She looked at Ryan with a brief smile.

"Yeah," Ryan interjected. "We have problems in our world, but we also have good things such as sports, books—"

"Chemistry!" Mel jumped in.

"Yeah, everyone has their hobbies."

"Speaking of hobbies," Gitchy said, "what time is it, Peaches? I need the time in order to accurately record this historical journal entry."

Peaches pulled out his pocket watch. "Almost eight o'tock."

"Eight o'tock?" Mel asked.

"Yes." Peaches smiled and recited a poem:

"Tickity Tock goes around the Clock
Twenty times a Day.
Tackity Tick clicks within each Tick
One hundred times each Way.
Now within each Tick,
Which moves around each Tock,
A Tack will beat the Rate."

"Sorry, you lost me!" Ryan said in a befuddled tone.

"As you can see"—Gitchy appropriated Peaches' watch for the impromptu lecture—"there are ten numbers circling the parameter of the watch. We call these tocks. When this dial *here* rotates past each tock twice, it means that one full day and night has passed. Within each tock, this dial *here* clicks ten times between each number; these are known as ticks," He harrumphed importantly. "Now within each tick, this other dial *here* will click five times. Hence, that is how we tell time in Enchantas." Gitchy took a deep breath before reciting another verse:

"Fifty Tacks a Tick,
One hundred Ticks a Tock,
Ten Tocks a Clock.

77

Two Clocks a day,
To help you plan your way."

Mel was fascinated. "Oh wow, we use hours, minutes and seconds to tell time in our world. That's totally different than—"

"Shhh," Peaches interrupted quietly, taking out a lasso. "Can ya feel that?" He knelt down to the ground. They all could feel it shaking.

"What is that?" Sally asked, looking worried again.

"Vegetables," Peaches replied. "Sounds like a good herd, too."

"Herd?" Mel's eyes widened.

"I'm huntin' for cabbage, and if I'm lucky, I'll get a carrot or radish," Peaches noted.

The three kids were stupefied. Could this place get any stranger?

"It is the season for cabbage and carrots. My favorite huntin' season is turnip. I'll be makin' a stew later."

The rumbling beneath their feet became stronger. "You'd all better take cover. This herd is a biggie!" The rabbit clapped his paws rapidly and hopped toward a violet-leafed maple tree.

"Hurry! Take cover! STAMPEDE!" Peaches swung his lasso over his head, ready to catch his dinner.

"Oh, no!" Sally yelled as she turned around to see hundreds of little green, red, and orange creatures charging down the hill.

The others ran for the closest blue-leafed Lixy fruit tree, intent on climbing out of the way. Sally tried to run, but her knee hurt too much to cover ground at more than a snail's pace. As the herd drew closer, she saw thousands of little vegetables charging rapidly toward them. The green and red varieties were round with little green legs, while the orange vegetables were long and skinny with green bushes of hair atop their heads.

Sally's knee buckled, and she went down hard.

"Sally, get up! Hurry!" Ryan cried from the topmost branches of the Lixy Fruit tree, but it was too late.

The herd of little vegetables trampled over her body one after the other in a red, green, and orange swarm and promptly disappeared from sight over the hill.

Wasting no time, Peaches hopped after the herd, swinging his rope into the air. "You're not going anywhere, ya bloody buggers!" He whipped his lariat with admirable accuracy, catching a few in one fell swoop.

Sally remained face down on the ground. Ryan hastily clambered down from the tree calling her name.

"You haven't experienced anything until you've been run over by a herd of vegetables!" She laughed, raising her head to look up at him. "Their little feet felt like a massage."

"At least you didn't get hurt," he said, the intense relief he felt showing on his face.

"It tickled." Sally stood up, and Ryan helped her brush off the dust that blanketed her after her run-in with the rogue veggies.

"Where's Peaches?" Mel looked in the direction where their rabbit guide had disappeared.

"I'm right here!" Peaches hopped toward them, a handful of screaming vegetables firmly ensconced in his right paw.

"There you are." Sally smiled as she looked down at the veggies. "Is that your dinner?"

"Yes." Peaches inspected them all. "Looks like quality game, too. I have enough for everyone, that is, if y'all don't mind raw veggies."

"NO! Not dinner!" the veggies cried. "Don't eat us; we have family!"

"Oh, shut up!" Peaches yelled, silencing them. "These bloody varmints never stay quiet. They'll say anything to get you to let them go."

"*Don't eat us!*" they screeched.

One screamed in terror as Peaches took a bite out of his leg. Peaches smiled and held up the screaming veggies. "Y'all are welcome to some."

The three were sickened by the thought. "Thanks," Ryan replied politely. "I think we've all lost our appetite."

"Alrighty. More for me." Peaches chewed vigorously and swallowed as he placed the rest of the loudly protesting vegetables in his satchel. "Besides, if you think they are screaming now, you should hear them being boiled or fried."

"So how far is the Great Owl now?" Mel asked, more than ready to change the subject.

"It is a ways yet." Gitchy pointed toward the forest in the distance. "We will be there soon enough."

It felt as though days rather than hours had gone by when the sun finally set.

The group entered the forest, which smelled of dew and leaves. It was dark and a more than a little eerie.

"It's getting pretty black in here," said Sally uneasily as she grabbed Peaches' furry arm.

"Yeah." Mel tried to hold his composure, but fear of the dark had haunted him since infancy. "I wish I hadn't thrown away that miner's helmet."

"I can help with this," Gitchy reassured as he rubbed his hat.
"Mystic Forest, late at night,
turn these leaves into light."
Suddenly the forest lit up, every leaf glowing neon in the dark. An astonishing colorful illumination of blue, pink, purple, and green illuminated the path for the five travelers.

"Wow!" Mel was astonished. "I have to learn that trick."

"This will also ward off any predators that hunt only at night," Peaches noted.

Together, they journeyed through the leaf-lit forest. The smell reminded Ryan, Sally, and Mel of a fresh spring morning. Fireflies and glowing butterflies fluttered around the forest. It was quiet and delightful, and surprisingly, they felt safe. A sudden gust of wind ruffled the leaves as they came to a massive clearing. Many yards away, in the middle of the clearing, grew an enormous twisted tree with dark red bark.

"Holy cow," Sally said in awe. "That tree is huge."

"This is the home of our Grand Majestic Sage." Gitchy opened his arms toward the tree. "The Grand Redwood!"

As they moved closer to the tree, the significance of its size became apparent. The trunk of the tree was about fifty yards in diameter, and the circumference tapered all the way up as it twisted toward the night sky. Gitchy rubbed his hat, and instantly a red glowing door appeared. The doorway itself was about four times the size of the teens. The rabbit guide knocked three times, and the doors opened.

"There you go, kiddos." Gitchy bowed and smiled, gesturing the humans forward.

"We aren't joining them?" Peaches frowned.

"No, our Sage would like to see them alone."

"Alrighty." Peaches sat down and pulled out a cabbage, which cried out pitifully for help until he bit off its mouth.

"Just step up onto the stairway and let it do the work," Gitchy said as the humans walked in.

The door swung closed. Candles lit the interior of the gargantuan hollowed-out tree, and aside from the spiral staircase attached to the outer rim of the walls, the rest of the space was empty. They cautiously stepped onto the staircase, which began to move them up the tree like an escalator.

"This is cool!" Mel smiled excitedly as he watched the floor sink underneath them.

The escalating spiral stairway was fast, and they reached the top quickly. They stepped into a dimly lit room; immediately the lights were turned up and a deep voice called out, "Do not be afraid, children." A large owl with a distinct air of nobility stepped forward, its wings wrapped around its body like a cloak. The magnificent creature was about three times taller than Ryan. "I only eat Redwood." The owl chuckled warmly. "As you can see, I've been building my home for many Ages now. Come closer— let me see you all." He studied them for a moment and asked, "Where is John?"

"How did you know about John?" Ryan asked, puzzled.

The owl replied with an acute chuckle.

"He ran off and left us earlier," said Mel.

"I see," said the owl. "You will rejoin him soon. Now let us get down to business."

"Okay," Ryan said abruptly. "How do we get home?"

"My dear boy, I believe Fate has brought you all to Enchantas. Fate has a plan for you."

"We just want to go home," cried Sally.

"I understand your frustration" The owl ruffled his feathers. "However, when Fate plans a prophecy such as yours, it is very important that you fulfill that destiny."

"So what's this prophecy?" asked Mel.

"And when can we go home?" Ryan added.

"I believe you were all sent here to bring peace and balance to our world, and I am positive that this is Fate's plan. I have studied Fate for many ages. Analyzing and predicting Fate is very tricky." He turned toward Sally. "Sally, may I see your compass?"

She handed it to him without question. The compass floated up as the owl put on gold spectacles.

"Ah, yes. I haven't seen this compass in Ages." The owl squinted. "Many Ages ago, I had the Knights hide this very compass in the Forbidden Cave for safekeeping." He smiled and let it slowly drop back into Sally's hand. "Looks like Fate has given it a new home."

Sally looked up, "Will it show us how to get home?"

"Eventually, yes," the owl said sternly. "However, the secrets of opening the Forbidden Cave have been lost with the banishment of our founders, the Knights." He paused and straightened his back. "I was the first Enchantian to meet the Knights of Minerton. I was a very young and curious owl. One day, a very long time ago, I flew around Cumberlake Valley, looking for food, when suddenly a magical doorway from another world appeared. A couple of humans stepped through, and because I was a brave and gregarious owl, I befriended these new travelers. In turn, they taught me how to speak. Later, more humans came and helped build our world. They were a very noble group of humans who became the Knights of Minerton. For Ages they were the protecttors of our peaceful world. That was until two more humans came through the cave. That was a devastating turn Fate visited upon us.

"These Humans were gracious and kind at first. The Knights taught them the ways of Enchantas and all of its magic. Our world and lives were faultless until the day came when the two decided that they wanted to go back to their world. The Knights refused to let them leave. They believed that Fate had brought them to Enchantas for a reason. In our world, to keep Fate's plan from coming to pass would be blasphemy. The two humans became bitter and resentful. They separated from the Knights and moved to the deserted wasteland of the Mortible Mountains. They began a new faith that led them down an evil path, transforming themselves into the very wicked Witch and Warlock. This new faith contradicted Fate, and when word broke out, thousands followed them. Not long after, the wicked Witch and Warlock raised a large army and declared war against the Knights. These Crusades lasted for many Cycles, and thousands of Enchantians died. After the Knights ultimately lost the war, they were exiled by the Witch and Warlock and banished to an unknown land. They have never returned."

"What happened next?" Sally found the tale compelling.

"The wicked Witch and Warlock were still determined to go home. Ironically, once they realized that the secrets of opening the magical doorway were lost with the Knights, they appointed themselves the new rulers of Enchantas and remained here forever. Since then, Enchantas has never been the same."

"So I see that this so-called Fate is a big deal for you all," said Mel. "Why would Fate let this happen?"

"No one knows. That is another reason many more Enchantians became followers of the Witch and Warlock," the owl replied sadly. He looked back at Sally and continued, "Keep that compass with you, my dear. It will guide you all where Fate wishes you to go. I also believe that by following this compass, you will all find your way home."

"When will that be?" Mel became furious.

"Just follow the compass, my children." The owl's voice became soft. "Fate will lead the way. Fulfill the prophecy!"

The visitors nodded as the lights around them dimmed.

"I must go sleep now." The owl stepped backward. "This old body becomes tired easily. Good luck on your journey; I truly hope Fate has brought you here to restore peace to Enchantas."

"Wait, what are we supposed to do?" Ryan was frustrated. This visit with the owl only grew more questions than answers.

"Follow the compass, my children." The owl faded into the darkness, and his voice became quiet. "Gitchy the Herald will help guide you."

The owl disappeared into the darkness, and the three stepped back onto the stairway, which obligingly carried them down to the entry.

Mel shook his head, disbelief and confusion clouding his expression. "What prophecy? What was he talking about? We need to go home." The practical joker had lost his sense of humor.

"I know how you feel, but I don't think we have a choice, Mel." Ryan put a hand on his shoulder. "I guess we just need to follow the compass."

"Well, we need to find John first," Mel said, worried about his surly new friend. "We can't just leave him while we go . . . *fulfill a prophecy* or whatever."

"You're right," Ryan agreed. "Not sure where to look, though."

"Sally," Mel said as he turned to her. "What does your compass say?"

She pulled it out and opened it. "We should go *This Way*." She pointed to her right.

"Let's get to it." The door would not yield at first. Then Ryan knocked on it three times, figuring what worked to get them in might work to get them out, and it did. Gitchy and Peaches were waiting outside.

"Are you all ready?" Gitchy asked.

"Yep," they replied in unison.

"The owl said to follow the Compass." Ryan turned to Gitchy. "He said you'd help guide us to fulfill this prophecy."

Gitchy smiled. "I sure will, my friends!"

"Yippie! Another adventure." Peaches rubbed his paws together. "Where to?"

"*There Way*." Sally pointed in the direction she meant after putting the compass back under her sweater.

"Can you check again?" Peaches asked, looking worried. "That's toward Foxtown."

"Don't worry, Peaches," Gitchy reassured him. "It won't be that bad."

"That bad, you say? Let us go through Rabbit City. It is much safer, and we can stop at my place for a bite to eat."

"I'm truly sorry Peaches," said Gitchy, "but I must refuse the kind offer. We must follow Fate's compass. There is a reason Fate is taking us this way."

"Rabbit City?" Sally asked. "I'm all right with that. Besides, I'm a little hungry."

"How far is it?" Mel chimed in. "I don't want to get off track at all."

"Oh, it's not far at all," Peaches started to hop away. "There is an entrance right up here."

"Peaches, I truly believe we should follow the compass," Gitchy argued.

"We will, my Herald. It is only a slight detour."

The five of them stepped off the red cobblestone trail, approaching a bushel of large, bluish-green pine trees.

"Here is one of our entrances." Peaches grabbed a small stone from the ground and pulled it up. A large circular piece of the ground was connected to the stone, resembling a manhole cover. He quickly jumped in. His head popped back up. "Come on down. Use the ladder if you wish."

Without word, the four followed Peaches down the dark tunnel, wondering where they would end up next.

Chapter VI
Rabbit City

Peaches lit a glass lantern that hung against the red dirt wall, illuminating the narrow tunnel. The teens had to stoop slightly because of the low ceiling, but the tunnel was the perfect size for any rabbit, squirrel, or beaver. Gitchy held his pointy hat in place as they followed Peaches down the tunnel. The smell of fresh soil reminded Sally of the times she helped her grandmother in the garden. Planting flowers, fruits, and vegetables each spring was one of her favorite activities.

As Peaches led the way, Gitchy sidled up behind him. "As a matter of fact, Peaches"—Gitchy smiled—"I am quite pleased you convinced us to go this way. I have not visited Rabbit City for many Cycles. I believe the last time I came to visit was a few Snow Seasons ago. Although in that Season, it was fairly quiet."

"Yeah, that ain't the right time to visit. Many are hibernating. Not me, of course." Peaches chuckled. "I am awake and busy all Cycle long."

They started down a long, seemingly endless stairway. Sally's knee ached, but she remained quiet, gamely limping along, not wanting to slow the group down. As they finally reached the bottom, they saw a massive, round stained-glass door in shades of red, blue, and green. It projected an image of a rabbit soldier dressed in turtle-shelled armor and holding a long sword. Peaches produced a key from his pocket and unlocked it. As the door swung open, they entered a large, tall cavern lined with streets and buildings. The streets were filled with busy inhabitants, mostly rabbits but also few visiting squirrels, prairie dogs, and beavers. Many were walking swiftly, and a few rode tricycles. Large car-sized lanterns hung above the streets, casting ample light on the streets and buildings below. At both sides of each cross-street were blue clay walls lined with four stories of circular doorways, windows, and balconies. Shops covered the bottom floors while the other three stories were apartments and balconies. The streets were as long as the eye could see. The city was alive and hectic as the occupants prepared for the coming Snow Season.

Who would have known that beneath the silent, peaceful valley and forest lay a massive, industrialized town such as Rabbit City? Colorful rabbits hopped around the streets, some casually and some chaotically, but always greeting each other in passing. The residents were very cheerful and sociable.

"Good aftermidday, Nibbles," Peaches said as he bowed to a white and yellow rabbit.

"Good aftermidday to you too, Peaches." Nibbles bowed in return. "How was hunting?"

"Just grand." He lifted his pouch of screaming vegetables. "Going home to make a stew."

"How wonderful! They sound very fresh."

"Oh they are. These little rascals herded themselves into a stampede!"

"You don't say. That makes the hunt much more fun."

Gitchy smiled and introduced himself. "Hello, my name is Gitchy, the honorary—"

"Herald of Enchantas!" Nibbles became excited and quickly shook his hand. "Very pleased to meet you. I have heard many stories from you as a child, when you came down to visit our school. Very heart-warming and adventurous!"

"Why, thank you. I enjoy my visits to the neighboring cities and villages."

Peaches glanced at his companions and realized he was being rude. "Pardon me, Nibbles. Allow me to introduce Ryan, Sally, and Mel, three humans who came from the Forbidden Cave!"

"Hi." Ryan nodded. Mel tipped an imaginary hat. Sally waved.

"You don't say!" Nibbles tilted his head. "Humans? As in the Prophecy?"

"I guess so," Mel answered, still unsure of the whole prophecy theory.

"Wow, wait'll everyone hears of this!" Nibbles quickly hopped away, telling everyone he passed whom he had just met.

"I hope our presence isn't a bother," Ryan offered politely.

"Oh, definitely not! If anything, your presence will stir up a celebration." Peaches chuckled benevolently. "They'll grasp at any reason to add another holiday in Rabbit City."

As they made their way past pastry shops, restaurants, black-smiths, and tailors, the residents all turned to watch them walk by. It was as if Nibbles had informed the entire city in a matter of ticks.

Sally was reminded of the incident in the lunchroom when everyone had pointed at her with horror and disgust. "Peaches, is there somewhere else we could go that wouldn't attract so much attention? It's a little uncomfortable having everyone stare at us."

He stopped and looked up. "Why yes, my dear. My humble home is right up here."

A platform slowly descended from above, hovering at a height where they could step on with ease.

"Now if the boys would kindly help with this pullivator"— Peaches grabbed a rope connected to a pulley system—"that would be wonderful."

Ryan and Mel put some muscle into the process, raising the pullivator to the second floor, where they stepped off onto a small balcony. The pullivator slowly descended back to street level as Peaches unlocked his apartment door. As they entered the apartment, a dugout of sorts beyond any hutch imagined, flames crackled merrily in a fireplace to the right. There were a few comfortable looking wicker chairs on the left. The smell of cooked stew and spices filled their nostrils. A giant log sawed in half served as a table; a checkerboard lay out awaiting the next game. They could see a small stove with a pot on top in the adjoining kitchen.

"Please make yourselves at home," said Peaches as he hurried into the other room.

The four fit comfortably at his table.

Mel was eager to play checkers. "Want to play a quick game?" he asked Gitchy.

"Why, sure." Gitchy set his journal down. "However, I must make it quick. I need to document this historic day."

Ryan and Sally sat next to each other, quietly taking notice of Peaches' collection of books, watches, and paintings of his extended family. It seemed as though there was not an open spot without a picture of another rabbit.

Gitchy noticed the two looking at all the paintings layering his walls like wallpaper. "Peaches does have an enormous family, doesn't he? I bet he doesn't know half of them."

"Not true, my old friend." Peaches smiled as he stepped into his living room, holding a carrot and knife. "I could name my siblings, uncles, aunts, grands, and cousins if you wish."

"No, that's fine." Gitchy didn't want to get him started.

"Are you sure?" Peaches started shaving the carrot. "Second, third, and fourth cousins too!"

"AHH, not my skin!" the carrot screamed in terror as Peaches leaped quickly back into the kitchen. "Oh, it hurts! Stop the pain!"

"If their screams bother you, I could leave to do this," Peaches said as he finished peeling off the carrot's skin.

"Oh, no. That's fine with us," Ryan said, not wanting to be rude to their host. He looked sympathetically at Mel and Sally as they cringed with disgust and awkwardness. They remained silent, trying not to offend Peaches' hospitality.

"Great," said the rabbit, dropping the vegetables in the boiling water. "I'm almost finished."

"Ouch, it burns! Too hot! Too hot!" a cabbage yelled, trying to jump out of the pot.

"What did you expect?" Peaches said as he put the lid on.

"Let me out. *Please!*" A radish scraped its little hands on the inside of the pot, also trying its hardest to escape.

"Now we can finally acquire some bloody peace and quiet! It's always a bit of a pain to cook these vegetables." Peaches eagerly shook his spices into the stew. "They start to quiet down when they get soft. Also makes it easier to cut them."

Ryan thought a change of subject was in order and tried quickly to do so. "Gitchy, I don't understand why the owl believes we're prophets or whatever. We are just teenagers. We haven't even finished high school. How can we be expected to bring *peace and balance* to Enchantas?"

"Ryan, I understand that you are confused by your current situation. The perplexity of finding yourselves in our world and then being asked so much of, is a lot for anyone to deal with. However, before you ask yourselves *how*, ask yourselves *why*." Gitchy smiled as he jumped four of Mel's checker pieces. "You have not only entered another world; you have entered another state of beliefs. We Enchantians strongly believe in Fate, and that Fate works for a larger plan, which is Destiny. Everything happens for a reason. We just need to find out why Fate chose you to fulfill that part of Destiny's plan."

"Okay." Ryan was still confused but didn't bother asking any more questions. He believed that, for the time being, it would be best to follow the leader.

"I hope everyone's hungry," Peaches hollered from the kitchen.

"Oh, we are." Gitchy grinned. "King me, kind sir."

"Again?" Mel shook his head in frustration. "I never get beat this badly."

Peaches lifted the pot lid slightly, and a particularly tenacious radish sprang out, landing on the counter. "Ouch! That was hot!" it yelled, holding its left foot in the air and blowing on it to cool it down. "You're not going to get me, *Rabbit!*"

"Oh, geez. Not again. There's always one of these bloody vegetables that has to be a nuisance," Peaches said, grabbing a small net from a cupboard. "Come here, you little bugger!"

"You cannot catch me this time!" The radish laughed.

Ryan, Mel, and Sally had to laugh, too, as they watched the ridiculous scene, the radish dancing on top of the table and teasing Peaches. Peaches didn't laugh; he was too intent on capturing the runaway vegetable. Peaches jumped as fast as he could toward it, but the radish jumped out of the way and landed on the floor.

"Ugh!" Peaches wiped his forehead in frustration. "Why must you do this?"

"You will never catch me!" The radish made for the open door more rapidly than one would expect of a half-boiled veggie.

"Gosh darn it!" Peaches yelled, whipping the net across the room. "There always has to be one that gets away. I was saving that radish for dessert."

"It'll be okay, Peaches," Sally said as she patted him on the ear.

"Well, anyway..." Peaches marched back to the kitchen to fill bowls. "You ready to dine?"

They sat on the floor around the table, cushioned by a plush black rug. The table was varnished to a high gloss; if they looked closely, they could see their reflection. Contemplating the bowls of stew, all three humans hesitated. The screams emanating from the stewpot had been disturbing. They weren't sure they could eat it.

"Aren't you three hungry?" asked Peaches, contentedly nibbling on a carrot.

"Mmm," Gitchy said with a mouthful. "Try it. This is so good."

Mel scooped up a spoonful and sighed. "Well, it can't be any worse than my mom's cooking," he said before shoving it into his mouth. He chewed for a moment and swallowed. His eyes grew large with surprise. "Wow, Peaches! This is really good!" He began to eat with real gusto.

Taking Mel's lead, Sally and Ryan tried it. To their amazement, they liked it as well.

Not long after the kids emptied their bowls, and without a word, Peaches served them more.

"I am truly glad you like my cooking. I had to make sure I gathered enough during the Hunting Season so I am prepared for the Snow Season."

"Hunting season?" Mel asked.

"Harvest Season, or whatever you wish to call it." Peaches stood up, collecting dishes and cutlery. "I, for one, call it Hunting Season."

"Yes, there are four Seasons per Cycle," Gitchy explained. "Harvest, Snow, Mating, and Sunny."

"Oh, yeah we have the same type of—" Ryan started to relate but was interrupted by Mel.

"I think we should go find John." His belly was full and his conscience was calling. Was his friend going hungry? Was he hurt?

93

"John can take care of himself," Ryan muttered. "Besides, we will probably meet up with him eventually. We are all—even that jerk—trying to find a way home."

As they discussed what to do next, Sally stood up, stretching. She quietly walked down the hall, which led to another room. The room was full of multicolored bottles, neatly lined up on shelves displays that lined the walls, along with some free-standing shelving in the middle. As she strolled around the room studying the collection, one bottle in particular caught her eye. It hung in a glass case with a candle lit behind; it had a twisted neck and was sparkling blue with a green cork. The bottle glittered, emitting a captivating essence. Without thinking, mesmerized, she opened it and consumed the entire contents.

Instantly the room started to spin; hundreds of colors swirled around as the lights, walls, and bottles became one. The air clotted into a thick and humid mass. The red and blue dirt walls dripped with moisture.

"Sally," Ryan called as he walked into the room. "Are you in here?"

She turned to Ryan, but his face started to grow rabbit ears from his eyes. Mel stepped into the room, and Sally watched as his face turned into Gitchy. She had no idea what was real and what wasn't. She wasn't sure if she was hallucinating or not.

Sally's face had turned a greenish shade and her eyes glimmered a sparkly blue, reminiscent of the liquid she'd thoughtlessly chugged.

"Peaches!" Ryan yelled, as scared as he'd ever been. "Come in here! Please!"

Peaches quickly hopped into his bottle room and saw Sally swaying with dizziness, holding the sparkly blue bottle. "Uh-oh. Someone's gotten into my Lixyworm wine!"

"What?" Ryan asked. "What is that?"

"It is a very potent drink," Gitchy said from the doorway.

"Yes, it is." Peaches extracted the bottle from Sally's fist and held it up to the light. "All gone. And I was using it to ferment homemade Lixy Dust so I can give it out as presents for my next family reunion."

"Oh, no." Gitchy grabbed the bottle. "She drank the worm!"

"Worm?" Mel's eyes widened with curiosity.

"Yes. Lixyworms are very ravenous creatures, always hungry and obsessed with drinking potions."

"They will do almost anything to satiate their addictive cravings," Peaches added.

"You have met one before," said Gitchy. "Slippy from the Valley. He was asking for payment in the form of some potion. However, I do not contribute to an addiction like that. They have only one goal in mind: to drink from the bottle. You see, they have no real life. Their goal is to chase after their next drink. The potion makes them weak and selfish creatures."

"All that patient waiting and work for nothing." Peaches frowned at the empty bottle. "You see, the potion itself is Lixy Fruit Wine and can be very potent when the worm is cocooned in the bottle. During this phase, it becomes Lixyworm Wine. After the worm consumes every last drop, it traps itself inside the bottle and dies. Their remains can then be shredded and ground into Lixy Dust. However, if they escape, they grow into very large worms and bury themselves deep in the ground where their shedding can be mined."

Ryan really didn't care about Peaches' wine, only the safety of Sally. "Okay, well... Is she going to be all right?"

"Yes, she will be fine." Peaches laughed. "She may be a little intoxicated for a tock or two."

Sally opened her bloodshot eyes slightly and stumbled into Peaches' arms.

"Grandma? Grandma?" She lifted her head and looked around. "Grandma, where am I?"

"No, Sally, it's us," said Ryan.

Peaches put his paw on Ryan's chest and whispered, "Do not worry. I've got this, my boy."

"No! Where's grandma? What did you with her?" Sally's head was too heavy for her to hold up, so she put it back down. "Where am I?"

Peaches patted her head in an attempt to calm her down. "Don't worry, Sally. You're safe here. You're with friends."

"Grandma? Is that you?" Sally squinted, trying to focus on Peaches' face. "Oh, Grandma! It *is* you!"

Peaches moved back for a split second, hoping the girl could refocus. He moved toward Sally again so she would see who he really was this time. Mel handed Peaches a candle; shedding more light certainly wouldn't hurt the situation.

Sally gazed into the rabbit's face. "Grandma? What happened to your teeth?" she muttered like a lunatic Red Riding Hood. She waved a floppy hand at his two large and protruding buckteeth. "We should go to a dentist and grind down those dentures of yours. I may just call you Grandma Beaver from now on." She started to chuckle.

"I am no beaver!" Peaches exclaimed, clearly insulted. "I will try to remember that you are not yourself. Besides, I went to a tooth fairy not too long ago, and he said my two front teeth were perfect."

"Grandma, what happened to your face?" She started to pet his green fur. "Don't worry. This Christmas I'll buy you a set of good razors so you can shave that beard of yours!"

Ryan and Mel laughed, the chuckles a relief valve now that they knew Sally would come to no lasting harm.

Gitchy gently grasped her arm. "I think we should get her to bed."

Sally patted Peaches' head, giggling to herself, "Grandma? What happened to your ears?" she exclaimed. She took her hand quickly away from Peaches' head. "Why are they so long? You told me that your hearing was going bad, but to get these is outrageous!"

Now Peaches was offended. "What's wrong with my ears?"

She lifted her head and screeched. "Oh boy, Grandma! Why did you turn into a bunny?"

She quickly ran to the corner of the room, crouched and huddled. "My grandma's a bunny!"

"Believe me, I am not your grandmother."

"Sally," Ryan said as he approached her. "It's Ryan, remember me?"

She squinted again and seemed to snap back to normal, "Ryan! Where am I? What happened?"

"You drank something that's making you a little hysterical. Are you all right?"

"I think so. Wait." Suddenly the effects kicked back in and she felt a rush of euphoric ecstasy. She jumped up and down and twirled around, dancing by herself.

"My grandma is a bunny! I want to be a bunny!" She twirled closer to Peaches. "Can I touch the pretty bunny? Please can I? I would love to touch the pretty bunny."

"No." Peaches was obviously getting annoyed. "Please do not touch the *pretty bunny*."

Oblivious, Sally threw her hand on top of his furry head and smacked his ear with all her might.

"Ouch!" Peaches exclaimed. "Why, that hurts! Please stop."

Sally didn't notice she'd hurt Peaches and kept petting him over and over. "I like pretty bunnies!"

"Ouch! Stop it, Sally! I mean it!"

"Sally, come on." Ryan grasped her hand and held her.

She looked around frantically. "Ryan? What just happened?"

"My dear," Gitchy said, coming closer to her. "You have drugged yourself with a Lixyworm and are not yourself."

97

"I'll say." Peaches rubbed his bruise on his head. "I haven't been hurt like this since I was captured by foxes a few Cycles back."

"Foxes?" Still dizzy, Sally stumbled onto Peaches stepping on his foot. "What are these foxes like, Grandma?"

Peaches looked around for advice, wondering if he should indulge in encouraging the inebriated behavior. "Well, if you would truly like to know, foxes are brutal creatures that only care for themselves. They live their lives with one goal in mind: to hurt anyone they believe is lower than them. Particularly rabbits. The foxes have been enslaving us for many Cycles. They, like the Witch and Warlock, have some twisted belief that Freewill facilitates their destiny. Their needs and desires come before any. A selfish breed, if you ask me!"

A shadow of humiliation and hatred passed over Sally's face as she was again reminded of the kids at school. "They have no respect for us do they? They couldn't care less about our feelings or needs!"

"What are you talking about?" Mel was baffled and annoyed.

"Sally, are you all right?" Ryan put both hands on her shoulders, but she quickly batted them away, raising her elbows defensively.

"We have been bullied for far too long!" She marched angrily out to the balcony. "This has got to stop!"

She stood upon the balcony, gazing across the busy city. She suddenly cringed with disgust at the thought of foxes enslaving and brutalizing these harmonious creatures. They seemed so peaceful and welcoming, scurrying around so pleasantly. How could anyone do them wrong?

"My fellow rabbits!" Sally yelled from the top of her lungs in her most authoritative voice. "Come gather to me!"

The city suddenly grew silent as her voice resounded through the streets. Rabbits and a few other creatures gathered themselves hastily at the foot of Peaches' balcony, curious as to what this girl had to say.

"My name is Sally. I am the human from another world. The Great Owl has told me that we were sent here to bring peace to your lands!"

"Oh, no." Ryan raced to the door. "What is she doing?"

By the time Ryan and Mel met her on the balcony, it was too late. She had already gathered the audience of the entire city. The residents remained silent, waiting for this prophet to speak her words of wisdom.

"Sally," Ryan whispered. "What are you doing?"

"Don't worry." Sally bobbled her head toward him as her body swayed from side to side, a telltale sign of her altered mental state. "I'll handle this."

She turned back to the crowd and yelled, "I know your pain due to the unfairness put upon you by this world! I have felt it myself in my own world, *but*, in the words of my grandmother, 'We must all stay strong and fight for our right to be ourselves.' No more tyranny from these so-called foxes. I say we fight back! Fight for what is ours!"

The crowd roared with shouts and applause. This was what they had been waiting for: a leader to guide them, a leader to bring hope.

Mel became worried. "Sally, what are you doing? We are not here to start a revolution!"

Ryan turned to Gitchy and Peaches. "We need to get out of here. I don't want her to start anything."

"I think she already has." Gitchy leaned over the balcony to see the rabbits gathering weapons and armor. "I do not believe it is safe for them here anymore, Peaches."

"I agree. Follow me." Peaches pulled Sally as she was cheering on the crowd. "We will take my secret escape route."

"Where are we going?" Sally tripped on her own feet. "I wasn't done yet."

"We are getting out of here before you start more trouble." Ryan picked her up and threw her over his shoulders.

"Oh, fun!" She giggled. "I get a ride, too? What service."

"Up here, all of you!" Peaches opened a secret stairwell from a large bookcase. "This will bring us to the surface."

As they hurried up the stairway, the residents of Rabbit City prepared themselves for a confrontation with the foxes. It did not take much to rile up the already distraught rabbits. All it had taken was a drunken girl venting about her own similar issues.

Chapter VII
The Bandits

A dirty, partially broken wooden carriage traveled down a red cobblestone trail. The buggy was small but able to hold three foxes with four barrels behind them. At the front, in harness and pulling the buggy, were four purple rabbits wrapped in chains. The rabbits were unclothed, bloody, beaten, and tired.

They pulled steadily as the three drunken foxes stood in the carriage, swaying side to side, pushing each other erratically. They slurred their speech as they sang:

"We are the Foxes, the foxes, the foxes,
We are the Foxes of this New-Found Union,
We fight furiously with terror
And do it with pleasure,
We are the Foxes of this New-Found Union!
We are the Foxes, the foxes, the foxes,
We are the Foxes of this New-Found Union,
We sing our loud stories

And praise them with glory,
We are the Foxes of the New-Found Union!
We are the Foxes, the foxes, the foxes,
We are the Foxes of this New-Found Union,
We bring power with one hand,
And swift justice to the land!
We are the Foxes of the New-Found Union!"

After singing a few rounds of their song, they grew tired and sat back down on the wooden bench in the buggy. They wiped their foreheads and chugged their green drinks.

"I have not had this much fun in seasons!" one of them said with a lisp. He held his mug of beer up high and continued, "Cheers to my old friends!"

"Cheers!" they all cried, bumping each other's drinks and taking a few more gulps.

"Hurry, you stupid rabbits!" another yelled. He took a large swig from his mug and set it down.

The rabbits grunted as they towed the foxes and their buggy. Blood ran down their furry chests as they hopped as fast as they could.

The three foxes sat beside each other, laughing and joking, holding their large wooden mugs in each paw. They had orange coats of fur with white on their bellies, hands, and feet. They sat upright and wore sashes around their left shoulders. One had a dark green sash, and the other two were light green. Their eyes were bright yellow, and their rotten teeth were sharp as daggers. Behind each of them was a long, furry orange tail that stood straight up as they sat down. The foxes sat behind their precious cargo: barrels of Bitterleaf Beer, which they were pinching.

"Here's to my very good friends, Bop and Wizzle. May Free-will be with all of us Foxes, and come to you both!" One of the foxes lifted his mug high into the air and hiccupped. A bright green liquid splashed out of his mug as he moved it side to side.

"You are so drunk, Fizzle! I think you should shut up!" one fox said and laughed.

"Shut up, Bop. So are you." Fizzle punched him.

Fizzle and Bop slapped each other around and wrestled on top of the buggy. Wizzle moved in between the two and said, "Do I always have to break you two up?"

"Sorry, Wizzle." Bop sat down.

"Try to sober up! If the Duke knew we were drinking on the job, he would seriously kill us." Wizzle rubbed one paw against his dark green sash.

"Sorry, boss." Fizzle shook his head rapidly, trying to sober up. Fizzle took another swig of his green beer. "I really don't know why we're always assigned the stupid jobs. I'm sure there are better things than delivering the Duke's beer!"

"I am sure that if war ever breaks out again, we will be the first to be deployed," Wizzle replied.

"That would be the life," Bop added. "Maybe we could then do real work like fight the rabbits, beavers, and birds." Bop took the whip and struck the rabbits.

"Rabbits are useless!" Fizzle agreed as he poured another mug of beer. "What I think we need is some excitement. Let's see how fast this buggy can go!" He whipped the rabbits harder and yelled, "Faster! Faster!"

"Yay!" Bop and Wizzle clapped their paws with excitement.

The rabbits hopped faster and faster as they pulled the buggy behind them. Their bodies never grew accustomed to the constant whipping, and each stinging strike felt like the first. The buggy dashed down the red cobblestone trail as the foxes drank their beer. Unexpectedly, a small figure appeared and stood in the center of the trail.

"Watch out!" a voice cried.

The rabbits' eyes widened as they tried to swerve around it. It was too late; the rabbits tumbled to the ground while the buggy toppled over. The foxes leaped off the buggy as the barrels crashed to the ground.

***

It had almost been a tock since the travelers had left Peaches' place. Worried the inhabitants of Rabbit City were following, they hurried as fast as they could toward the end of the secret tunnel. They were not afraid of the preparing army that Sally had riled up, only nervous that they would be trapped in the middle of a battle.

Gitchy opened up the secret grass-covered rabbit hole exit from Rabbit City as the other four followed. "Sally, dear, which direction does your compass direct us to go?"

Ryan set her down from his shoulders onto a red cobblestone trail and took a deep breath. He was quite pleased with himself for carrying her up the entire tunnel. He'd missed football practice, so this was a good substitute.

Sally looked around, confused. "What's going on? Where are we?"

"Don't you remember?" Mel laughed.

"No. Why? All I remember is exploring Peaches' place. And why do I have this pounding headache?"

"My dear." Peaches laughed. "We will just have to tell you another time."

"Yes, more importantly," Gitchy said, stepping over to Sally, "where does your compass say to go?"

She pulled out the compass and squinted with her bloodshot eyes. "*That way.*"

They all looked down the forest, which looked dark and dangerous. It had an eerie feel and a silence that would spook even the most hideous and fearless of creatures.

"Where do you suppose the compass is leading us?" Sally rubbed her head.

"If we were to follow its direction, it seems we are heading toward Foxtown," Peaches huffed.

"Will we be all right?" Mel worried. After listening to the stories about foxes and how angry the rabbits below were, he did not want to be around any of them.

"We will be fine," Gitchy assured him. "We will detour around Foxtown."

They reached an area where the trees had been chopped down, and the life essence of the forest began to diminish. The forest was dying before their eyes.

"Licklelake Forest was once the most beautiful forests in Enchantas, but it has become more desolate each season," Gitchy said as they gazed at the empty patches of trees.

"Exactly." Peaches sneered. "Since the foxes came to our land, they chopped the forest down for themselves. Industry for their 'New-Found Union' they called it. The foxes took what they could from the land and made their own buildings and bridges. Their Duke makes us pay taxes. For Cycles we have bartered for our foods and clothing. We have no use for currency!"

As they walked farther down the red cobblestone trail, the absence of trees made the scenery even more dark and threatening. The only light emanated from the pale blue moon shining above.

"A rebellion broke out," Gitchy continued to explain, "but the foxes were very well organized and strong. We had no chance at winning. A treaty was then formed with our grand Sage."

"I still believe the treaty was impractical," Peaches argued. The kids could tell this was a touchy subject for him. "We did not get anything out of it!"

"Peaches, try thinking positively. Cumberlake Valley will remain untouched."

"Yes, but they executed many rebel prisoners and enslaved almost all of the rest!"

A rumbling sound erupted, and the group stopped to invest-igate. They could hear what sounded like three voices coming toward them, but the darkness of the forest prevented them from seeing anything.

"Don't worry." Gitchy turned and smiled. "I'll shed some light upon us." He rubbed his hat and chanted:

"Mystic Forest, Late at Night;
Turn these Leaves-"

Before Gitchy could finish his chant, the noise became louder and the ground began to shake. Peaches' ears lifted and then suddenly dropped as he saw a carriage hurtling toward them. "Watch out!" He tackled the three teens, throwing them into a bush behind them.

Gitchy turned to see what was coming, but it was too late; four rabbits tumbled to the ground, and the buggy they had been dragging toppled over him. Three foxes leaped into a bush as barrels of beer came crashing toward the other four. They dodged the barrels by leaping back onto the cobblestone trail.

"Gitchy!" Sally rushed toward the toppled buggy. His body lay on the ground, his neck twisted backwards. "He's dead!"

Tears streamed down her face as she dropped to the ground.

The three foxes stumbled back onto the trail. "What are you thinking?" Wizzle screamed. "There is traffic on this road!"

"You killed him!" Sally shrieked back.

"Whom did we kill?" Bop asked as they walked up to the body.

"A gnome?" Wizzle didn't seem worried at all.

He turned to whisper to the others as a deep, scratchy voice came from out of nowhere. "What is going on here?" it asked.

Another fox in a blue cloak stepped out of the bushes. His eyes were sharp and his posture intimidating. "Fizzle, Wizzle, and Bop." He shook his head as he stepped over to the broken carriage. "Is this your mess?"

"No, Sheriff, sir!" Wizzle replied as he frantically tried to think of a good lie. "These bandits stole our carriage of beer and ran over this gnome!"

"What?" cried Ryan as he and Mel approached the sheriff. "That's not—"

"Silence!" the Sheriff hushed them. "Stealing property from our Duke is a serious offense, but nothing is more heinous than killing an innocent Enchantian. This incident will certainly dampen our peace treaty with the Vallians."

The other three foxes nodded in agreement.

"This crime is punishable by death of course," he turned toward the other three foxes. "Chain them and take them to the dungeon!"

"What?" Ryan objected. "No! This wasn't our fault."

"Peaches! Help!" Sally cried. Peaches was down the trail freeing the other four rabbits.

"I am truly sorry, Sally." Peaches unlocked the last rabbit and hopped away. "I warned you all!"

"What about them, sir?" Bop pointed at the escaping rabbits.

"I am sorry!" Peaches bellowed behind him as the five rabbits scurried away.

"We will deal with those rebels later," the Sheriff snarled as he tied a chain around Ryan's neck. "These bandits must be punished."

"Yes sir!" they all replied, covering the captives' mouths with rope gags.

"Now march!" The Sheriff kicked Mel. "Hurry, you sly bandits!"

The chains were tight around their necks and wrists as they continued their journey as prisoners, terrified and unsure of what was to happen to them next.

Chapter VIII
The Dungeon

The roar of a marching army echoed in the prison cell. John jumped up to the barred window and watched hundreds of red-cloaked foxes marching down the red cobblestone street. The soldiers looked proud with their shields covering their fronts and their spears clutched up high. Each one of them snarled with hatred; their yellow eyes burned like flame and their rotting teeth stuck out of their pointy snouts as they hissed in anger. Their mouths dripped with drool, and they grunted with each step, intimidating any weary foe who happened by.

John slid back down to the floor and kicked a pile of dust underneath him. His frustration had not lessened after the Leprechaun had tricked him and sold him into slavery. His shirt was torn, and there were scratches covering his face and arms. Only hours before, he had been forced to fight in a gladiator arena as hundreds of drunken foxes watched.

The room was dark; the only light was a scant gleam from the small window. The walls and floor were cobbled rock, uncomfortable for anyone to sit, much less sleep. He could hear screams of agony, suffering, and despair echoing outside the locked wooden door. He sat down on the bumpy stone floor and began to think about his life at home.

He thought hard about his sister and was very concerned about how his dad might be treating her. Ever since his mother had left, his father had been drinking more and more excessively. When he drank, he became angry and violent. John was always the one to step in. He was the strong one, always protecting his sister. Now that he was gone, he was afraid his father would take his anger out on her.

He lay back, wondering what was to come to him. Were these foxes going to kill him? The arena was punishment enough. He fought a soldier who was said to be there because he'd missed his guard duties the previous day. Was this to be his fate, to die alone in a gladiator arena? He chuckled at the irony of dying alone. He had spent his entire life so far as a rebellious loner. He had friends, but they were just party companions, not real friends who would care what would happen to him. Mel came to mind; he seemed like a person John could trust. However, Mel was not with him now, and that was only because of John's stubbornness. He'd chosen to leave the group and find his own way home.

A sudden compassionate sadness came over him as he thought about Sally and how he had treated her so cruelly. If someone had treated his sister like that, he would have beaten him or her to a pulp. That was probably why Ryan had stood up for her. John wondered if he would ever see them again, because he truly wanted to apologize. He was never comfortable with apologies, always feeling as if he was in the right with any decision he made and never looking back, even when those decisions hurt others.

This present experience humbled him, and a new set of morals was forming for John.

As he contemplated his past behavior, feeling guilt and remorse, a guard strolled by and snarled. John reached into his pocket and lit a cigarette. Suddenly the door opened, and a light-green-cloaked fox stepped in and, surprisingly, shoved Sally to the floor.

"Stay in there," the fox snapped as he shut the door behind them.

"You're alive!" John stood up, relief and excitement flooding through his body.

Sally's surprised reaction was far from ecstatic, however. "And I thought it couldn't get worse. Now I'm stuck in here with you," she huffed.

John ignored the comment, hiding his relief that he was no longer alone.

"Where are the other two?" He tried to help her up.

"Why do you care?" She pushed his arms away and rubbed her head. It still hurt; an after-effect from drinking the wine. "They were put into another cell."

She sat up and put her head between her knees. John began to feel awkward, as helping others was a foreign concept to him.

"All I want is to go home!" she sobbed.

"Join the club." He pouted and sat quietly across from her. He put his hand on her knee and spoke softly, "Look...I—I'm really sorry for being a jerk earlier at school."

She slowly lifted her head and gave him a hesitant smile. As she took in the veracity and sincerity in his eyes, she was reminded of her grandmother. *No matter what anyone does to hurt you, you must always learn to forgive and forget,* her grandmother's voice rang in her head.

She smiled put her hand on his and said, "Thank you. You are forgiven." She wiped a tear from her cheek and stood up. "So what happened to you?"

"Don't even ask." John sighed. He was embarrassed by how he had been tricked and abducted. His pride was a little shattered, so he didn't want to talk about it.

"What's going to happen to us?" Sally walked to the door. "We need to find a way to escape."

"No use," John replied. "This place is locked tight."

"Why would Fate put us here?" She opened her compass, which pointed toward the window.

"Now you're sounding like one of them." John said with irritation in his voice.

"What if it's true? You know, Fate."

"The problem with Fate is that nothing should control our own destiny but ourselves."

"Either way, I don't get how we got here in the first place. I wish my grandmother were here."

"Why's that?"

"She's a really strong, independent woman, and she always seems to know what to do or say."

John smirked. "That sounds like my mom." He sighed. "Probably why she left my dad."

With that said, a comfortable conversation grew between the two. They were finally becoming friends.

***

Down the prison hall in a similar cell, Ryan and Mel paced quietly, contemplating what to do next.

"This place reeks!" Ryan kicked the wooden door.

"This reminds me of the detention hall last year." Mel put his hands on the cold stone wall. "Have you ever had detention?"

"Of course not!"

"Well," Mel snorted. "I got into trouble last year for super-gluing Mrs. Phelps to her desk. That was hilarious!"

Ryan suddenly remembered that incident from last year. He was not impressed. "That wasn't funny at all! I had to help scrape her arms and butt from that."

"Wow, that makes it even funnier."

"We're in high school now. I don't see how that could be funny. You should grow up."

"Gosh." Mel shook his head in annoyance. "You sound like my stepfather."

"I doubt it. You should realize that high school isn't all about juvenile pranks and getting in trouble."

"I disagree! High school should be all about having fun and trying to get away with things. Wow, you really sound like my stepfather."

In a bizarre way, that hit home for Ryan. As he thought about his own parents, he resented being compared to any parental figure. "Well, I guess we just have different ideas about what is fun."

"I guess so."

"Hey, freaks," a menacing voice called out from the small window.

They looked up to see a reddish-orange furry face with ugly jagged teeth staring at them. He looked as if he were a prisoner himself, because he was so beat up. The fox opened the door and tossed a large, purple furry leg onto the floor.

"What the heck is that?" Mel squirmed up against the wall. Flies hovered around the leg as the stench of it filled the cell instantly.

"Dinner!" The fox growled as he bit fiercely through another leg. "Day-old rabbit foot!"

"We're not going to eat this!" Ryan kicked the leg out the door and charged the fox.

The fox reacted quickly, tripping Ryan, causing him to fall to the floor. "Aha! A feisty one, eh?" The fox picked up Ryan, holding his arms behind his back. "I have the perfect spot to bring you."

Ryan tried to squirm his way out of the fox's clutches, but it was no use. Another guard came up and seized one of his arms. The foxes pulled him out to the hallway and punched him a few times, but Ryan became tired and stopped fighting back. They dragged him down three flights of stairs until they came to another doorway. The sounds of excited, violent chanting came faintly from the other side. As one of the guards unlocked the door, the atrocious howling became louder and louder. Surrounding the room were hundreds of ferocious foxes banging their paws and wooden mugs of green beer against a steel-caged arena. The arena was about as large as half of a basketball court, and there was blood smeared all over the stone floor.

"Get him, Trox!" a cheering fan called out to the fearless fox.

An unclothed, bloody red rabbit hobbled around, trying to avoid the vicious and dominant fox. The rabbit fell to the ground as Trox slowly strolled toward it, swinging a spiked ball and chain over his head. Trox wore a metal vest with an armored helmet covering the top half of his face and ears. He stopped to observe and enjoy the crowd, which was taking much pleasure in his brutal and cruel victory. He lifted his other, most bloody paw. The crowd knew what he was about to do and counted his fingers.

"One!" The crowd cheered.

"Two!" The crowd roared with anticipation.

"THREE!" The crowd was shaking the cage and screaming for the kill.

Without a breath, the fox whipped the ball over the rabbit's head, spewing pieces of furry skull, ears, and blood into the crowd.

Ryan's eyes widened in sheer terror and disgust. "You're not expecting me to get in there, are you?"

"Yes we are!" The fox snarled as another opened the cage door and pushed Ryan in. "Good luck!"

Ryan fell to the stone floor. He lifted his arm, sickened by the amount of blood covering it. He looked over to his opponent with panic. Trox threw the ball and chain to the ground and sneered as drool slithered down his mouth. Ryan stood up and looked around; realizing his only way out would be to beat this treacherous fox.

Trox didn't waste any time, his adrenaline had already been pumping. He hurtled himself toward the boy, digging his claws into Ryan's back. Ryan screamed in agony as the fox bit into his right shoulder. Ryan punched him in his side as hard as he could. The fox yelped and let go of his fearsome grip.

"Another spirited one, eh?" He winkled his pointed snout and charged the boy again.

This time Ryan was ready and quickly moved out of the way, tripping the fox so that he slammed into the side of the cage. Trox shook his head, dizzy for a moment, then stood up to retaliate. "That was a lucky one, you freak."

"Bring it on!"

Trox leaped at Ryan a third time when suddenly Ryan's wrestling instincts kicked in, and he threw Trox to the ground in a very maneuverable chokehold. Trox was trapped with no way out. Ryan held onto the gladiator with all his might, not once giving in to his squirming and pleading. Ryan slammed Trox into the ground one last time, knocking him unconscious.

"Kill, kill, kill!" the crowd chanted.

Ryan looked at them, perplexed. Did they really want him to kill their own kind? Ryan walked quietly back to the door and yelled. "Let me out! I beat him!"

"Boo!" The crowd roared and clanged their mugs, but the guards opened the door.

"Let me go."

"Fine!" One guard chuckled as the other punched Ryan in the back of the head.

Ryan was instantly knocked unconscious and dragged back to his cell.

***

The atmosphere in the room had not changed. It was still dark and gloomy, but John and Sally laughed hysterically as they talked. If one were to look at them and not their surroundings, they would have never guessed that they were locked in a dungeon cell. Surprisingly, as they got to know each other a little more, they found their differences amusing.

"This might sound weird to you, but I like school." Sally laughed. "I really don't like the people, but I still love going to class."

"Really? You have got to be kidding!" John shook his head. "I'm the opposite. I hate my classes but like hanging with my friends. Besides, I think most of the teachers hate me."

"They don't hate you." Sally squinted and shook her head. "They probably want you to work harder."

"No." John smirked. "I really think they hate me."

"I doubt that, John. I think you're looking at school the totally wrong way."

"What do you think is so great about school?"

"I like knowing I've accomplished something every day. It's a good feeling."

"I kind of wish I had that feeling." He looked down. "I don't know. Maybe I'm just too lazy to do homework and pay attention."

"I was sick for one week. I didn't do homework and I got lazy," she said. "You know, I think it becomes a habit not to do homework. Once you start slacking, you get too overwhelmed and don't want to start up again. That's why I don't slack off. I stay ahead of the game."

"Yeah, but I'm not good at anything. I hate math. I hate science and history. I do like art, though."

"That's a start. Why don't you try to be creative with your homework?"

"How can I be creative in classes like math?"

"It's all in your imagination, John."

"I don't know." He shrugged his shoulders. "I think you're thinking a little too deep here."

"You should get a tutor or something. You know—" she started to say, but John interrupted her.

"I don't want a tutor." John shook his head. "You know Sally, you kind of remind me of my sister."

"Thanks, I think."

"Yeah, it's a compliment. Again, I'm really sorry about being a jerk earlier. I'm not the kind of person to apologize, but I think that you deserve it."

She smiled as she looked into his eyes. Her eyes watered slightly as she watched him lift his head slowly and started to smile with her.

"We're friends, right?" he asked.

"Of course."

"I think Fate must have put us here to make amends with each other."

"I can't believe you actually believe in that Fate crap. Like I said, the problem with that belief is that nothing should control our own destiny but ourselves."

"You sound like the Witch and Warlock," a voice familiar to Sally whispered from the window.

John turned to see a fuzzy green creature putting his head through the bars.

"Who the heck are you?" he asked.

"That's Peaches!" Sally jumped up, excited and happy to see the big rabbit. "I thought you left us back there!"

"I did, and I am truly sorry for that, Sally." Peaches sighed with guilty remorse. "Your presence in Enchantas has started something spectacular! Rumors have spread around the Valley and hundreds of Enchantians have come to rise up against the foxes. Fate has truly turned the tide of our world."

"Can you help us get out?"

"Already on that. Bubbles is coming to open the door."

"Bubbles?" John shook his head in wonderment.

"He is our most precious ally. Bubbles is a covert snuffball trained to break into highly secured places."

"Oh, great, a snuffball." John grumbled, remembering his last encounter.

The wooden door swung open. A larger-than-usual, black snuffball rolled in, urgently whispering in a dark, stern voice, "Hurry! We must find the others." Bubbles was the deepest shade of ebony and as large as an exercise ball they use in gym class or a weight room.

"Follow me." Sally ran out the door and down a flight of stairs.

She opened another wooden door to find a wounded Ryan and cellmate Mel sitting forlornly on the hard floor. "Come on, guys. We're getting out of here."

It was a struggle for Ryan to get up, but he tried to push past the pain of his injuries. In the meantime, Bubbles rapidly rolled around to all of the remaining cells, releasing all of the non-fox prisoners.

As they caught up to John, Ryan glared at him, still fuming from their earlier confrontation and John's idiotic idea to strike out on his own. He felt like making a snarky comment about how well that had worked out but quickly brushed it off. There was no time for a war of words; it was more important to escape.

"Hey, John." Mel smiled as they all ran down the hall. "Long time no see."

John grinned back as he tried to catch his breath; smoking was once again his enemy.

A red-cloaked guard turned the corner in front of the escapees, screeching, "Stop right there!"

Before the guard could point his spear at them, Bubbles bounced up and knocked his head against the stone wall. The guard dropped like a rock. Ryan grasped his spear.

They sprinted up yet another flight of stairs, finally reaching the front gate. Three guards braced for the encounter. "Hold this line," one guard snarled, staring at the group with his piercing yellow eyes. "They must not escape!"

John and Ryan charged the outer two while Bubbles slammed into the middle guard. It proved an effective strategy. In seconds the guards were splayed on the ground.

As they opened the door to the courtyard and the street outside, hundreds of hostile fox soldiers turned to sneer contemptuously, victoriously.

"Great. What do you suppose we do now?" Mel muttered. Without warning, the large iron gates of the town crashed open, and legions of large, fuzzy balls rolled into the courtyard. The balls were four times the size of the foxes and easily crushed them as they rolled freely around the crowd.

"We're being attacked!" one of the soldiers cried. "Rebels!"

After the large group of snuffballs rolled through, decimating the troops, another wave of warriors followed: a rabbit battalion armed with long swords and turtle-shell shields. From the sky above came swarms of fluitenducks, abnormal-looking birds with the feet and bills of a duck and a large, pouched potbelly, which carried vegetables. As they flew over the skies above, they hurled exploding powder-filled vegetables at the scattering fox soldiers fleeing through the streets. The vegetables screamed horrifically, animated missiles plummeting to death, exploding over the soldiers. A few brave foxes tried to stay and fight, but their loyalty was futile. They were overpowered in a matter of tacks. They retreated toward the Duke's castle.

"Come," Bubbles told the kids. "I must get you out of here!"

"Heck no!" John, who had managed to acquire a spear, turned back toward the remnants of the battle. "I want to finish this fight!"

"John." Ryan limped toward him. "Let's go."

"Why?"

"Come," Bubbles rolled up between the two, urgently imploring. "We must hurry!"

"Fine. But I really hate those foxes." John stayed with the group as they ran toward the city gates.

A doddering old fox frantically blocked their way, shakily pointing his walking cane at them and exclaiming, "Rebels! These four are rebels! Guards, stop them! G—" At that moment, a large blue snuffball efficiently steamrollered over the rebellious curmudgeon.

"Talk about close calls!" Sally yelled.

"I know," Mel, said, with an involuntary shudder.

Behind them the legions of rabbits and snuffballs flowed like a rapid river in the direction of the castle. The sky above was filled with fluitenducks and howling vegetables. The foxes were defeated, no doubt.

As they distanced themselves from town, the loud thundering sound of the battle and accompanying death cries became fainter.

"I've never been that close to war before." Sally looked at the skyline, where huge clouds of smoke were rising up through the air. Foxtown was on fire. "This is scary!"

As they scrambled up a small hill, Ryan turned to Bubbles. "Where are you taking us?"

"Don't worry. You will be safe."

As they reached the hilltop, they paused underneath a massive, turquoise and green-leafed oak-like tree. A short-haired white snuffball bounced up the hill.

"Rollaround. How goes the battle?" Bubbles asked.

"The foxes are nearly defeated and have retreated into the castle," he announced in a deep voice, rolling to a stop in front of Sally, Mel, Ryan, and John. "I am Rollaround, Captain of Fate's Army. I would like to personally thank you for bringing hope to our kind."

"Hope?" Sally asked, deeply moved. "What about poor Gitchy the Gnome? I wouldn't call his death any kind of hope. Why did he have to die?"

"Gitchy knew he had an important role in Fate's plan," said another deep voice from behind them. The Great Owl stepped out of the shadows. "Without the death of Gitchy, word of your arrival would not have spread so quickly through the land. Hence, this rebellious battle was sparked very quickly. Gitchy's death was not in vain. He was a great apprentice as well as a great friend. He will always be remembered as a hero."

"So are we done?" Mel asked. "Can we go home now?"

"I am afraid not, my boy." The Great Owl took a deep breath. "Our war has just begun. We have a long way to go before our lands are restored. You do not need to fight this war for us. Only inspire our lost and hopeless allies to join our cause."

"What?" Mel sulked. "What more do we need to do?"

"Patience, Mel," whispered Ryan.

"Do not worry, Mel. You will return home." The owl turned to Ryan. "Ryan and John, I would like you both to meet with the Gargoyles."

"Gargoyles?" John's eyes widened.

"Yes. The Gargoyles were once the Nightwatchers, the guardians of the Knights of Minerton. If we are to ever win the lands of Enchantas back from the Witch and Warlock, we need their help.

They have lost more hope than anyone of us combined. At the time of the Crusades, the Gargoyles blamed themselves for failing to protect our founders. When the banishment of the Knights came, the gargoyles secluded themselves in dishonor and humiliation. I realize now that it was vindictive and unforgiving to place all of the blame on them. I was also at fault." He sighed and continued, "That was a long time ago, and now we must move forward to restore our lands."

"Are you sure they will meet with us?" Ryan interrupted.

"Yes, they know as well as I that our fate rests in the hands of the four humans prophesied to save our land. If they meet with you, they will be much more willing to join our cause."

"Do I really have to go with him?" John asked, his reluctance clear. Both guys still held a grudge against each other.

"Yes, John," Owl replied. "I have another mission for Mel and Sally."

Bubbles rolled up to the owl and spit out a small chest. It magically opened and four bracelets floated from it.

"These magical bracelets were once owned by four of the Knights, they were given to me many ages ago." The owl nodded, and the bracelets moved forward of their own volition, each stopping to hover before one of the young humans. "They were crafted from the finest Lixy Dust and metals Enchantians had ever mined. They are very powerful."

The bracelets were made of sparkling gold, each with an emerald gem at the center of the wristband. They were V-shaped, coming to a point in the middle of the top of the hand as well as a V shape coming to a point on the underside of the forearm. Dragon engravings glittered on top. As they donned the fabulous, magical pieces, each felt a sense of rejuvenation. Sally's knee stopped hurting; Ryan's and John's scars quickly vanished.

"These bracelets were originally created by the Knights out of respect for all living creatures of Enchantas. It is said that humans were at the top of the food chain in their world, and the Knights did not want that to happen here. Among other things like bringing protection and magic, these bracelets will keep you healthy and nourished; you will never be hungry, and every scratch or scrape will be healed—within a reasonable time period of course."

"How does the magic work?" Mel asked excitedly.

"In times of danger, your Persona Weapon will emerge for protection. They are different for everyone, so I really cannot enlighten you on that. As for Magic, the bracelets have the power to control the four elements of nature: wind, water, land, and fire. Each creature in possession of a bracelet can control one element more than any of the others. Nevertheless, it may take many Cycles to master these elements, and I do not have time to teach."

"So how do we find the Gargoyles?" Ryan asked, admiring his bracelet.

"You must follow the blue cobblestone trail. That should lead the way. However"—the Great Owl pulled out a scroll—"given that Sally and Mel will be using Fate's compass, here is a map to the old Minerton Castle. The map is very old, so some of the checkpoints may be out of date." He pulled out another scroll. "Also, please give this letter to the gargoyles. It is of a personal matter."

"Okay." Ryan grabbed the map and the letter. "I will. Thanks."

"Now, Mel and Sally." He turned toward them. "I would like you both to visit Gitchy's wife and bring this letter. Again, it is of a personal matter."

"Sure." Sally took out her compass.

"Yes, good. You remembered your compass. It is your most valuable asset. Follow it carefully."

"Yes, sir." Sally gripped it tightly.

"The compass should direct you two down a green cobblestone trail. This trail should lead you to the Gnome Village." The owl took a deep breath and spread his enormous wings. "I must go now."

The intimidating size of the Great Owl multiplied as he ruffled his feathers. "Rollaround and Bubbles, thank you for all of your help. Please go finish what you have started and bring the Duke to my Redwood so we can reevaluate our treaty."

"Yes, sir!" they said, jauntily rolling back down the hill toward the remnants of the battle.

"Good luck, my young humans." The Great Owl flapped his wings, creating a wind tunnel beneath him. The four of them were flattened to the ground by the velocity and strength of it. "I hope to see you all soon."

As he flew into the distant sky, the four teens stood up, brushing themselves off.

"We should probably pick a meeting place," said Ryan.

"After we deliver our letter to Gitchy's family, we will meet you at the gargoyles'," Mel suggested. "We have the compass. It should guide us there, no problem."

"Good idea." Ryan started to walk. "The quicker we get this done, the faster we can go home."

"Sounds like a plan." John rushed to get ahead of Ryan.

"See you guys." Sally called as she and Mel walked toward the green trail.

John smiled as he waved to them both.

Ryan gave John a puzzled look, wondering why Sally was being so kind to him. He remembered how much of a jerk John had been to both of them. Considering the business at hand, he shrugged it off as the two continued to travel down the blue cobblestone trail.

Chapter IX
The Gypsy

The sky was dark gray and the sun brick red behind the smoky gray clouds. Stone mountains enfolded a gigantic black castle, much taller than any of the mountains surrounding it. The land between the castle and mountains was empty and desolate. The air smelled of burning sulfur. Smoke covered the land like a thick fog. A few dead trees were scattered across the landscape; clearly, not many could survive the polluted air.

In the second highest tower of the castle, a young human girl stood out on a balcony, gazing over the land. She was tall and thin; her shoulder-length hair was straight, brunette shot with light blonde highlights. Her eyes were bright purple, gleaming and hauntingly evil. Her stunning face was pale from the lack of sun, but even that could not diminish her beauty. The loneliness she felt could not be seen behind her poised appearance. She seemed confident and assertive. To herself and her Godparents, her name was Lexis, but to the fearful Enchantians of the land, she was known as the wicked Gypsy Princess.

She wore a dark green velvet dress with a dark purple hood wrapped around the back of her head. The dress sleeves flowed wide and long, flaring at the wrists. Dark purple high-heeled boots, visible in the thigh-high slit up the right side of the long skirt, climbed up past her knees.

She was a beautiful young lady around twenty human years of age. She had lived in the castle for many Cycles and was never permitted to leave. Her Godparents, the Witch and Warlock, forbade it. They were neurotic—paranoid—and did not want her to be influenced from the outside world by the ideals of Fate. Chance and Freewill were the lessons she had been taught every day since she had been abruptly transported to Enchantas.

Ages ago in her home world, she'd lived peacefully with her uncle. She had just graduated high school, beginning her new life as a flourishing young woman. She had just begun a new job as a secretary at her uncle's law firm when one day, on her way home from work, a portal opened, and she was forcefully transported into Enchantas. The Witch and Warlock found and adopted her as if she were their own daughter. She was very thankful at the time; however, as time passed, loneliness consumed her.

Over the Cycles she became obsessed with finding a true friend. She had many great friends in her past life. Now she had only the Godparents and hired guards to keep her company. She could never share her true feelings with anyone. What she wanted was a true friend who would listen to her hopes and dreams. She longed for a companion or someone to be there for her when she was sad or lonely. Her obsession became severe, and she blamed herself for her secluded life.

Not long ago, she'd come across a room of mirrors on the other wing of the castle. She would sit in this room for tocks as though the comfort of others surrounded her, even if they were only reflections of herself. One day, by chance, she discovered that the mirrors could teleport her anywhere in Enchantas, though out of fear her Godparents would find out, she had only used them a few times. She was terrified of being locked in the dungeon like the rest of the traitors, as her Godparents called them. The Witch and Warlock would curse any being who didn't have the same beliefs, either locking them in the dungeon or executing them in the courtyard.

There was a bright side; her Godparents had taught her magic. She wasn't as evil as they were, but her malevolence came in dissimilar ways. Over time she became avaricious and intolerable of all the creatures of Enchantas, only because they were free to do what they wished. She despised her Godparents for preaching Chance and Freewill, while hypocritically prohibiting her from exploring and making friends. Her jealousy of their army was also significant, for she believed they loved them more than her.

Curiosity triumphed over fear on the few occasions she'd traveled via the magical mirrors. During these times she'd come across many travelers and struggled to befriend them. She had lost all knowledge of hospitality, and intimidation was her only method of communication. It was obvious to all but her, and the friend-ships didn't last long. When her patience quickly grew thin, she'd become irate and fearful. In turn, she'd turn them into stone statues so that they would forever accompany her whenever she wished. Rumors of a mystical Gypsy princess bustled over the land, dimin-ishing her chances to befriend more Enchantians. Nevertheless, she believed it was not herself, but the reputation of her God-parents that frightened the Enchantians away.

After many Seasons of trial and error, she grew tired of traveling and accepted the fact that she would forever remain alone. She hired a few servants to traverse Enchantas and return to relay stories of the outside world.

She left her balcony, striding through a large set of bay doors twice her size. The two doors, trimmed in gold and fitted with beautiful stained glass in the middle, swung open, slamming against the walls as she stormed into the dark room.

She lit a candle with a flick of the wrist and sat on her bed, which had a bright red thin-clothed canopy draped from the ceiling. Her bed itself was covered in fluffy blue pillows and was as soft as a pile of feathers. A black brick wall surrounded the room, effectively imprisoning her. It was empty except for a few books on a shelf, an hourglass filled with glittering Lixy Dust, and an old wooden desk holding a glass volleyball-sized orb.

She glanced around and sighed. She wished for her life to be a little more than a few books, a bed, and a bunch of mirrors. Some days she'd lie on her bed and wonder what it would be like to have true friends again.

Suddenly, there was a knock at her door, and she leaped out of bed, wondering who it was. She never had visitors aside from her Godparents.

She turned the knob of an old wooden door slightly and asked in a soft yet scratchy voice, "Who is it?"

"Gypsy Madam, it's me, Slippy!" a small squeaky voice called out from the other side. "Please open the door."

Wonderful! she thought to herself and excitedly opened the door. She yearned for the days when she could hear a story of the outside world.

"Thank you madam." The blue worm slithered rapidly across the stone floor. "I'm afraid the Imps will eat me!"

"The imps won't eat you, and neither will the gremlins." She chuckled as she closed the door. "What news from the land?"

"Yes, madam." He slithered up the bed. "You promised payment."

"You will receive the usual once you tell me," she replied with an irritated voice. "Now, what news?"

Slippy was suddenly intimidated by the sound of her voice and quickly continued. "Oh Madam, you wouldn't believe what my eyes have seen the other day." He gulped. "I saw four humans in the Valley!"

"Humans?" she repeated, shocked. "Are you sure of this?"

"Yes, they had the same skin as you!"

This is wonderful! she thought. *The perfect chance to befriend another of her kind. Other humans!*

She sat at her desk and rubbed her soft hands on the glass orb. "I need to see for myself," she muttered. "My crystal ball will show me."

The crystal ball had been a gift from her Godparents, a part of one of her lessons in magic. She closed her eyes and put both of her hands around the sphere.

"Crystal essence of this Sphere,
Show me who is drawing near."

The crystal ball illuminated into a twirling spectrum of colors before an image appeared. Slip jumped up onto the desk and watched the movement of colors, which cleared to reveal Ryan and John walking down the blue cobblestone trail.

"Are these the ones you saw?" she asked the blue worm.

Slippy slithered closer to the ball and opened his eyes. "Why yes! Yes it is! They were in my orchard eating my fruits!"

"These are very handsome young men." She stood up and stumbled toward her closet. "I must meet them. What are they like? Did you talk to them?"

"I—" Slippy was going to explain when he was rudely interrupted.

"Never mind!" She grabbed a purple bottle of potion and gave it to the worm. "I'd like to find out for myself."

"Thank you!" The worm smiled, wrapping his long body around the bottle.

"Good job, Slippy," she added absentmindedly, which was in fact the first compliment she had ever given to a servant.

Slippy took his bottle and slid down the outside castle walls. He wiggled away with his payment, happy and content.

The excited Gypsy continued to watch the two boys. She couldn't wait to meet them. She rubbed the crystal ball again, but this time an image of Sally appeared. Sally looked sad as she walked down the green cobblestone trail. Immediately, the Gypsy mourned for her. Even though she did not know why Sally was sad, she felt as if she could relate to her misery.

"This girl looks sad," she mumbled to herself. "I must meet her. We could help each other."

Excited by this opportunity to make a new friend, she rubbed the ball briskly, but the colors cleared and the image faded. She glided back to the door and slowly opened it.

Out of nowhere, an imp trooper stood upright, staring straight up at her since he was a foot and a half shorter. His sordid, brown scaly skin was oily and disgusting. Although she was immune to the breed's stench, they were always an annoyance to her. His arms and legs were muscular, but his knees were bent the opposite way, allowing him to jump higher than any other Enchantian. His eyes were like black beads, and his small, pointy nose wheezed when he breathed. His pointed, floppy ears drooped toward his shoulders. Imps also possessed small bat-shaped wings, which helped them hover and descend slowly. Their sharp, triangular, scale-tipped tails helped to defend from behind. The imp had the characteristic claws of his kind, sharp as fillet knives. He carried a shield in one arm and a small spear in the other.

The princess stared back into the soldier's beady eyes. "May I help you?"

"Madam Princess. The masters Witch and Warlock are summoning you to dinner. They expect you to come in one tick."

"Tell them I'll be there in a few ticks," she pulled the door shut behind her with a bang, pouting out loud, "I swear, they have no patience!"

As the imp accompanied her down the hallway, a gremlin trailed behind. Gremlins were a half-foot taller than her and had slippery green skin. They didn't have wings or large muscles. Their legs were long and skinny. They wore green, pointed helmets, handy for ramming enemies. Their feet were as long as their lean calves, which made them very fast runners. The gremlins were the ground troops of the army and were among the fleetest runners in all of Enchantas. Their heads were shaped like a frog's, but they had long pointy ears. The protruding flaps weren't floppy like the imps'; they pointed outward, away from their squinty, black, fearless eyes. Their noses were much longer than the imps', and their sense of smell was remarkable. A characteristically wicked smile showed the gremlin's sharp teeth and long, orange, virulent tongue, which could stretch out to thirty feet, spewing poisonous venom on any living being it touched. Their arms were long and gangly; their fingers sprouted with razor like claws. Like their imp counterparts, each gremlin was armed with a short dagger and a small shield. They wore the green-and-black-armored suits that protected every infantry warrior. The armor was especially light so as not to hinder their speed.

The Gypsy Princess dismissively shoved the imp aside, stomping past him down the long spiral staircase. With royal indifference, she never noticed any of the guards posted throughout the castle. It was a normal routine for her. It was sad for her to know the only privacy she really had was in her bedroom. Even then she always felt as if she was being watched.

She reached the dining room and took her normal seat opposite her Godparents. The focal point of the high-ceilinged room was a sinister stained-glass window. Each panel vividly depicted a horrific battle from the Crusades, which had taken place Ages ago.

The table, stretching nearly the full length of the room, was adorned with flickering candles placed every few feet.

Her Godparents wore dark black robes that covered their entire bodies. Voluminous black hoods hid what was rumored to be deformed, gruesome faces, the devastating effects of dark magic. Only their gleaming red eyes blazed in the cloaked darkness. Only the Witch and Warlock knew the truth of why they hid their faces. Not even the Gypsy knew why. The Warlock, her Godfather, was tall. He carried a small scepter with a twirled gold shaft, a disproportionately large blue diamond mounted on the top. Her Godmother, the Witch, was a little shorter. She carried a small spiked wand rendered in the same design as the Warlock's scepter.

Though the Witch and Warlock were the most powerful sorcerers in Enchantas, they still had trouble keeping their Goddaughter in line.

"Lexis! Finally!" The Warlock placed his scepter next to his plate. "Your dinner is getting cold."

The Witch sat next to him, remaining silent as she sipped her goblet of Lixywine.

"Sorry," Lexis muttered as she looked down at her food. She stared at the plate of unfamiliar meat and vegetables. It could have been bird, rabbit, or fox. The carrots and celery were soft and silent, so she knew they were cooked well.

"Please eat your dinner. You will have studies to do later," the Witch said sternly. Her voice was crackled but clear.

"Studies?" Lexis erupted. She stomped her feet hard on the stone floor. Even the guards in the other room could feel it. "I already had my studies today. Six tocks' worth! Must I really do more?"

"You need to learn the materials, my child!" the Warlock yelled.

"My dear," the Witch spoke up. "You must understand that learning your studies each day will shape you into a respected and powerful leader. It is necessary to learn our magic to keep order in Enchantas."

"Yes. We have just heard rumors of an uprising in the valley," the Warlock added. "It is this chaotic Fate that needs to be diminished. That is not what we teach!"

"What happened?" Lexis asked.

The Warlock snarled. "Foxtown was destroyed."

"It was probably that dreadful owl," the Witch growled. "I never liked him. Why didn't we banish him?"

"The Foxes were no less a nuisance, my dear," the Warlock argued. "Their ideals of Freewill make it as if Destiny worked for only them. Which is ironic if you ask me." He chuckled as he bit into a carrot and continued. "You need to learn the necessary magic to keep the Enchantians from revolting and to bring order to this land. Chance doesn't happen every day! And we all need to be prepared for the unknown."

"I don't care about Chance!" she shouted back. "I care about Freewill, which makes you both hypocrites! What about my needs, my dreams?"

"Silence!" the Warlock yelled. "You will attend to your studies immediately after dinner."

The Gypsy's face turned red with anger and frustration. All of the Cycles of being locked in her room with no attachment to the outside world had been compressed into one huge ball of rage. She stood up, kicked her chair behind her, and blurted out, "When was the last time we spent time together as a family? All I am to you is a pupil."

"We know that. We are not your mother and father," the Witch said calmly.

"If you won't be my family, at least be my friends. You have no idea how lonely I have been." She paused as a tear rolled down her cheek. "I am locked in my room with no place to go. No friends to talk to."

The Witch and Warlock sat in silence as they listened to her complaints. They really didn't know that all she wanted was attention and appreciation.

"Sit down and eat your food," the Warlock demanded.

"There you go again, commanding me." She wrinkled her nose and marched out the door. "I don't need this! I don't want this! I never asked for this!"

A gremlin guard stepped into her path.

"Get out of my way!" She snarled as she flicked her wrist and sent the guard smashing through a stained-glass panel, whereupon he was hurled to the ground outside.

"Well, we cannot say that she isn't learning her magic." The Witch smiled beneath her cloak.

"Dear, this is not acceptable behavior! She needs to be punished. Ten lashes!" He pointed to the guards, and they swiftly marched toward the door.

"No!" the Witch objected. "That punishment is for traitors and scoundrels."

The Warlock contemplated for a moment, then nodded in agreement. Perhaps he had acted rashly.

"I think she has the right to have a little more freedom," the Witch added, as they both stood up and exited the room.

***

Lexis's heart pounded with adrenaline as she swung open the door to the room of magical mirrors. Another tear rolled down her cheek at she thought of her Godparents' cruelty. She did not agree with their ideals, and they punished her for it. She was alone again with no one to help her through these hard times. She ran toward a mirror and stood there, concentrating deeply. "I need to leave my life and find a new one. I need someone to talk to. Not myself anymore. I need a friend, a companion."

She stared intently into one particular mirror and chanted her spell:

"*Reflected Ripples of this Magic Mirror,*
Bring me a Friend, and away from Here."

The mirror obediently began to form ripples, as if a drop of water had fallen into a still pool of water. Suddenly a picture of Sally and Mel formed in the diminishing ripples. "There we go." She smiled as she stepped into the mirror, vanishing from the chamber. The mirror's surface stood undisturbed by the time the gremlins kicked down the door. Imps leaped onto the windowsills. The Witch and Warlock marched in behind their guards.

"Where is she?" the Warlock howled.

"I am not sure, sir," an imp replied. "We will find her!"

The imps leaped from the windows as the gremlins hurled themselves down the hall in search of the errant Gypsy Princess.

Chapter X
The Gnome

The night was freezing, and the icy road home wasn't safe to drive. Nevertheless, a green four-door station wagon sped swiftly down the highway. Frost covered the windows, and the wipers were not working correctly. A woman with long, curly brown hair drove as her husband held her free hand and smiled, watching the trees pass by.

"I had fun tonight, sweetie," said the woman.

"Me too." The man smiled from the passenger seat. "I wish we could have stayed longer."

"Richard, we have other obligations. Besides, it's not considered good etiquette to be the first ones to leave the company Christmas party."

"I know, but we really don't get out much, and I think we should."

"How would we do that? Get a babysitter every weekend?" she asked. "I don't like the thought of some stranger taking care of her all of the time. Tonight was an exception."

"I know, Susie, but every once in a while it's okay, right?"

"Sure. And I did have a lot of fun," she conceded as she looked at him again. "We haven't had that much fun in years."

"You're still a good dancer. I missed that."

"Thanks. You haven't lost your touch either."

They traveled quietly for a moment, reflecting on their night. They'd both had a spectacularly good time. It may have been just another company party to most, but for them it was a break from the everyday hassles at home and work.

"I can't see a thing," Susie complained, peering closely at the roadway ahead. "We need to fix these wipers."

"Hon, could you slow down please? The roads are pretty icy tonight." He was becoming uneasy; conditions seemed to be degrading.

"Richard, I'm not that drunk. I know what I'm doing."

"I know you're not, but—" he began.

"Richard, seriously. I'm okay!" She raised her voice. His fussing irritated her. She was the type of person who never liked to worry; if someone made her worry she vented in anger.

"Sorry, sweetie." He kept his focus on the road. The car heater was beginning to warm up the interior. The ice on the windshield turned to small beads of water that ran up the window. After a few minutes the window was cleared, much to their mutual relief.

She drove down a steep hill, at the bottom of which was a bridge that spanned a 100-foot-deep ravine. At the bottom of the ravine flowed a narrowly corkscrewing river boiling with frigid, turbulent rapids.

"Look, the sign says, *Caution: Bridge May Be Icy*, so that means slow down."

"Richard, I *am* slowing down. Why can't you—" She glanced over at him.

"Watch out for the rabbit!" cried Richard

A small white and gray rabbit had jumped out of the forest into the road. It hopped leisurely in front of the car, and Susie swerved in attempt to avoid it. The car came within inches of the rabbit as it hopped to the other side of the road.

As the car veered on the icy road, its back tires slid sideways. Susie turned the steering wheel in the opposite direction, trying to correct it, but the car had fishtailed with too much momentum.

"I can't control it!" Susie yelled.

"Turn right, turn right!" Richard screamed.

She turned the wheel to the right as quickly as she could, but the vehicle continued to spin out of control.

"What do I do? What do I do?" she yelled.

Suddenly, the station wagon rammed into the guardrail, snapping it in half. The car's front end dangled off the bridge.

"Oh my God! What do we do?" Susie's body shook in terror.

"All right, just breathe deep and let me think." Richard also inhaled and exhaled deeply, trying to restore calm. "Look out your window and see how close we are to the bridge."

She turned her head slowly, afraid that any sudden movement would send both of them hurtling to their deaths. The edge of the bridge was about a foot away from the front doors.

"Is it close enough to jump?"

She shook her head no and looked down toward the river.

"Don't look down," Richard instructed. "We need to climb through the back and out the hatch."

"You're kidding, right?" She closed her eyes immediately and started to cry. "I can't do this, Richard. I'm too scared."

"Yes, you can!" He gently eased his arm around her. "I know you can."

She looked at him with tears streaming down her face. "We can't die now."

"I know; we have to get home to our daughter." He smiled, trying to give her hope and encouragement. "Are you ready to try this?"

She nodded her head again and was slowly turning her body when suddenly the car nudged down a couple inches. The undercarriage groaned alarmingly.

"Richard!"

"Okay, let's try something else. On the count of three, we are both going to open our doors and jump out," he said.

She nodded again, too shaken to speak.

"Ready—" He paused, gathering courage. "One, Two, THREE!" They flung open the doors and catapulted themselves toward the bridge. Neither managed to reach the main structural surface—it was simply too far away.

Richard realized as soon as he jumped that he wasn't going to make it. He grabbed the first thing that came to hand, a metal strut on the underside of the structure. He'd seen Susie jump and heard the sickening sound of the door swinging back and hitting her while she was still airborne. She had thrown it open with too much force, putting her in the direct path of the ricochet. With a loud, rusty creak, the car listed forward, descending into the cold, churning rapids below.

"SUSIE!" he screamed desperately. And then he saw her underneath the bridge, hanging on to a small metal pipe shaped like a hook. "Oh, God! I'll be right there sweetie!"

He tried to pull himself up but didn't have the strength. The metal was starting to cut his fingers, and the ice was causing him to lose his grip.

"I don't know how long I can hold on!" yelled Richard.

"I love you!" she hollered.

"I love you too, Susie!" He watched her beautiful brown hair blow in the wind as tears formed in his eyes and ran down his face. Susie's body was shaking with cold and exertion. Her grip was loosening.

"Tell Sally I love her." She looked down. "I'm not scared anymore, Richard."

"Susie, what are you talking about? I'll be right there!" he exclaimed. "Don't do anything till I get there!"

"RICHARD!" Suddenly her frozen fingers slipped from the metal pipe, and she plunged into the rushing river.

"SUSIE!" The sound of the splash echoed in Richard's ears. He began to cry in disbelief and horror. With all his strength he tried to pull himself up. He had one foot over the railing when suddenly his fingers slipped and he fell. His scream of terror echoed throughout the ravine as he, too, splashed into the cold river.

***

Sally woke up abruptly, wiping her sweaty forehead. Her body shook as if a bolt of lightning had struck her. She turned her head rapidly back and forth trying to remember where she was. It did not take long for her to realize she was still in Enchantas. The sun was rising, casting an orange hue over the forest. It was cold and quiet.

"Are you awake?" Mel asked, crawling over to her.

Exhausted, they had stretched out underneath two large bluish-purple maple trees. It was surprisingly comfortable. Sally nodded her head yes and stretched.

"Well, it sounded like you had a nightmare. Want to talk about it?"

"No." She rubbed her eyes. A feeling of regret came over her; she kind of wished Ryan was with her instead of Mel. She missed talking with him. "Just another one of my recurring nightmares."

"I hate those. I always seemed to have the same one, where my parents turn into werewolves." Mel shut up; he knew he had an annoying tendency to talk too much and volunteer too much information, especially in the morning. That's when others slower to wake up appreciated a bit of peace and quiet. "Never mind. How much farther do you suppose we should go?"

"I'm not sure." Sally checked her compass. "It only says to go *This Way*."

"Okay. Are you ready to keep on?"

Sally stretched again, looking around the blue-leafed forest. "In a minute, okay? I need a little bit of alone time. It will help me forget my dream."

"All right." Mel sat back down, in no hurry to get up. "I'll just take a power nap."

Sally wandered off the green cobblestone trail, enjoying the smell of morning. For years now she'd been haunted by the same dream: the death of her parents. As if being acutely aware of her loss every day wasn't bad enough, she had to be reminded at night too? Life truly wasn't fair. And the only way she'd found to shake off the nightmare was to walk alone.

Sally stepped over a few branches and stumbled over rocks when suddenly, she was startled by a flashing purple light. A beam shot up from behind a yellowish-green spruce tree. For a moment she thought lightning had struck the tree, but no rain clouds were in sight. However, this was Enchantas, and she now knew full well that anything was possible.

"Hello?" she called in a quivering, hesitant tone, feeling rather foolish. "Is anyone there?"

A figure peeked around the tree and swiftly ducked back. A soft cry came from the tree, instantly worrying her.

"Hey!" Emboldened by the thought that someone might need her help, Sally moved closer. "Are you all right? Do you need help?" On the other side of the tree a beautiful brunette woman in a long, green velvet dress hunkered against the trunk, whimpering. The woman looked to be only a few years older than her.

"Are you all right?" Sally repeated loudly, kneeling beside her. "What happened?"

"It's nothing." The woman looked up with tearful purple eyes. Sally wasn't sure if you'd call them beautiful or just weird. Either way, her violet gaze was mesmerizing. "Oh my goodness, you're human?"

"Seems I'm not the only one," Sally responded. "You are too, aren't you?"

"I am." The woman looked directly at Sally, amazed. "I thought I was the only one! What's wrong? What happened to you? How did you get here?"

"Wow," the woman said, apparently regaining some composure, wiping her damp face and straightening her shoulders. She brushed off the folds of her skirt. "You have a lot of questions, don't you?"

"More than you think." Sally sat beside her. "Especially since I got *here*. I don't think I could ever run out of questions here."

"This place *is* a little different." The young woman actually laughed. "How did you get here?"

"Through some kind of portal called the Forbidden Cave."

"Really?" Those fantastic purple eyes lit up. "It is open?"

"Not exactly," Sally explained. "That's why we're trying to find another way home."

"So you're stuck here like me?"

"Yep."

"Never mind." The woman's mood abruptly changed again, and she broke into sobs. "Not like me," she wept. "I have been trapped in isolation by my Godparents. They imprisoned me in their castle, denying me any chance to experience the outside world."

"That's horrible!" Sally put a comforting arm around the crying woman. She was sure she'd be unbalanced emotionally, too, if she'd been shut up in some gruesome, moldering old pile of bricks and mortar. "How did you escape?"

"I, too, found a portal of sorts. One that brought me here."

Sally thought for a moment. "Well, Fate must have brought you here to me. We were meant to meet!"

"If you say so." The woman shook her head, unconvinced. "My Godparents aren't really believers in that sort of stuff."

"Well, whatever it is that brought us together, I'm glad you found me instead of a fox or something creepy like that." Sally grinned cheerfully, the nightmare forgotten.

The girl smiled. "Me too."

"My name is Sally." She said as she put her hand out.

"Hi, Sally. I'm Lexis. Some Enchantians call me the Gypsy Princess, or Gypsy. But I'd rather like it if you would stick to Lexis."

"Sounds good," Sally said, and they shook on it.

"So where and how are you going to find your way home?" Lexis asked.

"I'm not sure." Sally was about to show her the compass but hesitated, remembering the owl's words: *This is your most valuable asset.* Perhaps it was wiser to keep a few things to herself. After all, she barely knew this moody woman.

"Well, good luck, Sally. You'll need it—and then some. I, for one, have given up on trying to find a way home."

"You can come with us!" Sally exclaimed. She was eager to have another female in the band of travelers.

"No, I mustn't."

"Really, I'm sure it wouldn't be a problem."

"Hey, Sally! Where'd you run off to?" Mel cried from a distance.

"I—" Sally started to holler back, but Lexis stopped her.

"You mustn't mention me. Not yet."

Sally was curious. There was a look of real fear in Lexis's eyes. "Okay, we can keep this between us for now." She smiled reassuringly. "And I want you to know that I am totally trustworthy. You can trust me."

"I can?" The Gypsy smiled back. "So we are friends?"

"Yes," Sally replied with conviction. "We are friends."

"Great! For now I must go." Lexis quickly stood up, preparing to dash into the forest.

"Lexis, what's the hurry? Where are you going?"

"I must go," she repeated. "But I will see you again!"

The Gypsy quickly passed a few trees and disappeared into a vapor of purple smoke, the funneled smoke lit from within, like harnessed lightning.

"Sally," Mel called as he caught up with her. "Who were you talking to?"

"Oh, no one," she said, quickly fabricating a harmless white lie. "Just some random chipmunk passing by."

"Really? Wow." Mel chuckled. "It's so weird that you can say that with a straight face."

"Yeah, I know." Sally started toward the trail, venturing one look back to the spot where Lexis had seemingly evaporated into thin air. She remained silent about her encounter with the whimpering woman. She had a promise to keep. "Are you ready to get this show on the road?"

"Yep."

As they made their way down the trail, Mel admired the extraordinary forest. Everything around him seemed so alive and joyful; it felt like paradise.

"You know," he said, breaking her reverie. "I really wouldn't mind staying here."

"Really?" Sally found that puzzling. "Why?"

"I don't know. It just seems so peaceful," he said. "Except for those foxes, of course. But yeah, it beats life with the freaks officially known as my parents. My stepdad always nags me about school. I never know what my mom is going to cook next. It's as though she creates a flavor of 'bad' with every dish. I wonder what she'd make of these vegetables?"

Sally laughed. The way Mel talked about his parents made her miss her own all the more. He had no idea how lucky he was.

"So what about your parents?" Mel asked. "I'm sure they aren't as bad as mine."

Sally paused for a second before blurting the uncomfortable truth. Saying the words should have gotten easier, but it never did. "They died a few years ago."

Mel's jaw dropped. A rush of sorrow came over him. He felt horrible for bringing it up.

"Don't feel bad. You didn't know. I live with my grandmother now." She smiled at the thought of her grandma. "And she is a wonderful lady. We're two peas in a pod, as she would say. I'm very lucky to have her."

"So what are your hobbies?" Mel asked quickly, anxious to change the subject as quickly as possible. "What do you like to do?"

"I don't have many friends," she replied. "That's obvious. I usually stay at home, read romance novels, cook or garden with my grandmother, and do homework. Pretty lame. What about you?"

"That's not lame. I don't have many friends either." He snorted. "Nobody gets me. I usually just stay in my basement and play with my chemistry set or build robots. You know—invent or concoct stuff."

"Robots sound neat." She smiled, quite intrigued. "Concoct stuff? Like what?"

"Well, most of the stuff I make usually has a practical joke theme. This one time in seventh grade I made this egg launcher and egged people from a tree."

Sally's eyes widened, "That wasn't on Spruce Street, was it?"

"Yeah, how'd you know?"

Sally shook her head. "You egged me."

"Oh my gosh. I am so sorry." Mel put a conciliatory hand on her shoulder. It was time to change the subject again. "Here's one better. I was the one who stink-bombed the school to get classes canceled for the day."

"That was you?" she exclaimed. "Again, you got me on that!"

"How?" Mel gave her a puzzled look. "I didn't—oh, wait. I must have spilled some on you when we bumped into each other."

"Yeah, well..." She sighed as one used to being the butt of jokes. "Now everyone at school is going to think I don't shower or something. I'll always be the stinky girl."

"I am truly sorry for that, Sally." Mel sighed with her again, shaking his head at his thoughtless behavior.

"That's all right." Sally's grandmother's words rambled through her head. "I forgive you."

Mel smiled as they passed a couple of green and yellow maple trees. He couldn't believe how both of his most masterful pranks had directly affected Sally. He kept quiet about all of his other inventions and concoctions, just in case she'd been in the firing line, so to speak, for any of those. He especially didn't want to mention the incident at their spring dance in middle school, during which he'd spiked the punch with his homemade laxative. He let out a mild guffaw as he remembered all of the kids and chaperones racing to the bathrooms. That would, for now, remain his little secret.

A small clearing appeared as they rose over a hill. Only a few large trees surrounded it, and the morning sunlight shone through the treetops. A small stream of smoke arose from the clearing, and as they drew closer they noticed a large fire pit still smoldering from a recent fire.

They approached it cautiously and heard a quiet voice say, "Hello." A short, plump gnome carrying a pot and spoon waddled toward them. She was the same height as Gitchy and wore a light green dress that reached just above her ankles. "How may I help you?" She flashed a comfortable smile reminiscent of Gitchy's.

"Hi," Sally replied. "We are looking for the Gnome Village. Would this be it?"

"You've presumed correctly, little lady." The gnome smiled as she placed the pot by the smoky fire pit. "How can I help you?"

"We are looking for the wife of Gitchy," Mel added. "We have a letter from the Great Owl."

"My name is Seara, and I am the wife of Gitchy." The gnome stepped closer to them.

Sally pulled out the letter and handed it to her. The two stood silently as Seara opened and read the letter. Mere seconds went by before a tear dropped from her chin. That tear turned to two, and the two turned to many as Seara crumpled to the ground, weeping for her late husband.

Sally quickly dropped to her knees, hugging the little woman as hard as she could. "It's okay," said Sally, rubbing her back. What a morning it had been. It was the second time that day she had comforted someone.

"I told him that it was dangerous outside our village!" she sobbed.

Sally continued to hold her as Seara shakily rose to her feet. She glanced at the letter again and looked at them with her now dry, red eyes. Quickly pulling herself together, she said, "Welcome to our home. It says here that I am to supply you with some items for your journey." She turned and walked toward one of the large trees.

"Wait, Seara!" cried Sally. "It's okay; you don't need to do anything right now."

"Yeah, we have time," Mel added. They were both surprised and confused by her sudden change in demeanor. It was obvious she was trying not to allow the news of her husband's death to affect her.

"That is quite all right," she pronounced, wiping her eyes with her dress skirt. "Everyone mourns differently. I like to keep my mind busy." She hurried toward an old oak tree and opened a round door that started at the base of its trunk. "I believe you both will be too big to come into my home, so please wait out here."

Sally and Mel watched the plump little gnome scurry into her hole and waited patiently.

"I can't believe the owl made us deliver that letter," Sally said, irritated. "That was more than a little insensitive. He should have told her himself."

"You're right," Mel replied in the same tone. "I feel very uncomfortable. What should we do?"

"I don't know," Sally whispered, uncertain. "We can't just leave."

"Here we go," Seara said as she stepped out of the ground and dropped a large chest in front of them. "Gitchy has been the Herald for our grand Sage for many Cycles." She laughed melodically as she opened it. "If you ask me, this job made him a bit of a pack rat!"

"So what is all this stuff?"

"Well, the letter states you will need to give the gargoyles this bracelet." She handed a sparkly silver bracelet to Mel. "Not quite sure what the significance is. I am afraid that Gitchy was supposed to be the one to pass these belongings to you, but he is now gone." She paused, smiling sadly before continuing to rummage through the items.

"What is this?" Sally pulled out a large rolled-up cloth that was twice the length of her. "We can't carry this."

"You won't be carrying that, my dear." Seara smiled. "It will be carrying you. This is Gitchy's Magic Carpet. He acquired it from the Sphinx a few Seasons ago. He loved to ride it."

Seara set it on the ground, took a step back, and said a quick spell.

"Magic Carpet of the Sky,
Unroll Yourself and Let Us Fly!"

The carpet glittered with magic as it quickly unfurled.

"Go ahead and give it a whirl," Seara encouraged them. "It doesn't talk much, but it is fast as the wind. Gusto is its name." The carpet had an old-fashioned design on it—dark maroon with teal trim.

"Maybe when we leave," Sally said, looking uneasy.

"It will make any trip around Enchantas a speedy one." Seara went back to the chest. "Aha! Here they are." She pulled out four red chainmail jackets.

"These are Dragon Sheaths," she explained, holding one aloft for inspection, "made from the scale sheds of the mighty Red Dragons. Frightening beasts, they are, but they do craft the strongest armor in Enchantas. It will protect you from almost any weapon."

"Cool." Mel took one and put it on. "It fits!"

"But of course! The jackets will fit anyone worthy of wearing it." Seara closed the chest. "I believe that would be all."

Sally and Mel stood up, sensing that Seara needed them to leave. They did not want to outstay their welcome, especially since it had been only moments ago that Seara found out her husband was dead.

"Would you like some brunch?" Seara asked, going through the motions of being hospitable.

"Oh no, but thank you very much, Seara," replied Mel with a smile. "You have been kind enough."

"Yeah, thank you," Sally chipped in. "The owl told us that our bracelets will keep us from hunger. I haven't been hungry yet."

"Well then, I wish you a safe journey." Seara turned back toward the fire pit.

"Thank you," they both replied and stepped onto the carpet.

"Just one more thing, Seara," Mel called to the tiny, retreating figure. "How do you start this carpet?"

"Just yell, '*Go, Gusto, go!*'" she responded, and at that moment the carpet lifted and took to the air. It weaved back and forth, dodging trunks and branches until it found an opening above the tree line. Sally and Mel held on tightly as they ascended upward into the beautiful blue-green sky.

"Whoa, Gusto!" Mel grabbed the two front ends of the tasseled trim as makeshift reins and pulled back. "Hey, Sally, where are we going?"

Increasingly comfortable in her role as navigator, she pulled out her compass and pointed. "Go left and straight on from there!" She smiled, leaning on Mel for extra support. "Wow, this is fun! Scary, but fun."

Mel nodded as they soared through the clouds. Their eyes watered from the wind and the salty liquid brushed across their faces as they made their way toward the gargoyles.

Chapter XI

Gypsy Encounter

It had been more than a full day of hiking for John and Ryan before they finally sat to rest. The forest was becoming more of a marsh and the beautifully colored trees, once so abundant, were scarce. John and Ryan were two very different kids, but they had one similar admirable quality: determination.

The blue cobblestone trail had diminished miles ago, and their only guidance was the trusty map the owl had given them. Unluckily, the owl had been right: the checkpoints were outdated, and the boys seemed to be lost.

"I'm not sure if I'm reading this map correctly," said Ryan. "We should be in Butterfalls Forest according to this map. I don't see anything around that would give this place that name."

"Give me that map," John snapped, all too willing to put the jock who thought he was so smart in his place. "I told you we should have turned the other way back there."

"Shut up! That's not what the map said."

"I think you're just too stupid to know how to read a map."
John tried to grab it from Ryan's hands. "Now hand it over, loser!"
"No." Ryan started walking. It seemed like every time they
stopped, they argued. He wondered why the owl had put them
together on this trip. "Why? Do you think you can read it better?"
"As a matter of fact, yes I do. I'm not as brainless as you." John
ripped the map out of Ryan's hands. "My dad and I used to go on
hunting trips, and he taught me how to read maps."
"Yeah, right." Ryan snickered condescendingly. "I could just
imagine your dysfunctional family outing: beer, smokes, and
guns."
"Shut up, jockstrap!" John threw the map to the ground. Fueled
with anger, he gave Ryan a push. "Don't talk about stuff you don't
know about."
"That's the sixth time you've called me stupid, dumb, or
jockstrap on this trip." Ryan pushed him back. "Just to let you
know, I have one of the best GPAs in our class. So that definitely
proves I'm not stupid. At least I'm not a dropout like you!"
"I'm not a dropout!" John pushed back a little harder. "I just
missed too many days last year."
Ryan laughed. "Sure. Whatever makes you sleep at night,
loser."
"Cake-eating jockstrap!"
They jumped on each other like two hyenas fighting for the last
leg of lamb, rolling around the muddy ground as they'd done at
school. Punches continued to fly evenly from the both of them
until Ryan got John in a chokehold.
"Do you give up?" Ryan grunted into his ear.
"No," John snarled back.
Ryan held him for a few moments and then let him go. John
rolled away trying to catch his breath.

"I really hate you," John said, his voice muffled since he was lying on the ground with his face still buried. "I hate all of you pretty-boy jocks."

"Well, don't think I'm going to give you a break." Ryan stood up and kicked dirt at him. "I don't like you either. So let's stop the fighting until we can get out of here."

John picked up the map and realized Ryan was right; he was never going to get home if they kept fighting. "The owl did say this map might be outdated. Let's just find a trail."

They continued on their way until the muddy ground became more water than earth. "Where do you suppose the trail is?" Ryan stepped into an ankle-high puddle.

Before they could search the area, a strange voice came from behind them.

"Do you two need help?"

They both turned to find a young, beautiful brunette woman standing beside a leafless birch tree. The boys' jaws dropped in astonishment. She was a tall, purple-eyed beauty with a creamy complexion. They ogled her velvet green and purple dress as she walked confidently toward them.

"Who are you?" John asked in a charming voice.

"My name is Lexis. Do you two need assistance?"

Ryan was a little troubled by her presence. "How did you get to Enchantas? We thought we were the only humans."

"Ryan," John whispered. "What are you doing? This girl is sizzling! Don't interrogate her."

"Something doesn't seem right."

"That's not true at all; I've been here for many ages. I have just escaped the imprisonment of the Witch and Warlock. They kept me locked up for a long time."

"Oh, no." John walked closer to her. "That sucks. Are you okay? Can we help you?"

"Right now, I am only in search of true friendship and companionship."

"Well heck," John smiled. "I'll be your friend."

"John, hold on." Ryan stopped him. "How do you know we can trust her? Doesn't this seem a little sketchy to you?"

"If you don't believe me, then I will prove it to you." She waved her arms horizontally above the ground and turned the marsh into solid earth.

"That was amazing!" John exclaimed.

As the Gypsy walked closer to them, a glowing gold sword emerged from Ryan's hand, which grasped the weapon of its own volition. "What the—What's this?" He shook his arm frantically but couldn't get rid of the sword. "Get off me!"

"What is this?" The Gypsy stood back. "You don't trust me?"

"That's not it," John replied. "I don't really like this kid anyway. I'll be your friend." John moved in and found himself in the same predicament as Ryan. A four-foot, glowing gold spear emanated from his wrist, clutched in his unwilling fist. "Shoot, it happened to me, too!"

"Why is it that every time I meet someone new, they turn on me?" The woman's voice deepened to a growl, eyes glowing bright with anger. "All I want is to have some friends!" Her arms were suddenly bathed in a purple aura, also glowing as she clenched her fists tightly to her supple body.

"Curse me Dead, Curse me Alone;
Turn this Human into Stone!"

Sad loneliness warped and coalesced with her magical power into a vibrant purple beam aimed directly at John. But the Gypsy had not bargained on the power of high school athletics. Before the laser reached John's body, Ryan tackled him to the ground. As the shaken teen glanced back, he saw Ryan falling into the path of the beam and, sickeningly, instantly turning to stone.

"Ryan!" John screamed.

156

A small, glowing blue orb dashed through the air in front of him and yelled:

"Evil Gypsy with your Ugly Moan,
Take your Temptations and Go back Home!"

The orb illuminated with a blinding light for a moment, then unexpectedly dimmed and went dark.

John rubbed his eyes; it took a moment for them to adjust from the blinding glow of the orb. As he looked around, it became clear that the crazy woman had disappeared.

"The wicked Gypsy Princess is as beautiful as she is deceiving." A small, beautiful, translucent woman glittered as she fluttered around him. She looked about ten inches tall and had long, shiny black hair that fell to the middle of her back. She wore a scant white dress of prismatic fabric that glittered in the sun. Glitter dusted her face, arms, and long, silky legs, sparkling and shimmering. "You should be happy I came when I did."

John stared at her, agape. "Who are you?"

"My name is Dyad. I am one of the four apprentices of our grand Sage."

"What are you?" He was curious as to what type of creature could be so small yet so stunning beautiful.

"I am a fairy of course, one of four left in Enchantas. Like many other creatures of Enchantas, we are an endangered breed, a dying species, thanks to the Witch and Warlock. But Fate works in mysterious ways, and my three sisters and I are the only fairies left."

"Where are your sisters?" John had thought the Gypsy was pretty, but Dyad touched his heart instantly like no other. The thought of love at first sight came to mind, but that idea was ridiculous, especially to John. However he could not control his thoughts and feelings. There was something about this dazzling fairy that was special.

"Nymph, Pixy, and Sprite are all on different missions summoned by the grand Sage. My mission was to make sure you found the gargoyles safely. I have been following both of you for a while now."

"Great." John was suddenly embarrassed about his actions and arguments with Ryan.

"I have to say, humans are very peculiar creatures." Dyad floated onto his shoulder, and his heart skipped a beat. "Why do you fight over such inconsequential ideals?"

"Yeah, we can be stupid sometimes."

"Nevertheless, would you like me to de-stone him?"

"If you'd asked me a few moments ago, I'd have said no." He laughed. "But yeah, I guess you should."

"All right," She smiled and turned to the blue orb:
"Witches Dress, Warlocks Formal,
Bring this Boy back to normal."

Dyad grew bright once again as the stone crumbled from Ryan's form. He emerged as if from a clay mold, transforming back to his living, breathing self.

"John! Watch out!" He fell to the ground before he realized things had changed in a second.

"Ryan, I'm right here." John smirked.

"You were turned to stone, my friend," said the fairy, hovering over Ryan. "Hello. My name is Dyad, and I have come to help you reach the gargoyles."

"Great!" Ryan stood up. "Who the heck was that Lexis girl?"

"That was the wicked Gypsy Princess, Goddaughter of the Witch and Warlock. It seemed that she was trying to seduce you two into friendship. However, I'd advise against any relations with her. She is emotionally unstable."

"I can tell." Ryan scanned himself to make sure he was fully de-stoned. "So you said you were here to help us reach the gargoyles?" He accepted the fairy's direction without question.

The strangeness was almost becoming ordinary. "Because I think we're lost."

"You are both on the right path, I assure you." She floated ahead as the two boys followed. "You have followed the map correctly."

John's and Ryan's weapons abruptly disappeared from their arms.

"What the heck were those weapons?" Ryan asked. "And how did we get them?"

"Those were your Persona Weapons. They originate from your magical bracelets," she explained as they continued to make their way through the dried-up marsh. "There is a great deal of magic in the bracelets for those who wield them. The Knights used these bracelets for many things; protection was one of them. When the bracelets sense a nearby threat, they fabricate a weapon that is suitable to the bearer. John, your weapon seems to be the spear, while Ryan has the sword."

"Not bad." John admired his bracelet. He'd been thinking it was a little girly but had gained a newfound respect for its power.

"There is much more magic; however, there is no time to instruct," the fairy noted. They came to another clearing, and the Minerton Castle came into view. The castle was dilapidated, walls and windows broken. The entire right corner of the ramshackle structure was rubble. Thick vines climbed the walls. Magnificent statues of grotesque and macabre beasts were stationed strategically among the outside pillars. The castle was clearly uninhabited.

"We're supposed to find the gargoyles here?" Ryan tossed a puzzled look at Dyad.

"Yes." She fluttered in front of them. "Gargoyles are nocturnal creatures. They will find you when the sun sets." As the beguiling fairy began to fly away, she blew a kiss. "Sorry, my friends. I must return to inform our Sage that the Gypsy Princess knows of your presence. In turn, we should all assume the Witch and Warlock know just as much. This will hasten our plans, and we all will need to prepare a bit sooner than anticipated."

John looked sad. "What plans?"

"War against the Witch and Warlock for freedom over the lands of Enchantas!"

"Don't leave so soon."

"Sorry, John. I will return," she said, and then suddenly transformed into the blue orb and whisked smoothly back into the desolate forest.

Once again the two young men were alone. John pondered Ryan's character. His generosity of spirit was far greater than John's could ever be. He was amazed at how dignified Ryan was and how passionately and immediately he had acted to protect John from the Gypsy, even after their countless arguments and fist fights.

"Ryan," John spoke softly, "I think I was wrong about you."

Ryan tilted his head back, astonished. "What do you mean?"

"We both know we don't like each other, but for some reason you still stood up for me and saved me from that Gypsy girl."

"I'm sure you'd do the same."

"No, that's the thing. I wouldn't have." John shook his head. A few days ago he wouldn't have been caught dead apologizing or saying sappy things, but for some reason, after his short time in Enchantas and sharing a cell with Sally, he had changed. "I'm stubborn like my father in that way. I admire how noble you are. I haven't had many friends over the years, mostly just acquaintances —people I'd hang out with at parties or during lunch—but nothing with substance. I would be honored to have someone like you as a friend. I am really sorry for giving you such a hard time these past couple of days. Truce?"

Ryan was shocked and felt uncertain about John's sincerity. Did John even know what it meant to be a true friend? Ryan believed in second chances, though. Everyone deserved one.

"Truce." They shook hands, grinning. Ryan wanted to clear the air. "Sorry for that statement about your family. So you inherited your stubbornness from your father?" he teased.

"Yeah." John was surprisingly comfortable opening up. "That's one reason he and my mom divorced. After that, his drinking became worse. He was never there for me and my sis."

Ryan nodded. "That kind of sounds like my parents. Lately, they've been taking trips around the world and leaving my brother and me. They're never around or available when we need them."

"That's not so bad. I'd rather have my dad gone than drinking and beating us up."

"Good point." Ryan sighed. "It wasn't bad this summer. My brother and I could have our friends come over any time, and we stayed out as late as we wanted. But their absence took a toll on us. It would still be nice to have them around more."

Ironically, the two boys were not as different as they had once thought. An epiphany came to Ryan as to why John was such a rebel. It was for the same reason Ryan joined all of the sports teams and did well in school. They both craved attention from their parents. He thought about his own family and his selfish parents leaving them alone for months on end. *It's not surprising*, he thought, *that I'm lost and they don't even know I'm gone.* His brother was probably having a large party at their house. He and his brother were more like guardians of one another, each taking care of the other and making sure they stayed on track with school and lives. He loved him very much and wished him the best. He wondered what he would do if his brother were here right now, in this crazy place called Enchantas.

"You know, John." Ryan said as they climbed the stairs to the castle ruins. "You're not that bad. Now let's go check this place out."

Chapter XII
The Gargoyles

A bedroom door swung open, and the Gypsy Princess stormed down the hallway to her Godparents' chambers. The old familiar rage grew within her as she stomped across the brick floor. Voices rose from down the hallway, and she knew she needed to be a little more inconspicuous. She slowed down and quietly crept in front of an open door so she could hear the conversation taking place inside the room.

"Sire, it was horrible," a large fox muttered as he knelt on his knees in front of the Witch and Warlock. He wore a long dark black hooded robe and carried a short sword strapped to his side. "My entire city was destroyed!"

"And how do you say this came to pass?" the Witch asked, looking down her nose at the pathetic fox.

"The rebellion is back, my lords!"

"How?" The Warlock stepped closer. "It has been Ages since something like this has happened."

"Yes," the Witch snarled. "Why now?"

"I was told that four humans have arrived in Enchantas, my lords."

"Humans?" they both shrieked.

"Yes, my lords. I have heard rumors of four humans prophesied to bring peace to Enchantas. Those were the rebels' words, of course."

"This can't be," the Warlock huffed. "The Forbidden Cave is locked. How did anyone get through?"

"I am not sure," the Witch hissed. "We can't have Enchantians running around believing in this. We have controlled order throughout the land for Ages."

"Duke, is there any proof of their existence?"

The Duke was afraid to mention that he had held these humans in custody before the siege of rebels attacked. That kind of sloppiness would get him executed, or worse, tortured before execution.

"Yes," the Gypsy Princess said as she entered the room. "I have seen them."

"Ah, lovely. Our ungrateful Goddaughter has returned," said the Warlock.

"Lexis!" the Witch cried. "Where have you been?"

"I have met these humans you speak of, and they're just as awful as the rumors propose."

"You have met them?" The Witch walked briskly toward her. Lexis basked in the attention she so desperately craved.

"Yes, two boys." She did not want to mention her newfound friend Sally. "They drew weapons on me, and I struggled to escape. There was also a fairy who helped them."

"Fairy? That means that Owl is at work here." The Warlock was now really concerned. He glanced at the Witch. "This is worse than we thought. It has begun: the revenge of Fate."

164

Without a moment to spare, the Witch rushed to the fox and lifted the startled creature up by his furry, sweaty armpits. "Duke, you must gather all troops that are faithful to our cause and direct them to our castle. We need to prepare."

"What's going on?" Lexis asked.

"Lexis, there is no time to explain. We need you to find the humans and stall them. Do not permanently harm them, for they may be of some use to us."

"Use? They almost killed me!"

"Lexis, do what she commands," the Warlock blurted sternly. "They may have the secret to opening the Forbidden Cave."

"Okay." She muttered and mumbled defiantly under her breath as she made her way back to the room of magic mirrors. She knew they did not have the means or magic to open the Forbidden Cave, but she needed to remain silent for Sally's sake. She was happy her Godparents had given her this assignment, for if they sent their army, Sally would certainly come to harm from their clumsy, barbaric ways. She was also pleased she would have revenge on the two boys.

After a moment's thought, she snickered. "I know exactly what I am going to do to them."

***

John and Ryan stood outside a broken brick wall overlooking the dense marsh surrounding the ruined castle. They weren't sure if what they were standing on was an actual balcony or an old room destroyed by war. Broken rocks, bricks, and other rubble scattered the floors throughout the castle. They had explored the ruins for what seemed to be hours, but there was still no sign of the gargoyles. It was difficult to imagine what the castle had looked like when it was new and in use, because the walls, ceilings, and foundation of the structure were utterly demolished.

The sun started to set, and John lit up another cigarette. He blew smoke high into the air and felt a sense of calm flow through his body. "That's the stuff. So when do you think these gargoyles will show up?" he asked.

"I don't know," answered Ryan. "I wonder where they're hiding?"

As the sun set on the horizon, the stars grew brighter and a cold chill came over the marsh. The stale smell of swamp water filled the air as the two leaned patiently against the ruins of the highest floor of the castle.

Suddenly a beastly statue started to crack beside Ryan. He watched the fissure run up the muscular torso of the crouching lion with lizard gills and dragon wings. There was a ruff around its neck that could have been a mane or a reptilian coxcomb.

"Ryan, what did you do?" John took a step back.

"Nothing!" Ryan quickly scooted closer to John. "I was just standing there."

Around the balcony the cracking of one statue became two, and then a dozen more shattered into small fragments of rubble. Inside the statues were enormous muscled beasts. As they emerged from the dusty rubble, they stretched their legs, arms, and necks. Their large-spanned, bat-like wings flapped briskly as they yawned.

Dust and the smell of gravel engulfed John and Ryan as they watch in awe the awakening of the monstrous creatures. The beasts stood twice as tall as the two boys. Their complexions were dark gray like the massive stone statues they cocooned themselves in. Their skin and kilts were the texture of wet plaster or cement. Their large heads resembled lions' skulls, and their breath smelled of old chalk dust behind their sharp, rock-like teeth.

John and Ryan were frozen with fear. They did not know what to expect from these intimidating, grotesque creatures.

"All right boys!" One gargoyle postured like a rock star as he stepped off the ledge. "Another night of celebrations. Let's make it a good one!"

"Good idea, Bion!" another followed. "Hey, Dex, are you coming?"

"Wait for me!" A third one walked by the two boys as they stood stunned and dazed, rooted in the same spot. "Hey, look guys. We have company. Are you two here for the party?"

"Party?" John asked. "What party?"

"Fumble," an even larger gargoyle said as he came from behind. "Get the rest of the brothers from the other wing and meet us over here. We will have tonight's celebration on this wing."

"Sure thing, Dex." Fumble jumped high and glided toward the other wing of the castle.

"Who are you?" Dex looked down at them as the three stood alone on the balcony. He was not at all surprised or even happy to see them, which was unlike any other Enchantian they had encountered before. "What brings you humans to our humble home tonight?"

Another gargoyle appeared and handed him a two-gallon mug. "Here you go, Dex."

"Thank you, Tromp."

"Would you two like an ale?" Tromp looked down at the boys.

"No thanks," Ryan replied. "Don't drink."

"I don't know." John contemplated. "I had a bad experience with Butchbark Whisky the other day."

"Ah, disgusting! The only Enchantians that can drink that stuff are Leprechauns."

"So I've heard." John remembered his embarrassing incident with Liddy.

"Trust me, our home-brewed Rottin Ale is much better. Come with me. I will get you one."

John felt an assured sense of relief and security that these gargoyles were not as ruthless as they looked. Curious, he followed the gargoyle who was moving toward the others. A large circle of gargoyles held each other as they swayed from side to side, singing their drunken songs:

"Ninety-nine Mugs of Ale on the Wall,
Ninety-nine Mugs of Ale;
Take one down, pass it around,
Ninety-eight Mugs of Ale on the wall!
Ninety-eight Mugs of Ale on the Wall,
Ninety-eight Mugs of Ale;
Take one down, pass it around,
Ninety-seven Mugs of Ale on the wall!
Ninety-seven Mugs of Ale on the Wall,
Ninety-seven Mugs of Ale;
Take one down, pass it around,
Ninety-six Mugs of Ale on the wall!"

Back on the balcony, Ryan and Dex stood silently, studying each other. Ryan was still a little weary from the trauma of watching the gargoyles break from their stone cocoons, but in no time he regained his brave and gregarious attributes.

"Sorry, who are you?" asked Dex. "And what are you here for?"

"My name is Ryan, and that's John. The Great Owl sent us here. He told—"

"Oh, great." The gargoyle sighed and took a drink from his mug. "The Great Owl? He most likely wants us to join some ridiculous rebellion to retake the lands of Enchantas. Right?"

"Yeah, I think so. How did—"

"That is a useless pursuit." He took a large swig of his ale. "I told him that not even on a tri-moon eclipse would we ever partake in another hopeless war."

Dex took a few more drinks from his mug as Ryan looked around. More and more gargoyles staggered into the room. They guzzled their beer as if they had been in the desert for days without water. John was enjoying their company as he held a gallon mug aloft in both hands, trying to drink it.

"I see you notice our love for the ale." Dex sighed and finished his drink. Another gargoyle came quickly to refill it. "I'm sorry. I do not share the same optimism as the great Sage. We once did a very long time ago when we, the Brotherhood of Gargoyles, were the night-watch guardians of our founders. The Knights of Minerton were a noble group of humans, unlike the twisted Witch and Warlock." His speech was beginning to slur, and he covered it with another drink. "We had protected them for Ages, up until we were betrayed by our counterparts, the Griffins. The Griffins were the Daywatchers. We awoke from our sleep to find the castle deserted. We searched for the Knights for tocks, only to discover the betrayal."

"So what happened?" John had come back to the conversation with his mug of ale. He tried to drink as fast as he could, but there was so much.

"Ale." Dex finished another mug and again, it was quickly refilled. "And a lot of it."

"That was probably not the best decision," observed Ryan.

"We have consumed more ale than any other Enchantian since that dreadful night we lost the war. At first, we drank to have fun, party together as a brotherhood, and forget our horrific tragedy. We loved the sudden escape from reality and sense of indifference it gave us. It took a while, but as the nights of merriment diminished, our depression increased. A terrible pattern emerged. We needed to drink not to be merry, but to just feel normal. We continue to chase the feeling of euphoria, but it is no longer attainable. Over time, our depression had become greater and our loss of hope became debilitating. Soon our mission with the ale turned from chasing the euphoria to chasing normalcy. Now most of us are so deep in misery and hopelessness, it doesn't matter if we are sober or drunk. We will never feel normal again. So here we are, living our days as stone and our nights as hopeless pilgrims, journeying toward our deaths."

A tear fell down the cheek of the atrocious gargoyle. Ryan felt sympathetic and wished he could help, but he wasn't sure how.

The story made John think of his father and how he'd lost everything and had turned to the bottle. John turned and walked back toward the others, not wanting to be a part of the depressing conversation.

"Our lives once had a purpose. We lived proudly every night, fulfilling our duties as protectors; but now we've failed and must pay the price for our incompetence."

"It's not your fault that you were betrayed, Dex." Ryan tried to comfort him. "How were you supposed to know?"

"But it was my fault!" he cried more. "IT WAS!"

"How? How is it your fault?"

Dex ignored Ryan's question; he was consumed by his drunken sadness. "To make matters worse, we have lost more lives after the war than during it. Body quakes and suicide have been the causes of our demise since the war. Fate has wronged our kind for far too long."

Ryan didn't know what to do or say. Dex was tumbling down into his own sorrow. Ryan ran over to John, who was now immersed in the social conversation and songs of the gargoyles. They were singing, laughing, talking, and cheering as their mugs clanked together in celebration.

"Here's to John, a true lost man,
He came to us to find his land;
We searched up and down, and all around
But still no sign of anything found.
As Luck was fading,

And his patience waning;
The hope of discovering his way
Was surely slipping away.
Depressed, mad and all alone,
He cried, pouted,
screamed and shouted;
'All I want is to get back home.'
As we wept for the loss of our new found friend,
We knew our bond could never end.
So raise your mugs way up high
And cheers to us until we die!"

"John, I need your help," Ryan whispered as he walked up behind him.

"Chug, chug, chug!" the gargoyles chanted while John finished his jug.

"John," Ryan tapped his shoulder.

"Ryan?" John was definitely feeling the effects of the ale. As he turned, his eyes were glossy with drunkenness. "Have I told you yet that you are actually a pretty nice guy?"

"Yeah," he said. "A little earlier."

"Oh yeah, about earlier..." John leaned on Ryan's shoulders. "I am really, really, really sorry about that."

"It's okay. I understand."

"No, no, no!" John slurred. "I am truly sorry. I really think we could be best friends."

"Cool." Ryan's patience was reaching its limit. "Can you do me a favor and talk to Dex? I really think you can relate to him, you know—talk about your father."

"I don't want to talk about my dad," he snapped. "That'll just ruin my moment. I'm finally having a good time here!"

"Come on, John." Ryan was desperate. This trip to the gargoyles was not going as smoothly as he had hoped. "I thought you were my best friend. Please?"

John gave an intoxicated grin and replied, "Ah, fine! Only because you're my best friend."

As John stumbled his way to Dex, Fumble asked Ryan, "Hey, would you like a mug too?"

"No, thanks. I don't drink."

"Prude!" another gargoyle shouted from the crowd as they all laughed and went back to their drunken songs and conversation.

John lit up another cigarette as he continued to talk to Dex. "My father wasn't the best father before the divorce, but he did care more about himself and our family. When my mother left, he blamed us and started to drink more. He lost all hope, which destroyed any chance of salvaging a relationship between him, myself, and my sister."

"Did you feel betrayed?" Dex was starting to relate.

"Yes, I did! I felt betrayed by my mother and father for not getting the help they needed to keep our family together."

"I feel the same way, brother!" Dex put his arm around him.

Ryan listened to the conversation, worried that this was not going to work. He wondered how Sally and Mel were faring and if they were having as much trouble as he and John. He put his hands in his jeans pockets and pulled out the letter the owl had given him. "Oh, yeah! I almost forgot," he exclaimed, striding up to Dex. "Dex! I have something for you."

Dex turned to Ryan but noticed something was flying in the moonlit sky toward them. "Brothers!" he shouted, pointing toward the sky. "We may have intruders!"

John and Ryan both looked up but didn't see anything.

"Our eyes are made to see better than most creatures at night," Dex explained, stepping in front of them, an instinctual move to protect humans.

The gargoyles lined up in battle formation against the balcony wall as the unknown flyer came closer to the castle. Ryan leaned over and squinted, trying to get a better view of the intruders.

"I don't see a thing." John also tried to squint, but in his intoxicated state he was looking the wrong way.

"It's Sally and Mel!" Ryan exclaimed, stepping toward the edge of the balcony.

"Mel?" John slurred. "I miss that kid. Where is he?"

"They're not intruders, Dex." Ryan pointed up in the sky. "Don't worry. They're our friends."

The group of gargoyles slowly turned and returned to their playful bantering among each other, ignoring the newcomers, a little disappointed it was not a real threat.

"There are two more of you humans?" Dex moved aside to give the carpet room to land.

"Yes," Ryan replied. "Only two more."

As Sally and Mel touched down, they tried to conceal their fear of the large, grotesque beasts by focusing only on Ryan.

"What's this?" Ryan asked, indicating the carpet. "And what are you two wearing?"

"Long story." Sally tossed the Dragon Sheaths to them. "Where is the leader of the gargoyles?"

"There is no leader anymore, my dear," said Dex. "However, if you are referring to whom the previous leader was, that would be me."

"Great." Mel approached Dex and gave him the bracelet. "I believe we are supposed to give this to you."

"Is this what I think it is?" Dex sounded very excited. "Is this Fate's lost Bracelet of Hope?"

"I'm not sure." Mel took a step back from the creature. He was a little leery and intimidated by his size and looks.

"What does it do?" Ryan asked.

"This bracelet has the magical power to bring hope when all is lost. It will provide the bearer with the true destiny of Fate's plan. Where did you find this?"

"This was one of the items the Herald left for us," said Mel.

Dex put the bracelet on his massive gray finger and wore it as a ring. Suddenly a flood of positive energy filled his body. He looked down and closed his eyes and started to shake.

"What did you do to him?" Bion yelled as he looked back from the crowd.

The other gargoyles ran to Dex's side as he lay on the ground, looking like he was having a seizure.

"It is quite all right, Bion." Dex stood up and wiped the drool from his mouth. "I feel better now. This ring has taken away my hopelessness."

"This is for you." Ryan handed him the letter. "This is from the Great Owl."

Dex read the letter, and another tear rolled down his gray cheek. He looked at the four kids and then back at his fellow brothers, who were now silently sipping from their mugs and watching him. "We must help these four humans and join the Sage."

The gargoyles looked confused, obviously not sharing the same bit of optimism as Dex. "A new war is beginning to develop, and the revenge of Fate's Army is at hand."

"Dex," Bion said, a little worried. "You said yourself that more battles would be pointless and a waste of lives."

"Yeah," Tromp added. "Are you bewitched?"

"What did these humans do to you?" Fumble grabbed Mel and Sally.

The rest of the gargoyles started to murmur amongst themselves, becoming restless. This was not looking good.

"Silence!" Dex shouted. "I am not bewitched or enchanted, only enlightened by hope."

"What do you mean?" another gargoyle asked from the crowd.

"This here is the Bracelet of Hope, forged by one of the Knights. We once fought, died, and held their secrets with honor. I ask, can we bring our honor back by fighting alongside our old allies?" Dex took off the bracelet and put it on Bion.

Bion shook and quivered on the stone floor as the pessimistic drunkenness poured out of his soul.

"I understand now." Bion smiled as he looked up at Dex. "They're gone. The demons inside are gone." He looked around with wide, happy eyes. "You must all try this! I feel so much better." He looked at Sally and Mel and said, "Thank you so much."

One by one, the gargoyles put the bracelet on their fingers, and the demons of hopelessness lifted from them.

"You four must go and inspire more Enchantians," Dex said, smiling gratefully at the kids.

Mel sat cross-legged on the floating Gusto. "It was our belief that you would be our last stop, and then we could go home."

"Mel," said Ryan, walking up beside Dex. "I don't think it would have been that easy."

"Fine. So where do we go next?"

"My suggestion would be," Dex continued, "that is, if we were going to win this war, to ask the Griffins to join our cause."

"The Griffins?" Ryan was shocked. "Didn't you just tell me that they were the reason you lost the war in the first place?"

"True, but they could also be the ones to help turn the tides of this war. You must go soon. I am sure time is of the essence."

"Aren't you gargoyles coming with?"

"The Griffins have moved out to Cloud Island, and it is too far for us to fly. If we tried, the sun would rise before we reached the island. We would turn to stone over the sea and drown. Besides, our mission is to meet up with the troops gathering in Bootprint Forest."

"Gusto," Sally asked. "Do you know where Cloud Island is?

Gusto's answer was a negative shake.

"Cloud Island is a city in the sky above the Pink Sea. I suggest you make your way to Ruphport, a small town at the edge of the sea. There is a pirate named Max the Ferocious, and he knows the sea better than anyone. You may be able to charter a ride with him. It has been a few Cycles since we last met. I lost a barrel of ale to him in poker."

"That might work," said Ryan. "Gusto, do you know where Ruphport is?"

Gusto shook yes.

"Befur we go anywhure," John said as he stumbled over. "I thunk I need to threw up."

"Oh, gross," Sally exclaimed.

"Yeah, he drank a lot." Ryan shook his head in embarrassment. "I'm surprised he hasn't puked already."

"So are you two getting along?" Sally looked worried because she knew how much they hated each other.

"Yeah." A smile of relief came over Ryan. "We are."

"Oh, that's great to hear," Mel said, holding John up. "This whole experience would be crappy if you two were butting heads the whole time."

"Butting heads?" John lifted his head. "We ain't buttin' heads no more. Did Ryan tell you that we ur best friends now?"

"Yeah, he did." Mel sat him down on the Gusto.

"What am I sitting on?" John bounced experimentally, testing the surface.

"It's a magic carpet." Mel said, becoming irritated.

"A whut?" John put his feet up. "Can you believe this? I'm on a margit carpec. This place is just out of this world," John said and immediately passed out.

Gusto shook indignantly, aggravated that someone was snoring on him. John rose from his five-tack nap, lurching toward the edge of the balcony. He couldn't hold it in any longer, and he vomited over the side.

"You all right, John?" Ryan laughed as he climbed aboard Gusto. "Hope you've learned a lesson."

"Good luck, humans!" said Dex as he gathered the brothers. "Once you arrive in Ruphport, find the Husky Sled Saloon. Max the Ferocious has been known to spend time there."

John staggered back to Gusto and plopped onto the carpet next to Ryan and Mel. With the quartet comfortably on Gusto's back he slowly lifted, rising above the castle.

"Go, Gusto, go!" Sally shouted, exhilarated, and they flew up into the night sky, heading toward Ruphport.

Chapter XIII
The Wrath of the Gypsy

The wind ruffled briskly through their hair, the white sun beaming directly above. They had been flying the entire night and into the morning. It was Mel's turn to maneuver Gusto while the other three slept. Worn out from his escapades, John had been sleeping the entire trip. A blast of turbulence rippled over Gusto, rousing the slumbering travelers.

"Whoa!" Mel clenched Gusto harder.

Sally rubbed her eyes. "What happened? I was having a really good dream. Finally…"

"Just turbulence. I think Gusto is getting tired."

"Should we stop so he can take a break?" Ryan asked, stretching his arms over his head.

"Oh, my head!" John covered his dry, bloodshot eyes. "Why is that sun so bright?"

"You had quite a bit to drink." Ryan laughed, not unkindly. "Hope you learned a lesson."

"What happened? Where are we?"

"We are on our way to Ruphport to meet some pirate and travel to the Griffins."

"Griffins? Wow, I must have been really drunk. I don't remember any of that." John squinted his eyes as he rolled over, peering at a dreadful sight of the ground, miles below. "Holy crap!" He curled up to Ryan like a baby seeking comfort from his mother.

"What's wrong?" Ryan sniggered. "You afraid of heights?"

"No!" John straightened up in a vain attempt to hide the fact that he really *was* afraid of heights. "I just didn't know we were flying. What are we flying on?"

"Gusto the Magic Carpet. How many times do I have to tell you?" Mel shouted over his shoulder. The sound of the rushing wind filled his ears, so he wasn't sure who could hear him.

"Oh. Okay." By now John was accustomed to, if not at ease with, the strange and unusual.

"Let's take a break and land down there," Sally said, pointing at a prairie of yellow grass.

"Yeah, good idea." John tried to mask his intense desire to get to safe and secure flat ground.

Mel steered Gusto adroitly, and the carpet veered slightly right, angling down toward the prairie. A foot above the ground, Gusto came to an abrupt halt, hovering steadily as Mel, Ryan, and Sally simply stepped off. John, on the other hand, rolled off, landing on the ground with a thump. When he thought no one was looking, he fervently kissed the ground.

The knee-high, bright yellow grass swayed gently in the wind. The terrain was flat as far as the eye could see. The air smelled like a meadow full of lavender.

"I gotta do my exercises," said Ryan, beginning his warm-up with vigorous jumping jacks.

"Wow." John rubbed his aching head. "How can you do that this early in the morning?"

"It's not morning, John." Ryan dropped down to plank position for push-ups. "The sun is directly above us."

"Well, it's morning for me."

"I wonder how much farther we have till we reach Ruphport?" Mel sat on Gusto, petting the rug's soft nap. "Our magical friend here is getting tired."

"Hopefully not too much longer." Sally bit her lip. "We've already been here for a long time. My grandma is probably really worried."

The three of them nodded but could not really relate; John's and Ryan's families wouldn't even realize that they were missing, and Mel believed his stepfather would be relieved to have him out of the house.

"We'll get home soon," Ryan said, finishing with a set of sit-ups.

"I hope so." Sally glanced around. She had that funny feeling that someone was watching her. Lo and behold, a tall, striking beauty with long dark hair materialized behind her.

"Lexis!" Sally jumped up and down with excitement. She looked at the guys, eager to make introductions. Her joy was abruptly interrupted. Lexis was actually sneering, very much in an imperious Gypsy Princess manner, glaring at them with her penetrating purple eyes, fists clenched. Her malevolent magic charged a purple glow that pulsed from her hands.

"Lexis!" Ryan's sword appeared in his hand.

"Ryan," Sally chirped anxiously, looking at his weapon. "What are you doing?"

"What do you mean, what am I doing?" Ryan stepped forward toward the Gypsy.

"Lexis is my friend."

"What?" John and Ryan exclaimed, exchanging astonished looks.

Mel scratched his head. "I think I'm more confused than all of you put together. I've never seen this woman—uh, girl—before."

"You know her?" Ryan questioned Sally. "How?"

"I met her in the forest the other day. Why would you want to hurt her?"

"Because, Sally, she's the evil Gypsy, Goddaughter of the Witch and Warlock." Ryan spoke slowly, as if tutoring a very slow student.

"What?" She turned to the imposing, glaring female who was watching the scene with detached amusement. "Lexis, is this true?"

"Yes, it is," she snarled with resentment. "I ran away, and these boys tried to harm me!"

"We didn't! We—" John started to explain, but Lexis cut him off.

"Sally? Are you going take their side?"

"I haven't even heard their side. I didn't know there *were* sides." Sally was completely confused. Here was Lexis, materializing out of nowhere and inexplicably on bad terms with her other friends. She was stuck in the middle of the feud, and she didn't like it.

"Sally, I thought I could trust you!" The purple magic continued to throb and undulate as Lexis reflexively tightened her fists. "I thought you were my friend!"

"I am."

"Really? Then what are you doing with these good-for-nothings?" Her eyes pierced them in her anger. "They tried to hurt me."

"Hurt you?" Ryan narrowed his eyes. "No, we didn't! You're the one who hurts people! You turned me into stone."

"Lexis! Is this true?" Sally sensed that it was.

"Silence! All of you! There is no fairy to help you this time." The Gypsy shot a bolt of purple lightning at Ryan; Gusto adroitly blocked it, erupting in flames.

"Gusto!" Mel suddenly pointed at the burning rug, and a gush of water sprayed from his wrists. He aimed the jets carefully to ensure that every last spark was extinguished. Gusto flattened to the ground, half burnt. Mel turned to the Gypsy; now a glowing gold boomerang appeared in his hand. "What did you do that for?"

"Lexis!" Sally screamed. "What is wrong with you?"

"Shut up, Sally!" Lexis commanded. "We are not friends anymore!"

Sally sought shelter behind Ryan. "I don't get it. She seemed so nice in the forest. What's going on here?"

"I don't know." Ryan put out his arms, protectively shielding Sally behind him. "She turned me to stone yesterday. She's evil."

"That's right!" Lexis cycled her magic into higher gear. Now a green glow gleamed from her fists, undulating currents of voltage as visible as the bulging veins on her knuckles. "And there's no one to help you now!"

"Lexis!" Sally pleaded. "Don't do this! We can still be friends. Don't hurt us!"

"Too late, my dear!"

In a blind rage, Ryan stepped toward her, sword drawn.

"Pathetic." She snickered and then chanted:

"Gypsy Magic, Curse your Crown;
Steal your Strength, and Keep you Down!"

The green glowing beam shot from her fingertips, as cutting as a spear. Ryan crumpled to the ground, his strength lost.

"I can't move," Ryan cried weakly. "It's like she drained me. I can't feel a thing."

"What did you do?" Sally turned on her false friend. She ran to Ryan.

Before the others could retaliate, the Gypsy raised her arms high in the air and screeched:

"Hear no Evil, See no Evil, Speak no Evil;
Deprive Your Senses, without Retrieval!"

183

An explosion, a blue glimmer, erupted from the Gypsy's outstretched hands. Sally, John and Mel took the direct hit, flying several feet up in the air before they hit the ground, knocked breathless. "That should slow you down!" A wicked laugh bellowed through the air as the Gypsy Princess disappeared in a cloud of deep purple fog.

"Sally, John, Mel!" Ryan shouted as he lay on the ground. He'd recovered some power in his voice but remained paralyzed from the neck down.

Sally stood up, dizzy. She couldn't see. She tried to open her eyes. *Something's wrong*, she thought. Panicked, she ran her hands over her face, frantically searching.

"MY EYES! They're gone!" she exclaimed, terrified. "I'm blind!"

Mel staggered to his feet, equally frantic. "Sally? John? Ryan?"

"Mel!" Sally shouted tearfully behind him. "I'm right here!"

"Where is everyone?" Mel called. No one was in sight.

"Mel, I'm right here! Can you see me, or are you blind, too?"

Mel finally turned around. He ran to her. "Sally, are you okay? Oh my gosh, what happened to your eyes?"

He watched her mouth move.

"I can't hear you!" he shouted.

"Mel," she sobbed. "What is happening?"

Mel put his hands where his ears should have been. "Where are they? They're gone!" He panicked, rubbing the abnormally smooth sides of his head as if to coax his ears to reappear.

At last John collected himself and stood up to speak, but he could not move his mouth. It seemed to be missing entirely from his face. His eyes widened as he stumbled over to Mel. John managed a moan, but Mel couldn't hear a thing.

"Is that John?" Arms outstretched, Sally groped and flailed in the air, futile in her effort to get her bearings. "What's wrong?"

Mel screeched. "John, where's your mouth?"

"Can someone help me, please?" Ryan cried helplessly supine. "I can't move."

"Ryan, I don't know where you are. I can't see," Sally replied, repeating, "What is happening?"

Sally, roaming aimlessly, tripped over a large, purple glass bottle. As it shattered into small pieces, she stumbled and fell. Blue smoke seeped into the air above her and the ground started to rumble.

"Earthquake!" Sally braced herself. "Someone please come get me. I don't know where I am!"

"Sally!" Ryan yelled. "I can't move!"

"Sally? Ryan?" Mel's bewilderment grew as the earth shook beneath him.

"Mmm," John pointed to the rising blue smoke.

As it rose in a vaporous, twisting funnel, out of the smoke unraveled a school bus-sized blue worm.

"Oh, thank the lord of Enchantas!" The enormous worm stretched its tail and slammed it to the ground. The tremors knocked John and Mel to the ground. "I thought I'd be in there forever. Who do I thank for freeing me?"

"Hello?" Sally stood up, blindly groping for the creature who was speaking to her. "Who are you? What are you?"

"Who am I?" the worm giggled. "It's me, Slippy! I remember you, humans."

"Where are you? I don't want to step on you."

"Mmmm." John also stood up.

"Can you help us?" Ryan cried.

"Who was that?" The worm surveyed the scene.

"That was Ryan," Sally replied. "I can't see where he is, though."

Mel didn't know how much more he could take. "Oh, boy, a giant blue night crawler. What next?" He stepped backward just in case the thing decided to slap its tail again.

"Mmmmm. Mmmm!" John replied, waving his hands frantically.

"I can't hear what you're saying, John. As you can see, my ears have gone missing."

"Mel," Sally enunciated carefully, thinking he might be able to read her lips. "This is Slippy."

"What?" Mel tried, but all he could make out was, "He's going to eat you?"

"No. This is Slippy!" Sally exaggerated her lip sync and raised her voice several decibels.

Mel's frustration grew. "I STILL don't know what you're saying! It looked like 'He's going to eat me!'"

"I'm not going to eat you." Slippy giggled. "You did not eat me when you had the chance."

"What's it saying?" Mel took a few more steps back. "It's preparing to eat us or something."

"Mmmm," John argued.

"I'm not going to stand here and get eaten!" Mel turned around and darted through the long, yellow prairie grass. "Follow me! Run for your lives!"

Mel did not get far; John grabbed him firmly and pinned him to the ground, shaking his head and grunting for all it was worth, trying to reassure Mel that the now large, blue worm was a friend.

"Slippy, can you help us?" Sally asked. "We've been cursed by the Gypsy."

"The Gypsy?" exclaimed the worm. He thought for a moment and realized that he was the one who had informed her of their presence in Enchantas. Was he to blame for this terrible curse? Quickly, he showed his alliance to the humans by blaming the Gypsy for his recent travesty. "That wicked Gypsy tricked poor Slippy. She was the reason I was imprisoned in the bottle! She gave me potion for work that I did, but it locked me in there."

"So you will help us?" Sally asked.

"Yes." He was pleased to be of service, especially if he was to blame for the situation they were in. "As a matter of fact, I can. Growing and being in the bottle has given me the powers of Genie magic. And for rescuing me from that horrible prison, I will grant everyone one wish."

"A wish?" Sally exclaimed. "Really?"

Ryan didn't waste any time. "I wish to go back to normal and not be paralyzed," he pleaded.

Slippy slithered close as he blurted his wish spell:
"Curse be lifted, the Spell is Chanted;
Make his wish, Gifted and Granted."

The worm snapped his tail, which apparently worked as a wand as well as a wrecking ball.

Ryan sprang to his feet and rubbed his torso, arms, and legs laughing in relief and the sheer elation to be able to move again. "Oh, Slippy, thank you so much!" He had never been so frightened in his life. Having lost all feeling and movement for just that small amount of time gave him a new appreciation for the simple things he'd taken for granted.

It was Sally's turn to make a wish. "Please give me my eyes back. I would like to see."

"You must say, 'I wish.'"

"I wish to have my eyes back." At that point Sally feared she would never see again.

Slippy whisked his tail toward her and repeated:
"Curse be lifted, the Spell is Chanted;
Make her wish, Gifted and Granted."

She wiggled her glasses and squinted. Her eyesight was blurry for only a second when she finally gazed upon the mammoth blue worm. "Oh, my, Slippy. You're so huge!"

The Worm bowed, obviously pleased with his super new size, and turned toward Mel. "Now you. What would you like to wish for?"

Mel stared blankly. "What does the worm want?"

"Slippy," Sally explained, "Mel can't hear. He lost his ears. Can you give them back?"

"Of course, only he needs to wish for them."

Ryan and Sally yelled, pantomimed, and attempted every charade possible to convey to Mel that he must wish for restored hearing, but Mel couldn't understand their entreaty.

"What do we do?" Sally asked, stumped, and then turned to John. "And what are we going to do about you?"

"John knows what's going on, but he can't speak to make his wish," Ryan explained to Slippy. "Can we make their wishes for them?"

"I'm sorry," the worm replied. "My magic does not work like that. The one wishing must be the one requesting."

"What do we do?" Sally asked again, scratching her head.

After a moment, an idea occurred to Ryan. "Does anyone have a pen or pencil?"

John's eyes opened wide – *Eureka!* He brandished his spear. Using the tool as an oversized pencil, he carefully etched into the dirt at their feet: *I wish for my mouth back.*

Slippy scooted over to read the ground. With a nod, he twirled his tail and said:

"Curse be lifted, the Spell is Chanted;
Make his wish, Gifted and Granted."

"Oh, sweet release!" John immediately pulled out the battered pack and lit up a cigarette. "The worst part of not having a mouth was not being able to smoke."

"Typical." Sally laughed, rolling her eyes.

"Oh, I see," Mel yelled as he read John's note on the ground. "The worm is granting wishes!"

Everyone nodded in agreement.

"Okay. Then I wish to have my ears back so I can hear!"

Slippy once again flicked his tail.

"Curse be lifted, the Spell is Chanted;
Make his wish, Gifted and Granted."

"Okay, so don't everyone talk at once." Mel said, looking at his speechless companions. "Can someone say something so I know it worked?"

Sally laughed. "Hi, Mel. Can you hear me now?"

"Thanks, Slippy. Don't know what I'd do without you!" Mel threw his arms around the pliable end of the worm's giant tail, affectionately resting one cheek against Slippy's cool, blue skin. The other three snickered at his quirky behavior. "What? I hug when I'm grateful."

The shared laughter broke the tension cementing the forming friendships even more. All three could see that it was the little things that made them like each other more. They just needed to give each other a chance.

"Well, that was quite a feat. Thank you again, Slippy." Ryan sighed, sobered by the state of the seriously wounded Gusto. "Our next step is to find transportation. I don't think Gusto is up to a trip to Ruphport."

"Gusto!" Sally ran to the carpet, desperately stroking a charred corner. "Wish yourself better," she implored.

Gusto shook himself, feebly flapping around his edges.

"Sally," Ryan muttered. "Gusto can't talk."

"No! That's not fair. Gusto can't die! He didn't do anything wrong."

Gusto tried to pick himself up but weakly plopped back onto the ground.

"Gusto!" Sally sobbed. "Is he dead?"

"Sorry, Sally," Ryan comforted her. "There was nothing we could have done."

Sally cried, head bowed, leaning on his shoulder. She couldn't believe Lexis had turned out to be so bad.

Ryan put his arm around her as he looked to the others. "We do need to get going."

"We can't just leave him here," Sally cried.

"We can't just bring him everywhere we go, either," John said.

"That's so sad." Slippy sighed. "But I must go too. I have family to see."

Mel turned to the worm. "Slippy, are you able to get us to Ruphport?"

"I can't. My magic only works for one wish each."

"No, not a wish," Ryan said. "Give us a ride. We are on a very important mission for the future of Enchantas."

"What about Gusto?" Sally glanced at the carpet, still weeping. She wished she could bury Gusto or something. Closure would be nice. It reminded her of the lack of closure in her parents' death. Empty caskets left her hoping that someday they would be returned to her, but of course that was impossible.

"Sorry, Sally." Ryan put his arm around her again. "We really have to get going. There's no time." He turned back to the Worm. "So, Slippy, are you able to take us there?"

Slippy considered it for a moment and replied, "Why sure. I'd be happy to."

"Thank you."

"Oh, great," John spoke sarcastically, stubbing out his long-needed cigarette. "Now we're gonna ride on a slimy worm? Like this couldn't get any worse."

"Don't mind him, Slippy." Sally shot John a dirty look and chuckled. "He's always crabby."

"I don't mind." Slippy gave a huge grin. "Close your eyes, my little human friends. You may get wet."

"Wet?" the four questioned simultaneously.

As they gazed up at the large blue worm, Slippy allowed them no time to change their minds. He opened his mouth wide and scooped them into the cavernous hole. Instantly, Slippy picked up his pace, slithering fast as lightning from the prairie, leaving Gusto alone in his final resting place.

Chapter XIV

Raphport

In a matter of ticks, Slippy spit them out onto the middle of a yellow cobblestone street much like the one in Foxtown, but thankfully no foxes were in sight. Instead a mass of other Enchantians scurried aimlessly throughout the streets—mostly dogs and cats with a few pigs, goats, and other animals in the mix. The dogs walked on their hind legs in a similar manner to the foxes. There were a variety of different breeds: Wolves, Bloodhounds, Pit Bulls, Poodles, Maltese, German Shepherds, Terriers, Beagles, Huskies, Collies, Labradors, and Bulldogs. The cats, on the other hand, looked alike except for the colors of their fur. Most were black, but there were some white, blue, orange, green, and pink cats, too.

The humans remained silent as they brushed the sticky slime from their clothes. Their ride in Slippy's mouth had not been long; however, it had also not been pleasurable. They made their way down the cobblestone street, looking around with curiosity and amazement of the architecture. Each building was two or three stories tall, but the buildings themselves were not directly perpendicular to the streets; each was built on a slant, some angled more than others. Some buildings were even angled over the street, providing shade to pedestrians. No one seemed to notice the four humans as they made their way down the main street. That was until a naked, muddy pig with feathered wings trotted up to them.

"P-p-pardon me," the pig stuttered. The short, plump porcine specimen carried a satchel of red heart-tipped arrows on his back. He held a bottle of whiskey in one hand and an empty mug in the other. "Could any of you spare some Buttons for a helpless old Cupid?"

"Buttons?" Ryan was curious. "Why would you need Buttons?"

"I lost my Buttons in a game of poker, and I need a ride to my next destination."

"But why would you need Buttons?"

"I think Buttons are their currency," Mel guessed.

"Yes!" The pig stumbled. "And can you believe I lost it all? Stupid Leprechauns!"

"Leprechauns?" John remembered all too well how Liddy had stolen his jacket.

"Yes, Leprechauns." Cupid was irritated and held out his empty mug. "Now can you spare some Buttons?"

"Sorry. We have no Buttons," Mel replied. "But maybe you can help us. We're looking for a ride."

"No Buttons?" The pig swigged from his bottle. "Then what good are you?"

He stumbled away in a huff as he continued to suck at frequent intervals from his bottle.

"That was so sad!" Sally had always had a soft spot for creatures in need. She knew what it was like to be lonely and need help.

"That was weird, if you ask me," John said as they continued on their way. "Where are we going again? This place is pretty big."

"Dex said to find the Husky Sled Saloon because that is where Max the Ferocious will be," replied Ryan.

"Seriously?" John cracked up. "What's with the names here?"

As they made their way down the street, they glanced down the side streets only to find more buildings and more Enchantians scurrying to and fro.

"Hey, look." Sally pointed down a side street at a large coliseum. "Snuffball race track?" She remembered the time her parents had taken her to watch horse racing. She had loved horses as a child, but her parents had never had enough money to buy one.

As the four wandering humans turned a corner, they found themselves at a street market with many vendors selling assorted products. Everyone was hollering at the same time, attempting to catch the interest of any passersby.

"Come get your selection of beer, wine and liquor!" a dark black wolf yowled. "We have every selection Enchantas can offer! Only five buttons a bottle, with a deal of five bottles for twenty."

"No thanks." John may have been tempted if he'd had buttons.

"Fresh Lixy Fruit, vegetables, and flavored Squeaky Chews or Yarn Balls!" a yellow rabbit yelled out to the four. "The veggies are guaranteed: no whining."

Sally surveyed the selection and found that the vegetables' mouths had been shaven off.

"That's a lie!" an overlooked carrot screamed. "Help me! Help me! I need to get—"

Without hesitation, the rabbit quickly grabbed the screeching carrot and chomped him whole. "Sorry about that. There always seems to be one that gets away. Would you like to purchase?"

Sally quickly shook her head no. Repulsed, she moved on to the next booth.

"Turtle slaves! Get your turtle slaves!" a tall brown and black weasel bellowed into the street. "Hello, little miss. Would you like to purchase a fine turtle as a servant or slave? Turtles may be a little slow, but they are extremely loyal followers."

She took one look at the three turtles and was instantly distressed. Their heads, arms and legs were bandaged up. One looked as if its shell had broken. If only she had buttons, she'd buy their freedom.

"No thanks," she looked down, mortified as they moved to the next booth.

"Luck Charms and Lixy Dust!" called out a soft and familiar voice. "Get your Luck Charms! Good or bad!" The booth was filled with small colored stones, rabbit toes, horseshoes, amulets, four-leaf clovers, old keys, diamond jewelry, and small hourglass-shaped vials of shimmering bluish-gold Lixy Dust.

John looked up and saw a tall, shiny black-haired humanoid creature with butterfly wings standing behind a booth. Her face and body were covered in sparkly glitter. He froze in his spot, enamored of her beauty. His heart skipped several beats and his forehead started to sweat. "Dyad? Is that you?"

"Hello, John!" Dyad exclaimed sweetly.

"You're so tall!"

"Yes, I change my size every now and again." Even her laughter twinkled with shine.

Mel stepped up to the booth. "Hey, want to introduce me to your lady friend?"

"This is Dyad," Ryan said. "She's a fairy that helped us when we first met that nasty Gypsy. By the way, Dyad, where were you just a little bit ago? She put a curse on us."

"Oh, Ryan." She laughed softly as she sold a Charm. "You cannot expect me to be everywhere." She looked at the other two. "And you two must be Mel and Sally. It's a pleasure to make your acquaintance."

"You too." Sally smiled. She was excited to meet a real-life fairy. As a child she had always wanted to dress up as a fairy for

Halloween, and she loved fairy tales. A childhood dream had finally come true. "These Charms are really neat."

"Why thank you, Sally," Dyad smiled. "Please help yourself to one."

"Really?" Sally was beaming from ear to ear. "How wonderful!"

Ryan leaned over her to peruse the selection. There was so much to choose from. Suddenly a sharp glimmer of sparkly diamond earrings caught his eye. He picked them up and gazed.

"These would be gorgeous on you!" Ryan told Sally.

"Gorgeous?" Sally blushed.

Ryan suddenly realized how he sounded and also became bashful. "I mean they would look real nice."

"Okay." Her discomfort lightened as she turned back to Dyad. "May I have these?"

"Morning Star diamonds." Dyad grinned. "Very good choice, my dear."

"Thanks so much!" Sally put them on and hesitantly turned to Ryan. "Thank you, too, Ryan. Good choice."

She had not worn earrings for a very long time. Her mother had pierced her ears when Sally was a child, but since their death, she had never felt the need to wear them. That was until today, surveying the generous fairy's wares with Ryan. Slowly, he had been restoring her self-confidence. He had a way about him that brought joy and happiness to her life.

Ryan was experiencing similar feelings for Sally. He wasn't consciously flirting with her, but there was something about her, especially during the last couple of days, that triggered a feeling of warmth deep inside. In fact, he had never picked out earrings for a young woman before. Was there something about Enchantas that enhanced his attraction for her, he wondered? Or maybe it was just the fact he was spending more time with her. No matter what the reason was, he was not complaining. She really was a great girl.

"So…" John was curious, gawking at the dazzling fairy. "You are selling charms now?"

"No, not really. I'm incognito. Every other Enchantian sees me as a Phoenix. I think it's a perfect disguise. I was sent again to check on your progress. So where are you all heading now?"

"Dex sent us here to find a ride to Cloud Island so we can meet the Griffins. He believes they will help us," Ryan explained.

"The Gargoyles are sending you there?" She thought for a moment. "I guess that could be a good idea. They would be great allies for the cause. However, be very careful. I am not sure they can be trusted."

"Dyad," Mel piped in, "do you know where the Husky Sled Saloon is? We are supposed to find some pirate there."

"Why, yes." She pointed down the street. "It is right over there. Sally, did you lose your compass?"

"Oh, I totally forgot."

"Always keep this in mind. Bad luck may come about if you veer off course, even slightly. However, those new earrings should help."

"Thanks, I'll remember." Sally pulled out her compass and looked toward the end of the street. "I think I see it."

Sally pointed to a small building next to a large harbor where hundreds of ships were docked. This town was definitely the central hub of trade and economic development for Enchantas.

"I had better be going now," said Dyad as she compressed with a flash back into a tiny form, fluttering in the air. Her booth disappeared as she floated away. "Be careful, please. This town has been known to be a little rough."

"I'm sure we can handle anything after the foxes," Ryan said, remembering his cage fight.

"But where are *you* going?" John was once again disappointed. He really wanted to spend more time with Dyad.

"I'm sorry, John. We will meet again soon. Goodbye for now!" With a dainty wave, she zipped away.

As they continued down the sidewalk, they couldn't help but notice the diversity of the Enchantians. Some were rich, sporting golden buttons and charms on their clothing; others were poor, dressed in rags.

"But you cannot take away my houseboat," an orange cat pleaded with a bloodhound dressed in fine clothing. "It is everything I own! It is my life!"

"A bet is a bet!" the bloodhound said around the cigar stuck in the corner of his mouth. He coughed several times before continuing, "You should have thought of that before you bet your home in the snuffball races. You lost fair and square; now give me the deed or else."

"The race was fixed!" the cat wailed as he handed papers to the dog. "I will win it back. Just you wait and see!"

"It looks like some of these Enchantians have a real gambling problem," Mel whispered.

"A loss for one is a gain for another," John noted just as they reached the saloon.

The double swinging doors whipped open, nearly hitting them. A long-haired black cat and a red bulldog tumbled out of the saloon and into the street.

"You're a cheat!" the cat hissed.

"Liar!" the dog barked back as he drew his sword.

The cat struck back with his sword as the two dueled in the middle of the street. The cat was quicker with his sword, which eventually wore down the bulldog. As the dog fell to his knees, the cat jumped behind him, lopping off his head with one swipe.

"No one cheats in this town, and if you do, you'll answer to me!" the cat purred victoriously as he donned his double-horned Viking helmet. "I am the law of the town! I am the law of the sea! I am Commander Hisser!"

"Okay," Sally was frightened of the cat and disgusted after witnessing the grisly beheading. She stepped through the swinging doors. "You all ready?"

The guys followed her into the crowded saloon. Thick cigar smoke filled the air as the stench of hard liquor and wet dog engulfed their senses.

John smiled rakishly. "Now this is my kind of place."

"I can't be in here," Sally said, and she covered her nose and hurried outside.

"Okay," Ryan hollered to her. "Wait outside. We'll be right out."

"So which one do you think is Max the Ferocious?" asked John.

"Not sure." Mel glanced around the smoky bar. "Let's ask the bartender."

"Good idea," Ryan said through a cough.

As John looked around the saloon, he saw a familiar face in the dark corner. "Hey guys, I'll be right back," he told the others, and he started to make his way through the crowd, away from the bar.

"Okay, meet us outside," Ryan replied.

After a few tacks of pushing and shoving, John finally reached his target: a large, round table where a bloodhound, a bulldog, a beagle, a black cat and a leprechaun sat, the latter of whom blurted a greeting full of familiar blarney. "Well, hello stranger!"

"I want my jacket back!" John said, gritting his teeth.

"Well now, me fine fellow." Liddy took off his green top hat. "That is no way ta treat an ol' acquaintance."

"You drugged me, sold me into slavery, and stole my jacket! I want it back!"

"Liddy, sounds like you've been pretty busy," the cat meowed while the dogs howled with laughter.

"I did not steal. I purchased it." Liddy puffed on his pipe. "Check your pockets."

John looked through his pockets and found three golden buttons that he was sure had not been there earlier. "All right, if that's how you want to play this. I want to buy it back." He placed the currency on the table.

"Me dear boy." Liddy chuckled. "That is not how a business transaction works."

"Fine. Then I'll play you for it!"

"Ye want to gamble?" Liddy laughed out loud. "Ya only gots three Buttons; this is a high-roller table, me boy! Why don't ya try a wee little roller's table by the bar?"

"Will this get me into the game?" John slammed his bracelet on the table. "How much is this worth to ya, Liddy?"

Liddy paused for a tack. Then, hiding his excitement, he replied, "An antique bracelet, eh? That may be worth a pretty Button or two." A chair slid from across the room and in front of John. "Pull up a chair, me boy, and let us see what ye got!"

John lit up another smoke and countered, "Deal me in."

***

Sally waited impatiently outside the saloon. She had a funny feeling the residents were looking at her. It was half true; a few glanced at her, but they were only curious as to what she was and why she was there. In any case, this encouraged her to slowly move herself from the street and into an alleyway between two buildings. The buildings leaned against each other, making a large triangular opening and casting a shadow. No one seemed to notice her, except the voice from behind.

"Sally," a familiar voice whispered.

Sally quickly turned to see the Gypsy Princess standing less than a foot away. She seemed taller somehow, and her bright purple eyes penetrated Sally.

"Lexis?" Sally's eyes widened in surprise. "What is going on with you? Why did you hurt us back on the prairie?"

"You betrayed me, Sally!" Lexis scorned. "What do you expect?"

"No, I didn't. Those are my friends too. Why are you like this?"

"I am sorry, Sally. For ages my Godparents held me prisoner in that castle, so my social skills are not as good as they once were. Ever since I arrived in Enchantas, I can't seem to make friends. That was until I met you. After that, I got enough courage to try to befriend those two boys, but that backfired. All I want is a friend, Sally," the Gypsy said as a tear ran down her cheek.

"I'll still be your friend, Lexis."

"Really?" The Gypsy's eyes lit up with excitement. "Then I will give you one more chance to help me. Ditch these boys and become my friend. Together we can find a way home."

"No. Lexis, I can't leave them."

Lexis's eyes flashed. "Why? We are both strong women. We can take care of ourselves. We don't need men to help us—or parents for that matter!"

"I know, but that's not it." Sally gulped, fearful of what the Gypsy might do to her. "They are my friends."

The Gypsy narrowed her eyes, trying to read Sally's mind. It was easy for anyone to see why Sally really wanted to remain with the group.

"It's that boy, isn't it?" Lexis cringed.

"Who? Ryan?" She blushed and looked away. "No."

"I knew it!" the Gypsy punched the wall behind Sally. "You will never join me!" She turned and started toward the back alley.

"Wait." Sally took a step forward but stopped. "Where are you going, Lexis?"

"Back home! There is nothing for me here. Consider this your last chance, Sally." She wiped her tearful face. "I really thought we could be best friends...like sisters."

"We still can! Why are you so stubborn?"

"Because I don't like your other friends. It's either them or me."

"But—"

"This is your freebee, Sally. I will not harm you this time. My Godparents have sent out a hunting party for all of you. You had better watch your back," the Gypsy said as she conjured her magic. With that, she disappeared into her purple magical smoke.

Sally's heart dropped, and she wondered if she should tell the others. She slowly made her way to the Saloon doorway and leaned against the wooden wall. She decided not to mention her encounter. *Why make them worry more?* she thought.

***

Meanwhile, Ryan and Mel finally pushed their way through the crowd and up to the bar. When they reached it, they saw a German Shepard bartender busily running from one end of the bar to the other.

He stopped for a tick, clearly yearning for a moment's rest, and snarled softly at the sight of the two kids. "So what do you two want?"

"We're actually looking for someone," Ryan said. "Do you know Max the Ferocious?"

"Oh, yeah." The bartender looked around the saloon. "Don't believe I have seen him today. He might be at sea already. His charter was departing today."

"Bartender, give me another mug!" a beagle at the other end of the bar slurred.

"I hate my job," the bartender muttered before leaving to help the customer.

"Great." Mel crossed his arms. "Now what are we going to do?"

"Not to worry." The bartender came back and pointed out the window. "He's right out there loading his ship."

They looked out at the pier, where a few vessels were tied up.

"He's the black dog wearing an eye patch. Lost his right eye a few Cycles back. See right there? He's no longer a Pirate. He's now a profitable businessman. However, I don't quite know the difference. They all seem to steal something from someone. Anyway, he changed his name to intimidate other Buccaneers and Vikings. He says it makes for safer travels when he's doing business."

"Thank you!" Mel said as they headed for the door.

"Not a problem. I wish I had more customers like yourselves." The German Shepard shot down a glass of Sniffle Rum. "Not drinking. The nicest kind!"

Once outside, the two signaled Sally to follow. She promptly followed, pleased not to be alone. The ship looked large from afar, but it was even bigger the closer they got. They looked up at the enormous vessel in amazement. It had twenty-one large canvas sails strategically positioned from the three masts to harness the most wind. The three-level deck was outfitted with twelve large cannons, their barrels projecting from battlements below. Dozens of dog sailors swarmed above and below decks, attired in matching knee-length, black-and-white-striped shirts, each with a sword hanging from his leather belt. They sang loudly and cheerfully as they prepared the ship for departure. On the bow, at the very front of the ship, was mounted a metal molded dog skeleton. The gruesome figurehead had surely been placed there to intimidate any enemies.

They approached Max, a short Border Collie with all black fur except for his white paws and a white circle around his unpatched eye. Next to him was the plump, feathered-winged pig they had met earlier. He swayed as he suckled from his bottle and spoke to Max.

"He doesn't look that ferocious to me," said Sally.

"Please, Max?" cried the pig. "You do not understand! It is mating season over there, and my boss will kill me if I miss it again. I need to be there by season's end!"

"Cupid, I truly feel for you, but this is business, not charity," Max replied and then yelled out into the street. "Attention, all hands! Remember, this is a charter ship and you need money—Buttons, jewelry, or whatever you possess of value—to pay your way. This is not a charity!" He pushed the pig aside as he acknowledged the three humans. "Welcome to my humble ship, the sensational *Storm Glider*. How can I help you?"

"Dex the Gargoyle sent us," Ryan responded.

"Ahh, Dex! How is he doing? Last I saw him, he was in rough shape. You know—with the drinking." Max walked up behind the Cupid pig, who was trying to sneak on the ship. "What have I told you? Get out of here! Stupid, drunk Cupid!" He turned back to the threesome. "So how can I help you?"

"We need a ride to Cloud Island."

"Cloud Island?" Max considered it. "Hmmm... It has been quite some time since my ship went airborne," he glanced up at her masts and smiled. "Sure, not a problem. I'm always ready for an adventure. Besides, it is right on our way."

"Great." said Mel.

"So, how are you all going to pay?"

"Pay?" Sally asked.

"Oh, dear lords of Enchantas! Not again."

"Sorry," Ryan chimed in. "We just thought that since Dex—"

"Hey, Dex is a great gargoyle and all, but like I told this drunken Cupid here, this is business, not charity. Do you or will you have payment in"—he glanced at his watch—"two ticks?"

"Umm, I don't—"

John walked up then and handed the dog a paw full of golden Buttons from a leather pouch. "Will this be enough?"

"It sure will. More than enough."

"Where did you get that?" Ryan asked, shocked. He instantly thought John had stolen it but then saw his jacket. "And I see you got your jacket back."

"I beat a Leprechaun, three dogs, and a cat in poker."

"Ahh, you played Liddy, I see." Max grinned. "You must be a pretty good at cards to beat him. He is always cheating."

"Yeah, well, you can't always beat a straight flush." John smiled victoriously.

"Excellent." Max nodded. "Come aboard, then. This ship sails precisely on time."

"Wait," Sally said, considering the pathetic, dirty pig. He stood bereft on the sidewalk, with his shoulders hunched over, picking his nose in between drinks from his ever-present bottle. "Will that payment be enough for Cupid to come with us?"

"I suppose." Max sighed dramatically. "However, I will not be responsible for any damage he does or trouble he causes. That will come out of your pockets."

"Okay." Sally called to the creature, "Hey, you there! Cupid? We got you a ride."

"Really?" the pig staggered to his hooves. "How?"

"We paid for you." She gestured urgently. "Come aboard now – hurry, before it leaves."

"Thank you so much." He hiccupped. "You do not know how much I needed this ride."

"I know. You're welcome."

Max continued to greet and inspect his crew. He was a very proud captain and valued his men. He knew the importance of each mate's contribution to the efficiency of his ship.

"Hello, Butch!" Max laughed as he patted a long, skinny black Poodle on the back. "Nice haircut. Where is your matching dress?"

The entire crew erupted with laughter.

"Shut up!" Butch replied in a deep, scratchy voice. "I was a little drunk and went to the beauty shop instead of the barber shop."

"No." The Captain laughed uproariously. "I really think it's a good look for you."

"So how long is this trip?" Ryan asked. "And where do we stay?"

"We should arrive at Cloud Island sometime tomorrow," Max replied, rubbing his eye patch. "You will be staying below decks. Since you all are my last passengers, you may have trouble finding a berth. The sleeping quarters are first come, first served."

"That's fine," Mel replied. "We'll manage."

"Aye, then good." Max strode toward the bridge. "Now, you are all welcome to hang out on the upper deck, UNLESS—" He paused, making sure they were all listening. "Unless we are under siege by Raiders or Vikings or a storm arises. The last thing we need is an all-out search for a lost passenger when my crew should be doing more important things. Understood?"

"Aye, Captain!" Mel answered, snapping to a salute. Laughing, Sally and Ryan also saluted.

"What if you were being attacked and I wanted to fight?" John asked, his imagination captured by swashbuckling glories.

"That's fine with me, but you would be volunteering. You get no pay."

"That's all right." John grinned, excited at the possibility of a spirited battle.

"Prepare to cast off!" Max yelled to his crew.

The mariners let loose the lines—braided rope thicker than a man's arm—that held *Storm Glider* at the wharf. They raised the heavy bronze anchor, hauling in its chain. As the ship slowly left port, the captain maintained the wheel at the bridge with masterly ease. He was a very experienced helmsman and navigator, which made the four new sailors feel safe in his hands.

The ship was steady; the water was calm. They headed out of the harbor and into the open, pink sea. They were finally off.

Chapter XV
The Viking Bounty

Pearlescent pink seawater flowed beneath *Storm Glider*, and the dance of the gentle waves had a calming effect on the kids. The sky was still bright green with the white sun shining high above. The sea had a sweet smell, and in the humidity, every breath they took tasted and smelled of cotton candy. Ruphport was far behind them; there was nothing but open sea as far as the eye could see. Cupid stumbled around the upper deck nursing his bottle, oblivious to reality. He took frequent stabs at conversation, but his drunken babble was unbearable and incomprehensible to both crew and passengers. Both groups consistently avoided him.

The crew remained busy, inspecting rigging, adjusting sail trim, lashing down any loose items and setting up for the voyage. They passed the time mainly by singing loud sea chants and hoisting their bottles of rum:

"Yo yo, ho ho ho,
Yo yo, ho ho ho.

We drink, we fight;
We cheat and gamble throughout the night.
We are the Pirates of Sea.
Yo yo, ho ho ho,
Yo yo, ho ho ho.
Vikings come, Raiders go;
Courage begins with the sword or bow.
We are the Pirates of Sea.
Yo yo, ho ho ho,
Yo yo, ho ho ho.
Cannons fire, sails burn;
Defeat comes with no return.
We are the Pirates of Sea.
Yo yo, ho ho ho,
Yo yo, ho ho ho.
The ship floats, the ship flies;
Whatever the battle, it never dies.
We are the Pirates of Sea."

As the crew sang and worked tirelessly, making sure the ship made good time, Ryan and Sally leaned on the port side of *Storm Glider*, looking out over the water. John and Mel conversed with each other on the starboard side.

"This reminds me of sailing with my brother and parents when I was young," Ryan said. He was growing fonder of Sally. He looked forward to talking and laughing with her. "Have you ever been on a boat?"

"Actually," she said, feeling herself blush again, "this is my first time. I'm having a hard time walking straight."

"Yeah." Ryan nodded. "Your inner ears are adjusting. You'll get used to it."

"So did you take many trips on your parents' boat?"

"When I was younger, yes, but not lately. My parents usually leave my brother and me home when they travel. Right now they're in Florida or something."

"Really? That's weird. And school just started."

"I know. They don't act like real parents, if you ask me." He frowned. "They care more about themselves than about my brother and me."

"I'm sure that isn't true, Ryan." Sally touched his hand. Her heart skipped, and feeling bashful, she pulled it away. "I'm sure they love and care about you."

Ryan gave a cynical shrug. "They sure don't show it. But enough about me. What about your family?"

Sally sighed. "Well, it's just me and my grandma now. It's been a few years since my parents died."

"Oh." Ryan paused for a second and put his hand on hers. His heart skipped too, but he wasn't timid, so he left his hand where it was. "I'm so sorry. That must have been hard."

Her eyes watered. "Yeah. It was, but grandma and I are best friends. She really took care of me and still does."

"Did you and your parents ever go on trips?"

"Yeah, short ones." She smiled again, thinking back to when her mom and dad were alive. "We all loved to watch the horse races, so we would go every weekend during the summer. It was so much fun. They would bring me to the stables to see the horses after each race. My favorite was named Sunflower."

"Tell me more about them, Sally." Ryan scooted closer to her as his warm, luminescent blue eyes locked with hers. She silently gulped as her heart started to race.

"You mean my parents? Or the horses?" she teased. *Wow,* she wondered. *Am I actually flirting a little bit?*

As they stood on the teak deck, bathed in the warm sun, she started talking comfortably with him, not really paying attention to what she was saying. All she knew was at that moment, she had never been happier or more at ease in her life. Her attraction to him grew stronger every moment. Slowly but surely, their bond was becoming unbreakable.

***

On the other side of the ship, Mel and John spoke with Butch about the ship and its crew. They were very interested in the life of a pirate.

"So how will we get up to Cloud Island?" Mel was curious. "I heard the captain talk about flying."

"Flying?" John's eyes widened with fear. He couldn't escape his fear of heights. It seemed that there was no way he would avoid another adventure in the sky. He mumbled under his breath, "Man, I'm content at sea."

"Oh, yes. Many ships have the ability to fly," Butch said as he attached a new line to the mainmast on the *Storm Glider*'s starboard foredeck. "But the magic that produces flight comes at a very high price. Not sure how many Buttons it costs for Lixy Dust, but all I know is that the barrels are not cheap. That is why, to save expenses, the captain likes to sail on the sea instead of flying. He used to work for the Witch and Warlock, delivering Lixy Dust around Enchantas."

"Really?" Mel was intrigued. "So what happened?"

"Well, he was the best ship merchant in Enchantas. He had done it for many Cycles up until he had a heated disagreement with the Warlock and quit. I was with him for the last few Cycles, and let me tell you, it was a very stressful time. Anyway, after he quit, we started to loot and smuggle Lixy Dust to Anti-Freewill lands. We all became fierce pirates. That was also how we started to charter rides. It was our cover for smuggling. A few very profitable Seasons went by before the Witch's and Warlock's troops finally caught us. The Captain took all the blame and was tortured for an entire Cycle. That was how he lost his eye." Butch paused and took a large breath. "We tried to break him free but failed. When he was finally released, we devoted our lives to him for his brave and admirable act of taking the blame and protecting his crew. He quit pirating of course, due to the fear of getting caught. So we've remained a charter vessel ever since."

"Wow." John sighed. "That's horrible, what was done to him. Has he ever thought about fighting back?"

"The captain definitely has no love for the Witch and Warlock and is against everything they stand for. I believe he would fight against them if he had the opportunity."

Mel seized the opportunity to gather more Enchantians. "We're actually on a mission to enlist fighters for Fate's army. Do you think he would be interested?"

"You may want to ask him; however, my advice is to inquire after our trip. He usually prefers to focus on one task at a time."

"So do you see many battles out here at sea?" asked John.

"Well there are many Raiders, Pirates, and Vikings out here. They try to attack us, but they are no match for the *Storm Glider*. This ship is one of the strongest and fastest ships in Enchantas. Not to worry—you are in very safe hands with us. We are ready for any looters that storm our ship."

"Yeah." John pulled out his spear and grinned. "I'll be ready, too!"

"I am very pleased that we have an enthusiastic passenger on board if a crisis arises. Many flee to cower below decks." Butch patted him on the shoulder before hurrying to his next duty. "I'll be sure to call on you if needed."

"That's not fair! You got a cool spear, and all I got was a stupid boomerang," Mel exclaimed. "What the heck is this good for?"

"I don't know." John laughed. "Maybe the bracelet knew you like to play with yourself."

"Ha. Ha. Very funny."

"Attention, everyone!" the captain's bellowing voice resonated from his post at the wheel. "If I could get everybody's attention, please! It is that time!"

As crew and passengers gathered on the main deck, many muttering, most wondering what was going on. Sally and Ryan stayed in their spot by the railing, their hands almost touching. Ryan spotted the other two members of their foursome.

"What's going on?" he asked Mel.

"Not sure," Mel replied.

"Hope it's a battle," John proclaimed eagerly.

"Some of you are new sailing with me," the Captain continued. "So I will give you the rundown of activities on this ship. There is a casino and saloon on the bottom deck that is open all tocks of the day and night. And around midday, which is now, we will start snuffball races. You may place your bets with Butch and he will keep track."

"Sir?" Butch huffed. "Again?"

"Yes, Butch, again."

"Snuffballs?" John whispered, in case any were lurking around. "I hate those things."

"Snuffballs are cute," Sally said with a laugh. "What are you talking about?"

"Avast, ye swabbies!" The captain gestured grandly. "Bring out our snuffballs!"

A Pit bull sailor produced an intricately wrought iron key, which he inserted into a large mahogany chest. Six snuffballs rolled and bounced onto the deck, aiming for the edge of the ship. An orange one bounced out over the lifelines and tumbled into the sea.

"Oh no!" Sally exclaimed. "Can they swim?"

"No!" the captain slapped his knees, shaking with mirth. "I bought these snuffballs from the market. There is a wolf who traps them in the Valley. Not to worry. I got them at a good price."

"Poor things. They probably have family."

"Snuffballs, COME!" the Captain commanded. The remaining five: green, red, yellow, blue, and purple reluctantly rolled up to the commander as slowly as possible. They quivered in terror.

"We want to go home!" a squeaky voice cried.

"We don't like it here," another moaned.

"Trust me, my furry, round, little friends. You will all have a chance to win your freedom."

"Win?" The green snuffball bounced.

"How?" The red one rolled in quick circles.

The yellow one hopped. "Do we get to play games?"

"We love games!" the blue furball cheered.

"Not a game, a race! The winner of this race wins their freedom when we return to Ruphport."

"Yay!" The five snuffballs bounced with excitement. They adored all games, especially racing.

"There is the race track." Max pointed up to the three masts and gave a thumbs-up to his crew.

The sailors furled and bundled most of the sails, with only enough canvas left up to retain current speed. Meanwhile, sets of hammock nettings were unrolled to form a horizontal zigzag racecourse high above. The course contained a very complex set of net slides and resembled a marble maze.

"Snuffballs." Max walked briskly onto the bridge, parting the crowd of spectators as he walked. "You will start on top—here."

The snuffballs hurried up to the bridge eagerly. They could hardly wait for the race to begin.

"And you will roll yourselves onto the other side of the deck to enter the netted maze from the edge of the bowsprit. The track consists of four levels of labyrinth nets. You must be careful, because any wrong move could be a deadly one. The first to reach the watchman's post on the foremast wins."

A bulldog waved from the post high above.

Max turned to the crowd and shouted, "Everyone, please place your bets and move aside. The snuffballs need to pass through." He laughed. "I am sure they would not hesitate to knock you off this ship."

"Sally," Ryan said, putting his arm around her. "Let's make a bet. John, do you have any Buttons left?"

"Well yeah, but—"

"Good. Give us a couple."

"Come on, man. I won these fair and square."

"John," Sally said, giving him puppy dog eyes. "You owe me."

"Fine." He sighed, but after he gave her the buttons, a feeling of kindheartedness came over him.

"John, can I have a couple?" Mel was eager to place his own bet.

"Mel? Come on!"

"Please? I have a real good idea."

"Here, I might as well make a bet, too."

"Sally," Ryan whispered in her ear. "Which one do you wanna bet on?"

Sally thought for a moment and smiled. "I like the yellow one. It reminds me of a Sunflower."

Ryan ran up to Butch and gave him his bet. "Two Buttons on the yellow one."

"Okay, any others?"

"Put me down for five on red." John slapped five buttons in Butch's paw.

"What if no one wins?" Mel asked, his grin mischievous.

"What do you mean?" Butch was confused. "No one wins?"

"If they all fly off the ship and none finish, then who gets the winnings?"

"I guess you all would get it back. But that has never happened before."

"So what if I bet on no snuffball winning?" Mel asked.

Butch and Max were perplexed. No one had ever requested such a thing.

"Then you would win it all, I guess," Max conceded.

"Okay." Mel handed over a Button. "I'll take that bet."

The rest of the crew placed their bets with Butch and stepped back to watch.

"Ladies, gentlemen," Max cried as he marched back up to his overlook. "If all bets are in, let us get this race underway!"

The snuffballs dribbled themselves impatiently as they waited for the Captain's signal.

"The sound of the cannon will start the race." Max lifted his black furry arm. "Ready? On your mark! Get set!"

BANG! went the cannon, and the five snuffballs rolled and bounced as fast as they could to the opposite side of the ship.

They pounced on each other trying to take the lead, and a few accidentally banged into spectators. John was ready with his spear; he did not want to get hit by one again. As the racers reached the narrow bowsprit at the head of the ship, the red one jumped a little too high, and the blue quickly knocked him off the ship.

"What the heck?" John yelped. "That's not fair! I lost already!"

"Four more left." Mel laughed.

"Go, yellow!" Sally screamed as the crowd followed the exciting race. Sally rubbed her earrings for good luck, hoping for the best.

As they entered the netted maze, the green was in the lead while the purple, yellow, and blue followed close behind. They scurried up the nets and entered a cross-section by the mizzenmast. All veered right except the blue one, who took a detour and almost flew off the ship. Instead it bounced off the spanker and fell into the lead. The green snuffball did not like that move and at the next turn pushed the blue, knocking it off the ship from the portside.

"Help me!" the blue ball's squeaky voice screamed as it splashed into the water.

The crowd roared with excitement.

"Three more to go!" Mel cried and smirked.

The purple and yellow were side by side as they climbed another slide. Suddenly they came upon another cross-section near the middle of the foremast. The yellow quickly moved in front and deked to the right. The purple decided to swerve to the left, but it was a trap. The purple snuffball screamed extensively before it, too, splashed into the deep pink sea.

There were two more levels of track left, and the green and yellow snuffballs were the only two remaining. The green was ahead by a little, which made the yellow more determined to roll faster.

"Come on, yellow!" Sally, Ryan, and a few other spectators cheered.

"Go green! Go green!" opposing gamblers chanted.

At once, the yellow snuffball caught up, and they fought for the lead. As they passed the mizzenmast, they turned around and headed closer to the watch post. Bumping and bruising, the two snuffballs rolled as fast as they could toward the finish. The Bulldog quickly ducked down in his basket, afraid of being knocked from the crow's nest. The green ball bounced slightly, trying to make the basket, but the yellow came from behind and hit the backboard, falling directly into the post. The green flew high into the air and down into the sea.

"And the winner is—" Max paused. "Yellow!"

"We won!" Sally jumped into Ryan's arms. The thrill of victory rushed through their bodies. As they squeezed each other tightly and laughed, they were unaware of how close their faces were. Suddenly their eyes locked, and both of their stomachs began to flip-flop. Their hearts began to race as they looked at each other.

"Good job, guys," John muttered. "Beginners' luck, I'd say."

"Well," Mel groaned. "I still think I had a good idea to bet on everyone losing."

"Yeah." John laughed as the two walked away. "That was pretty crafty."

"So that was fun, huh?" Ryan whispered to Sally.

"Yeah." She smiled, looking deep into his eyes as he gazed into hers. "That brought me back. I'd forgotten how exciting races are. Thank you, Ryan."

Slowly their heads came closer together. She closed her eyes as he closed his. Time stopped for a couple ticks, their lips only inches apart. Suddenly a bell sounded from above, startling them. They quickly sprang apart and glanced around.

"Captain," the Bulldog cried from his watch post above. "I see a ship."

"A ship?" the Captain yelled. "What markings?"

The Bulldog patted the excited snuffball and took out his telescope. "A single-sailed Viking ship, sir! Their oars are out, and they are heading directly for us."

"Men, hurry and prepare yourselves for battle. Take down the race nets and set the sails."

"Captain, can't you fly to avoid them?" Mel asked.

"And what? Flee? Nonsense, my boy!" He grabbed a sword and smiled. "Can't miss the excitement of battle, we have only been out to sea for a tock."

"Yeah, but—"

"Don't worry, Mel," John said, gripping his spear. "This will be fun. I missed the battle with the foxes, but I am definitely not missing this one!"

"What's going on?" Sally asked.

"We are going to battle with some Vikings!" John was thrilled. "Come on, Ryan. Get your sword out."

"Wait, I'll be back." Ryan grabbed Sally's hand. "Follow me. I want to make sure you're safe."

Ryan and Sally raced down below to find a good spot for her to hide. Neither mentioned their near-kiss. Ryan wasn't afraid of a fight, but he was worried about her safety.

Mel paced the deck frantically while John gripped his spear, readying himself for battle.

"Are you going to fight with us?" Butch asked Mel.

"I—I don't think so."

"Well you'd better get down below with the other passengers. Or else you will be in my way."

Mel quickly took his advice and headed toward the companion-way steps.

"Mel, come on." John seemed disappointed. "Where are you going?"

"Sorry, John. I am not ready for this!"

"Ah, whatever."

Mel passed Ryan as he was racing to return to John. "I take it Mel isn't fighting with us."

"Nope."

"Well, I actually don't want to either. It's not our fight."

"Yeah, but it'll be fun." John grinned. "Besides, if I'm gonna be stuck here, I want to enjoy it somehow."

The Viking ship was very close. As John and Ryan watched the single-masted ship move closer, they could see the battle-enraged cats hissing and howling with determination. They raised their axes and swords high above, eager to fight.

"Ready the cannons!" Max barked.

A deck below, wooden window flaps opened, and loaded metal cannons were positioned.

"Oh, great." Max snarled as he saw a black cat wearing a Viking helmet and steering toward them. "Commander Hisser! I really hate that cat!"

The Viking ship drew close to the port side of Storm Glider, and dozens of invading black cats armed with axes, swords, and daggers leaped on the deck. As they charged the awaiting dogs, they hissed loudly, foaming at the mouth.

"Fire!" Max screamed, and the loud bangs of the cannons echoed from below. Smoke filled the air between the ships, but it did nothing to hinder the charging cats.

"Get the humans!" Commander Hisser hissed. "Get them all!"

"What the heck do they want us for?" Ryan asked John, when suddenly four cats charged after them with axes.

"I don't know." John stabbed three of them at once. "This sure is fun, though!"

"Typical," Ryan said as he threw a cat into the sea.

"There are two of them!" Hisser screeched. "Get them! Their bounty is worth a fortune!"

"Nice," John said as six more ran toward them. "We even have a bounty."

"The Witch and Warlock will give us treasure we could only dream of."

"Be silent, you hairball-coughing varmint!" The captain jumped onto Hisser with rage. "Get off my ship!"

"Max the Ferocious," Hisser snarled showing his stained feline incisors. "How pleased I was to find out the humans were on your ship. Better to kill two dogs with one stone, I always say."

"You wish!" Max punched Hisser in the snout. "What do you want with those humans anyway?"

"Word is out, my boy. A bounty from your old employers. I was surprised you never took it."

"I do not work for those sorcerers anymore. I'm a business dog now, not a sleazy pirate."

"That is a good thing," the cat said, putting Max in a chokehold and holding a dagger to his neck. "Since you retired, my profits have tripled!"

"Go ahead." Max clenched his teeth. "Kill me."

Hisser looked around the ship and realized his troops were losing. He laughed mirthlessly. "And spoil the fun for next time? Nonsense!"

The dogs stood their line and fought bravely. The cats had no chance against them. The side of the ship rained defeated cats as they splashed, meowing in a cowardly way, into the sea. Ironically, these Vikings despised water and swimming.

"Retreat!" Hisser let go of Max and leaped up onto a sail to claw his way onto his own vessel. "Back to the ship!" he ordered.

The few cats left in the battle obeyed. The rest, floundering in the pink depths, were left to drown.

"Stay and fight!" Max stood up and ran to the edge of the port side. "Scaredy cat!"

"Until next time, my old foe!"

The lines hastily pulled in, the Viking ship quickly sailed away.

"Sir!" Butch ran to his captain. "We have more loaded rounds. Permission to fire?"

Max sighed. "No. There will be other times. Save our ammo."

He pushed Butch aside and marched toward the two humans. "Could you two please tell me what that was all about?"

"I'm not sure, Captain," Ryan replied. "I'm truly sorry. I didn't know there was a price on our heads."

"Yeah, well, you're lucky you're on my ship. Any other captain would not think twice about cashing you in. Why do you have a price on your head? What did you do?"

"I'm not sure. We have been sent to enlist others to join Fate's army to bring peace back to Enchantas.

"You're kidding, right? I have not heard of this. Under whose orders?"

"The Great Owl," John confirmed. "He sent us to ask the Gargoyles, who in turn sent us to ask the Griffins."

"It's true," Butch added. "The cowardly one told me. He was going to ask you to join."

"Well any friends of the Owl and Gargoyles are friends of mine," said Max. He had been seeking the right opportunity to get back at the Witch and Warlock for what they had done to him. "Count us in this fight! But only after this journey. Other passengers have paid for this trip, and I do not intend to leave any behind."

"Thank you!" said Ryan and John, both pleased. The more Enchantians they found to help, the closer they were to finding a way home.

"No problem. Well, with that excitement behind us, I suggest you find a room before word of your bounty gets out and some greedy passengers decide to cash you all in."

"Okay, thanks," said Ryan. He was eager to get below decks and check on Sally.

"I'd find a room quick before they are all taken," Max advised, "or you all will have to sleep with my crew. Trust me, the smell is unbearable."

"Sir?" Butch and a few others seemed offended. They were busy dumping a few remaining dead cats overboard.

"I am only joking." Max laughed, but he wasn't really kidding.

As the crew swabbed up the blood on the decks and tended to the wounded, John and Ryan quickly went below to look for Sally and Mel, hoping they were okay.

They finally reached the small closet where they were hiding. Sally dove into Ryan's arms, bashfulness forgotten as she was so relieved to see him alive and unharmed.

"Oh, my gosh. You're all right!" She squeezed him hard. "I was so worried. I even rubbed my earrings for good luck."

"Really?" Ryan smiled as their eyes locked. "Well, I think it worked."

As they held each other intensely, their eyes closed once again. Their hearts dropped as their lips were again inches away from touching.

"Are you lovebirds ready?" John asked, pulling Mel out of the closet. "Hurry. We have to find a room. I don't want to stay in some smelly, wet-dog-stench room with the crew."

Ryan grabbed Sally's hand as they followed the other two through the corridors of the ship, searching for an available room.

Chapter XVI
Fate's Arrow

It was late at night and the rocking of the ship had lulled everyone to sleep, except for Mel. It wasn't that he was seasick; he'd just always felt uneasy in boats—especially when he was cooped up in a bunk room shared with four others. Earlier that day, after the battle, they had tried to find separate rooms, but there was only one left. So Sally, Ryan, John, Mel, and the pig, Cupid, had to share the same small space. Mel hoped this would be a one-night deal. He tossed and turned, finally opening his eyes to see if anyone else was awake. A single oil lamp hung in the room, swaying with the motion of the ship. Ryan and Sally shared a tiny rectangular berth across the room while John and Mel shared the other. Cupid had passed out in the middle of the floor earlier that day and had been lying in the same position since well before the battle.

"John," Mel whispered as he nudged him. "Are you awake?"

"Ugh," John moaned. "Now I am. What's up?"

"I don't know. I just can't sleep."

"So you decided to wake me up?"

"Misery loves company, I guess," said Mel.

"You are so annoying." John lit a cigarette. "Now that you got me up, you are going to have to get used to me smoking."

"That's fine, as long as I have someone to talk to. I'm really bored."

"So what do you wanna talk about?" John scooted himself upright.

"I don't know." Mel's mind raced with wild ideas as he tried to think of a topic. "Why did you end up repeating ninth grade? I mean, you're a smart kid."

"Well..." John sighed and took a drag. "The truth is that my dad is a drunk, and I missed a lot of school days because I needed to drive him around to work, grocery shopping, and crap like that during the day. He's really not supportive at all. My sister is too young to drive, so I became the man of the house."

"Wow. That really sucks. My stepdad usually tries to work me too hard." Mel didn't really want to talk about his family, but he desperately wanted John to stay up and keep him company, so he changed the subject. "What about girlfriends? Do you have one?"

"No," John said with a laugh. "I had one last year, but she dumped me at the beginning of summer."

"Why?"

"Because I had to retake my freshman year. She said she didn't want to date a loser freshman. Pretty dumb, huh?"

"Wow, that is pretty bad."

"What about you?"

"No, no one special. My parents kept me busy so I would never have time for a girlfriend. Not saying that I wouldn't like to have one."

"Yeah, girlfriends are real nice." John suddenly remembered Dyad and how unbelievably beautiful she was. "You know, to tell you the truth, I do kind of have a crush on someone."

"Really? Who? Do I know her?"

"Kind of."

"It's not Sally, is it? Because I really don't think you two are a good match."

John laughed. "No, not Sally. But you probably would think it's stupid."

"Oh boy. It's not that evil Gypsy girl, is it? She is kind of a b-"

"No, no, no!" John whispered in urgency. "She's pretty hot, but way too crazy!"

"Okay," Mel snorted and replied, "Then who? Tell me!"

John really couldn't keep his feelings inside any longer; he had to tell someone. "It's that fairy you met in the market yesterday."

"Dyad?"

"Yeah, kind of weird, huh?"

"A little," Mel said, trying to be nice. "She is a little—"

"Small, I know, but when I met her in the marsh for the first time, there was something about her. A little corny, but it was like...love at first sight or something."

"Well, she can change her size," said Mel, "but I'm not sure about the rules around here when it comes to relationships."

"You're probably right." John sighed as he put out his cigarette.

Mel glanced at Sally and Ryan as they slept. "Do you think Sally and Ryan have something going on?"

"What do you mean? Like dating-wise?" John thought for a moment. "I don't know. He did protect her at school when I was being a jerk."

"Yeah, and I swear they almost kissed in the closet. I don't know, it just seems like they like each other."

227

"Can you two please be quiet?" The pig had apparently awoken and was rubbing his bloodshot eyes. "I am trying to sleep."

"Shut up and go back to sleep!" John yapped back. He wasn't in the mood for any more of the pig's drunken babble.

"Hey Cupid," Mel chimed in, not giving the pig a chance to recover from his hangover. "What's the significance of your arrows? Do they make others fall in love or what?"

Cupid moaned for a moment and replied, "If I tell you, will you let me sleep?"

"Of course."

"These are Fate's arrows, and they do not make others fall in love. Only have a temporary infatuation with each other. The effects only last a tock or two. That is why I need my sleep, so I can do my work and the circle of life can continue. Okay? Good night." Cupid dropped his head and fell back to sleep.

"That's pretty cool," Mel whispered. His eyes lit up. "I've got an idea."

"What now?" John grumbled. "I think the pig has a good idea. We should *sleep*."

"No, this is a grand idea." Mel's trickster wits returned in full force as he considered the pig's arrows with a sly smile. "Are you thinking what I'm thinking?"

"Probably not. You're pretty twisted."

Mel inched his way over to Cupid, pulled out two arrows from his case and tiptoed back to John.

"We can use these on Ryan and Sally."

"Why? That is seriously mean!"

"Oh, come on. It won't last long. They'll probably only have good dreams about each other anyway."

"I wouldn't."

"It'll be fun. Watch."

"Mel, get back here."

Mel slouched low as he crept. Ryan and Sally were facing each other, only a couple feet apart. Mel quickly poked them in the shoulders with the arrows. They moved slightly but didn't say anything. Mel scurried back to his bunk.

"Sally," Ryan whispered, opening his eyes slightly. "Did you feel that?"

"Feel what?" She opened her eyes, and suddenly they couldn't take their eyes off each other. "I think I felt—something."

The same something came over Ryan, a feeling he'd felt before, but this time it was stronger than ever. His heart dropped, and he was at a loss for words.

"What is it?" Sally had the exact same feeling but didn't want to tell him.

"I—I don't know," Ryan gulped. "There is just something about you that I never noticed before."

Sally started to blush. "What is it?"

"I don't know. Let me—" He paused and took her glasses off, combed his fingers through her hair, and smiled. "You are the most beautiful girl I have ever met."

Sally was beet red by this time and had no idea what to say. She had never had a boy talk to her like this before. "Thank you." She looked down, feeling very shy.

Ryan tilted her head back up. "You don't need to be shy around me."

"Okay." She smiled slightly and replied, "Then I have a confession."

"What's that?"

"I've had a crush on you for a very long time."

"Really?" A feeling of regret came over him. "I hate myself for never noticing you before, Sally!"

"That's okay." She put her hands on his. "With all this talk about Fate and Destiny the last couple of days, I am really glad we fell down that well and got to know each other."

"I am too." Ryan kissed her on the cheek. "I really wish this moment could last forever."

"Me too, Ryan," she said as she snuggled closer to him. "Are we dreaming?"

"I'm not sure. If we are, this is the best dream I have ever had."

"Me too." She put her head on his muscular chest. "I am going to close my eyes and savor this moment."

"Good idea. Just in case this is a dream."

Ryan held her tightly in his arms. She looked up at him, and their eyes locked again, but this time there was nothing to stop them falling for each other. Ryan leaned over slightly and licked his lips. Sally closed her eyes and reached for him as well. The moment their lips touched, it felt like sparks jetting throughout their bodies, as if they were in a free fall, tumbling down the well once again. This time they were not afraid of the outcome. He rubbed his fingers across her cheek and then finger-combed her hair again. She wrapped her arms around him tightly, and for a few minutes, they were inseparable. She slowly let go of him and looked back into his eyes with a smile. Her dreams had finally come true; her new life had just started. As she placed her head back on his muscular chest, they both closed their eyes.

Mel and John remained silent for a while to make sure the couple was truly back to sleep.

"Oh, boy. That was better than television!" Mel chuckled. "I have to say, I am proud of this prank."

"You are so mean." John turned over. "What's going to happen in the morning?"

"Probably nothing!" Mel was a little irritated that John didn't share his enthusiasm. "They probably won't even remember."

"You don't know that! Placing stink bombs around the school is one thing, but messing with people's emotions is not cool at all."

"Ahh, you're no fun."

"I'm going to bed now," John said and turned over. "Night."

"Okay, fine." Mel pulled the covers over himself. "I think I can finally sleep, too."

It didn't take long before the ship rocked them both to sleep.

***

The morning had passed, and it was midday before Mel finally woke from a well-needed rest. Everyone else was already up. As he stretched, preparing to climb out of bed, the wooden cabin door swung open and John rushed into the room.

"Mel!" John said, oddly frantic. "You have to get out here. NOW!"

Mel quickly jumped to his feet and followed John to the upper deck.

"I think something's wrong," John whispered. "Aren't the effects of the arrows supposed to have worn off by now?" He pointed to Ryan and Sally, who were holding hands. "It's been half a day! What did you do?"

"I—I don't know. Shoot, what do we do?"

"What do *we* do? This was your idea, buddy." John started to walk away. "I just wanted to point out how much you screwed up. You'd better fix this!"

Mel looked around anxiously for Cupid. He spotted him a few feet away from Ryan and Sally, alternately drinking his bottle over the edge of the ship.

"Cupid!" he hailed softly. "How are those arrows supposed to work again?"

"Again?" Cupid gulped from his bottle, clearly bewildered. "What do you mean?"

"You told me last night that the effects of your arrows only last a tock or two." Mel glanced at Ryan and Sally and turned back. "Why did you lie?"

"I do not remember ever telling you such a thing." He counted the number of arrows and glanced at Sally and Ryan. "Did you use my arrows on them?"

Ryan looked over at them, obviously hearing the conversation.

"I didn't—"

Ryan let go of Sally's hand and marched over. "What's going on here?"

"Sorry, Ryan."

"Sorry for what, Mel?"

"Please come with me, you two," said the pig. He pulled Sally and Ryan aside and pushed Mel away from them.

"What's going on, Cupid?" Ryan said with a stern and serious voice.

"It seems that he used my arrows on you two last night."

"What?" Sally's eyes widened.

"That little—" Ryan started, ready to deck Mel.

"Before you get angry," the pig said, stopping him in his tracks, "let me tell you something about these arrows."

"Is this why we started to like each other?" Sally asked, worried that all of her desires of being with Ryan were nothing but a love curse. That none of it was truly real. If so, she would have been devastated.

"These are Fate's arrows. They are meant to be used during the mating seasons for Enchantians," he explained with a giggle. "I call it hunting season. Nevertheless, the effects of the arrows only last a tock or two. At least they should."

"So what are you trying to say?" Sally was more worried than angry. "When did he do this?"

"It seems that he used them on you two last night." He gave them a large grin and took a drink. "If that is the case, with you two, the effects will last forever."

"Forever?" Ryan's eyes were aglow with something that looked a lot like love. "Is that bad?"

"No, not at all! This is very uncommon. The main purpose of Fate's arrows is to bring two spirit-mates together."

"We're spirit mates?" asked Sally, relieved of her previous worries.

"Yes!" Cupid tossed his empty bottle into the pink sea. "This is great news! You two were destined to find each other."

Cupid hugged them both. "Like I said, do not be angry. This is a great thing for you both! Many Enchantians search their entire lives looking for their spirit-mates. You are very, very lucky."

"Well, we're still pretty ticked off about Mel's thoughtless behavior." Ryan glanced at Sally, searching for a sign that she agreed. "No one should mess around with other people's feelings."

"Yeah," Sally agreed. "This prank could break hearts."

As Sally and Ryan chatted with a surprisingly coherent Cupid, John approached Mel, who had retreated to the rear deck on the starboard side of the ship. He shot Mel a dirty look, shaking his head in disappointment.

"I still can't believe you did that to them," John said. "It was seriously mean. They're probably going to be scarred for life."

"Okay, okay!" Mel rubbed his forehead. "I feel so bad! I wonder if they will ever forgive me."

"I hope they don't." John slung his arm around Mel's shoulder. "But I'm sure they will. They're a lot nicer than you," he joked. "And anyway, they forgave me after I was a huge jerk to them."

"I know, but this little prank backfired."

"Mel!" Ryan called as he and Sally marched over. "That was not cool, what you did!"

"I know, I know." Mel rushed to apologize. "I am so, so, so sorry!"

The two glared at him for a minute, but they couldn't keep it up.

"But it's all right now." Ryan grabbed Sally's hand. "We do forgive you."

"Really?" Mel wiped his sweaty forehead. "That is so great to hear!"

"Cupid told us everything," Sally added. "And I guess the arrows' effects are supposed to be temporary unless they happen to strike two spirit-mates."

"Really?"

"Yeah, so we were destined to find each other," Sally said as she hugged Mel. "If it weren't for you, we may have never shared our true feelings for each other."

"Oh, wow. This is great news!" A sense of relief washed over Mel. For once, one of his pranks had turned out to be a good thing. "I'm really happy for you both! Honestly, it wasn't my intention to hurt you two. Just a bit of fun. But I'm really happy that you two found each other."

"I know. We are too." Ryan reached over for a small tray bearing four glasses of purple liquid. "Now to celebrate, I'd like to propose a toast to you, Mel."

"Me? Really?"

"Of course! Like we said, if it wasn't for you, we wouldn't be together now."

"Fate works in mysterious ways," Sally added as she raised her glass.

Mel grabbed two glasses and turned to hand one to John. "Here you go."

"No thanks. After my last hangover, I don't trust any drinks here."

"Come on. It's only purple grass tea." Ryan raised his glass. "Cheers."

The three clanked their glasses and drank.

"Wow, this is amazing tea!" Mel finished his glass and drained John's. "You should've tried some."

"No, I'll pass." John looked at the two and thought of Dyad. He wished he could be as happy as they were. "Congrats to you two, though."

Suddenly a physical and electrifying sensation came over Mel as he looked at John. He couldn't keep his sparkling eyes off him.

"What?" John wrinkled his nose. "Why are you looking at me like that?"

"John," Mel gulped as his heart dropped. "You are so gorgeous!"

"Oh my God!" John looked at Ryan. Sally was giggling. "What did you do to him?"

"Just a little payback." Ryan snickered.

"And you had to have him like me?"

"That wasn't the plan. But—"

"Don't say another word, John." Mel gazed deeper into his eyes. "Just confess your true feelings."

"Shut up, Mel," John said, quickly becoming irritated.

"John!" Mel wrapped his arms around him. "Hold me!"

"I don't know how long I can take this." John shoved Mel away, annoyed beyond belief, and began to walk away.

"John!" Mel followed like a lost puppy with his arms wide open. "Don't leave me! Hug me!"

"Get away from me, you freak!" John glared at the other two. "Thanks a lot."

Ryan and Sally burst into laughter, dropping to the ground. They laughed so hard tears poured down their cheeks.

"I hope he learns a lesson to never mess with us again." Sally scooted over closer to Ryan.

"I'm sure he did," he said, enfolding her in his arms.

"I think I am going to fly," the pig said when he approached them again.

"Fly?" Sally asked. "I thought you don't drink and fly."

235

"I don't usually, however, you four have given me hope to finally find spirit-mates in Enchantas. For many cycles now, I have been in a rut with my job. Consider me a brand new Cupid! Now that I am back on an upswing, I am going to cut down my drinking and concentrate on the important stuff."

"Like what?" Ryan asked.

"Love." The pig smiled and flapped his wings. He hesitantly lifted off the ground and bobbed in the air for a moment before he caught a good gust of wind and flew off. "Thank you all for bringing hope back into my life. Bye bye now!"

"Bye!" Sally and Ryan called and waved to him.

"That is so sad." Mel wiped a tear and looked at John. "You're not going to leave me, are you?"

"Oh, brother." John shook his head. "How long will this last?"

"Cupid said not long." Ryan laughed. "Unless you two are spirit-mates."

"In my heart I believe we are." Mel tried to grab John's hand, but John quickly moved out of reach. "Why do you deny my love for you, John? You know, I think I like this hard-to-get game you're playing."

"I honestly can't take any more of this." John turned to Ryan and Sally, Mel shadowing every move with adoration in his eyes. "Can I just tie him up?"

"Do whatever you want, buddy," said Ryan. "He's your problem now."

"Tie me up?" Mel smiled. "That sounds like fun!"

"Okay..." Sally covered her ears and walked away. "I've heard enough!"

A tock went by as Sally and Ryan conversed with each other under the sun near the bow, the ship smoothly plowing through minimal waves. John stayed busy helping Butch tie up loose lines and ignoring his puppy love-struck stalker.

Sally and Ryan held hands, grinning happily as they strolled to the bridge. She pulled out her compass and compared it to the direction they were headed. She did a double-take. "Oh boy! Ryan, we're going the wrong way."

"What are you talking about? I'm sure Max knows where he's going."

"That's not what my compass says!" She showed him. It was definitely pointing in the opposite direction. "Max! Max!"

"Captain, my dear," Max said as he pulled a line tight.

"Sorry. Captain, I think we are going the wrong way."

"What are you talking about? I know my way around this sea like the back of my paw."

"But we should be going that way." She pointed in the proper direction.

"My dear, where do you need to go now?"

"I'm not sure. I just follow this compass."

"Good lords of Enchantas, are you serious? You don't know your destination?"

"Not—"

"You told me you needed to be brought to Cloud Island. So that is where I am taking you."

"But—"

"No buts about it," Max said and started to walk away.

"Hey." Ryan stepped up. "Could you cool it a little, Captain?"

"Sorry, but you four are not the only passengers that paid a fare for this ride. If you really want to go that way, I can take you there on our way back."

"Captain, I beg you to reconsider," Sally cried.

In an instant, a rolling fog completely enveloped the ship, overshadowing her request.

"That's a little creepy," Ryan said uneasily.

"Remember what the Owl said about going the wrong way?" A bolt of lightning struck the water nearby. They both jumped. "Bad luck would arise."

"All passengers to their bunkers!" yelled Max. "NOW!"

The wind picked up, but the fog remained. Yellow hail shot from the sky as the passengers hysterically raced below. Max frantically leaped to the bridge and seized the steering wheel. To him it felt as if the ship was turning in circles. Max tried his best to gain control of the rudder and steer back to the original destination, but he was not strong enough. The wheel slipped through his paws, spinning rapidly.

"You'll never take me!" he cried to the storm, lashing himself to the steering column.

The wind rocked the boat from side to side, keeling it so far over that pink water gushed onto the decks. The crew hurriedly tied themselves to any handy rail, post, or stanchion to prevent being thrown overboard. The wind whipped the sails and the boat turned around.

"Drop the sails! All canvas down!" Max ordered, but as quickly as it had arrived, the storm ceased and the fog lifted. "Is everyone all right?"

The captain was relieved to see the entire crew accounted for. He'd jumped down from the bridge to check on the passengers when he spotted a large landmass directly ahead. Max ran back to the wheel with all haste. It was too late. Collision was unavoidable. *Storm Glider* was running out of water. Passengers and crew alike tumbled to the deck as the ship grounded on a crystal white sandy beach. Max snarled with frustration; as if things couldn't get any worse, they were now stranded.

Chapter XVII
Ghost of Enchantas

Merely a quarter of the ship's heavy keel was beached, with only minor leaks on the port side. The air was like a fresh, misty spring, but the island was thick with fog. No one could see past the beach. John, Sally, and Ryan climbed from their bunk while Mel peered anxiously from behind a barrel of rum, unsure if the storm was over.

"Where did this island come from?" Max shrieked as he desperately looked through all of his maps. "It isn't on any of the charts!"

Mel shivered from behind the barrel. It felt like his worst fears had finally come to pass.

"Mel, where are you?" Sally yelled as the three of them came up on deck.

"John!" Mel screamed with fear, jumping at him like a child in need of coddling. "Where were you?"

"What the heck are you talking about?" John looked puzzled. "I was down below where I was supposed to be. The captain said."

"No!" Mel's voice was stern. "You should have been with ME! Protecting ME!"

"Mel, come on now. This is stupid. You have been drugged by—"

"*Stupid?*" Mel climbed over the edge of the ship and threatened to jump. "You call my feelings for you stupid?"

"Mel!" Sally and Ryan ran toward him, but he had already jumped.

"Oh, great!" John followed them to peer over the edge. "Do you see what your so-called payback did?"

Mel had fallen harmlessly into a small pool of water and was running toward the island.

"Thank God he's okay!" Sally hugged Ryan.

"We have to go after him," Ryan said and started to hoist himself over the edge.

"What?" John refused. "No, I think you two have to go after him. For the first time in my life, I can finally say this is not my fault."

"John, I don't want to get separated. Remember last time?"

John instantly remembered Liddy and the foxes and replied, "Ugh, fine."

Ryan was tossing down a rope ladder when Max walked up. "Where do you think you're going? I suggest that you all stay on the ship."

"Our friend just jumped off and ran away." Ryan turned to him. "We have to go find him."

"Is that a problem?" John added as he helped Sally onto the ladder.

"Actually, it is." Max crossed his furry arms. "For one, I have no idea where we are, and if I do not know, then we could be on a very dangerous island."

"Yeah." Ryan also crossed his arms. "And our friend is on it. We can't leave him."

"If you head off this ship and do not return by the time of departure, you will all be left here. Without reimbursement."

"We'll take that chance," Ryan replied.

"Captain," said Butch, who had just approached. "We could help them."

"I will do no such thing!" Max handed Butch a hammer. "I do not want my crew placed in peril because some passengers chose to act irrationally. Looks like we only have a few minor repairs. We have just enough paws to quickly fix this ship. So we should be off in no time. I suggest you find a better way to help our passengers by getting back to work. That's an order!"

"Aye, sir."

Sally and John were already off the boat by the time Max finished lecturing Butch. Ryan stood waiting.

"I guess this may be goodbye then."

"Yeah, sure." Max softened. "Listen, kid, don't make a big scene. We will wait as long as we can."

"Thanks, Captain," Ryan said and nimbly climbed down the ladder.

"May good luck be on your side, young humans!"

As Ryan splashed into the small pool of seawater, he couldn't help but notice how the pink water glimmered. It enticed him to cup a handful and bring it to his lips. With astonishment, he tasted, spat, and cried, "Hey! You should all try this. It's not salt water. It's sugar water!"

"We already know that, Ryan!" John waved him over to the white-sanded beach. "The sand is pure sugar, too. Now hurry up. It was your idea to go find Mel."

As Ryan joined the others, the fog cleared to the point where he could see a vast forest. To their amazement, the trees, grass, and

241

other plant life were all green. A comfortable reminiscence of their hometown filled Ryan's mind as they raced through the forest.

"Wow." Ryan's eyes widened. "This reminds me of my parents' camp by the lake."

"Come on." John started to jog through the dense, still lightly fogged forest. "Let's go."

"I'm coming," Ryan said. He caught up, clasping Sally's hand. "Losing someone in a forest would be hard enough to track down, let alone a forest with the fog."

"Mel!" Sally yelled.

"Mel!" John hollered. "Where are you, buddy?"

In the distance they could hear a faint whimper.

"Can you hear that? Sounds like Mel."

"Sally—" Ryan put his arm around her. "Look at your compass. It might show us where he is."

"Oh, yeah. Good idea." She pulled it out of her dragon sheath and held it up. "It says we should go *Here Way*."

The three of them rushed as fast as they could through the maze of trees and bushes. The whimpering became louder and louder when finally, they saw a boy sitting on a large rock, head down and crying.

"Ugh, I think those effects are wearing off." The sound of relief tempered Mel's voice. "Finally."

"Thank God!" John agreed.

Sally kneeled next to him. "You all right?"

"Yeah, but I feel like my heart has been dropped off a skyscraper."

"Cupid said you may feel broken-hearted for a tock or so," Ryan explained. "It will go away."

"I'm sorry." Mel looked up at John with red, tearful eyes. "John, I'm really sorry if I embarrassed you."

"Embarrassed me?" He was too proud to admit that he was humiliated to be the butt of a joke. "I was flattered. No, I'm kidding. Besides, you should be more worried about yourself. You made a fool of yourself."

"I know. I probably said a lot of things to you that were way out of line."

"I was referring to your prank on Ryan and Sally."

"Oh, right." With a shameful look, he glanced at the others. "I am really sorry for my prank. That was mean, and I deserved—"

"It's okay now, Mel," Sally said, patting his shoulder. "We're even."

"Okay, so now that we're all good"—John lifted Mel back to his feet—"let's get back to the ship. I don't want to miss our ride."

The four of them surveyed the foggy forest with uncertainty. The disorienting haze remained; visibility was poor. They were lost.

"Follow me," said John. "I have a good sense of direction."

"Wait!" Ryan grabbed John before he could walk away. "Let Sally use her compass."

Once again, Sally took out her compass, which pointed in the opposite direction.

"Fine," John muttered. "Let's follow the compass."

They were continually amazed at how much the island looked like home. The plant life around them was as green as a midsummer's day. As they made their way deeper into the forest, they started to realize that the compass was taking them farther away from the ship.

"Sally," John argued, "are you sure you're following the compass right? I'm sure if we would have gone the way I said, we would be there by now."

"Yes, it's pointing in this direction."

Suddenly the fog started to dissipate, and a small house on top of a large hillside appeared in the distance.

"Look!" Ryan pointed up the hill. "Is that a house?"

The fog was completely gone now, and what had appeared to be a small house turned out to be a large, four-story, red brick mansion with four large white pillars supporting the roof and balcony. The mansion was so wide and long that it covered the entire top of the hill. Trees and bushes peaked out of parts of the roof as if the foundation were built around them.

"That's a mansion!" Mel was astounded.

"Are you sure we should be going there?" John tried to act brave but felt uneasy. "I mean, what about the ship?"

"The compass is telling us to go there," Ryan replied. "We have to go before we get struck by more bad luck."

"Wait." Mel was flat-out scared. "What if there are monsters or something in there?"

"Don't be a wimp." John laughed and tried to sound tough. "Of course there are going to be monsters or something in there. Look at where we are. This entire place is full of monsters. So again, don't be a coward, and let's go."

They climbed the hill, reaching the front door after only a couple of minutes. It was a large, wooden door about four times their size with a round metal knocker as big as a basketball.

Mel looked at the other three for guidance. "Should we knock?"

Ryan stepped forward and knocked three times.

Even from the outside you could hear the sound of the knocker echo throughout the mansion. As the door opened slightly, Ryan poked his head inside.

"Hello," his voice echoed. The front room was very spacious and clean, which was surprising since they had been expecting spider webs and dirt. The fireplace was lit, and the smell of fresh bakery filled their noses. Directly in front of them was a large willow tree growing from the ground beneath the floor. It reached the ceiling and its branches spread across its entirety drooping down around them. Candles were placed sporadically throughout the tree as if it were a Christmas tree. A few small birds hid among the branches, tweeting lovely songs.

"Sally," Mel said, becoming more and more uneasy. "Are you sure we're going the right way?"

She glanced at the compass and nodded yes. They stepped slowly and cautiously deeper into the front room as the door quietly closed behind them.

"I don't know." Mel shivered. "This is creepier than I expected."

"What do you mean?" John laughed at the thought.

"Well, I'm sure we all expected a gloomy, spider web-filled haunted house, right? Now it seems like something is luring us in. Ever read Hansel and Gretel? I am not into being someone's dinner."

The room went dark. Spider webs appeared all around them, filling every vacant nook and cranny, pushing them close together. The lights of the tree blew out, and the leaves fell off. Mel shook his head and ignored his trembling knees. He forced a grin.

"Now that was not what I expected either. I take back what I said. I'd like this place normal."

The surroundings immediately went back to the way they had been. Harp music began to play, accompanying the tweeting birds. The notes wafted from somewhere up the long winding stairway located behind the trunk of the willow. Without warning, a large green frog appeared before them. He was a little shorter than Sally. He wore a purple pointed hat and long robes which covered a few feet of the floor around him. He carried a crystal-balled scepter in one hand and a thick, old, octagon-shaped book in the other.

"Great." John shook his head in annoyance. "Another weird life form."

"John," Ryan snapped. "Have some common courtesy." He was getting a little tired of the increasingly bizarre characters they encountered, too, but hostility wouldn't help anything. "Hi. My name is Ryan, and this is Sally, Mel, and John."

"It is my pleasure to finally meet the four of you. We have been waiting for your arrival for many Ages now."

"You have?" Sally questioned. "We aren't even sure where we are or how we got here."

"That's fine; Fate has its ways of bringing the plan together. By the way, my name is Firp, and I am the current wizard tyro of the beings once named the Knights of Minerton."

"The Knights of Minerton!" Mel blurted enthusiastically. "Where are they?"

"They are here. However, they wish not to show themselves unless they are certain you are the four prophets."

"I don't believe we are any sort of prophets," John said with some of his old arrogant attitude. "But what other humans have passed through here lately?"

"John," Ryan warned again. He wasn't surprised at John's attitude. He could sense his frustration. "Be a little more polite."

"Honestly, I just really want to go home. I am tired of being tossed around this Enchantas." He put a cigarette in his mouth. "Maybe I just need another one of these."

"Let me get that for you." Firp pointed his long, slimy finger at the cigarette and lit it. "I need to practice."

"I feel your frustration, young ones," a deep voice interjected. "We have been trapped on this island for many Ages now." A transparent figure of a man appeared before them. His eyes glittered with a vibrant green glow. He was a tall, dark-haired man with a long beard that reached his stomach. He wore a dark, hooded robe and carried a long crystal ball scepter. "My earth name was Brian," the ghost said, "and I was the first human to step into Enchantas."

Sally stepped forward. "Nice to meet you, Brian. Are you dead?"

"It does seem that way, doesn't it?" Brian smiled serenely. "But no, becoming a spirit was part of the banishment curse that was put upon us. We are unable to use magic in this state."

Mel gasped. "Wow. As if banishment was not enough, they had to do that to you."

"I believe it was their way of ensuring their curse was unbreakable."

"Brian," Ryan piped in. "Sorry to cut to the chase, but what are we doing here? Enchantas, I mean."

"That's quite all right. I figured you'd all be anxious to return to your home. We believe you have been sent here by Fate to help change Enchantas back to its original form."

They all stood looking at him curiously, still not getting the answer they wanted. Ryan spoke up. "And that would entail?"

"Well," Brian replied, "I may as well start at the beginning."

"Fine." John took a seat on a nearby couch and relaxed with his cigarette. "This will probably take a while."

Brian continued. "Enchantas was created by an entity that we named Destiny. We once believed Destiny consisted of two elements: Fate and Luck. After this entity created the land, it also created the three elemental types of natural life: plants, animals, and Mythics. These native inhabitants were primitive and barbaric; however, Destiny itself was too proud to teach them morals and how to live, so it had Fate find beings from another world to teach them. It picked our world; Earth. One day while working in the mine, I noticed an odd type of metal. It was red and scaly, exactly like your dragon sheaths," he said, indicating their armor. "I was very curious to understand its origin and composition, so I blasted it. After the blast, a bright and blinding light came over the tunnel, and that is how I found this world. My brother James and I walked through, in awe of the colors and the out-of-worldly inhabitants. We befriended the Owl, whom I believe you've already met."

They nodded, fascinated.

"We taught him to speak, and as time progressed, we learned that these inhabitants weren't as primitive, dumb, or barbaric as we once thought. We were astonished at how intelligent these creatures were, so we took it upon ourselves to teach them how to live civil and productive lives. At this time we had no idea about Fate, Luck, and Destiny. We were just as ignorant as the inhabitants. Anyway, we taught them how to speak, write, build, sew, cook, clean, play games, have fun, and live in harmony amongst themselves. The Enchantians were pretty bad at first; standing in line was even a problem for these natives. First come, first served was a difficult concept for them. But they eventually grew into a thriving society. We were very proud of our accomplishments here. And of course we needed to name this world, so we chose Enchantas. I thought it was a great name. Over time, many more miners came to help, loving the colors and freedom that Enchantas had to offer, especially to a group of miners that usually see only darkness day after day. We were all young and single, and truth be told, a miner's life wasn't that spectacular." He paused to chuckle.

"I believe there were twenty-six original miners who came to Enchantas, but only a few of us decided to stay and live our lives here. Thirteen of us humans became the fourth living element to reside in Enchantas." Brian floated around them. "Ages went by, and we set up a time system and calendar to help prepare for the different seasons such as harvesting and hunting. Slowly, day by day, we started noticing small magical powers coming from each of us. I remembered the first day I levitated a book—scared me half to death! Most of the Mythics had them too. As time went on, we mastered these magical gifts and helped teach others.

"Finally, the day came when one of us stumbled upon a pattern of social abnormalities. Sometimes things would happen for each of us perfectly, while at other times it would go terribly wrong. For instance, one day I was building a house for a gnome, and nothing went wrong. I mean *nothing*! The next day I was building another house for an imp, and everything was going wrong. That was when we discovered Destiny's plan and how Fate and Luck played a part. We started to believe that everything happened for a reason, and if something bad happened, we would just do the opposite and surprisingly it would usually all work out."

"That's pretty peculiar," said Mel. "How would you know you were doing the correct thing?"

"Trial and error." Brian sighed. "Which took many Ages to figure it all out."

"So where do this Witch and Warlock come in?" Ryan asked.

"Well, the time came when we believed Fate wanted us to close the Forbidden Cave because animals would cross over to our world. For some reason, Humans and Mythics could cross over without a problem, but if animals or vegetables crossed over, they turned into our type of animals and vegetables. They were not able to speak or think as they do here. Hence, they would lose their way and not come back."

"Oh, that is so sad," said Sally.

"Yes, it was. Many families were destroyed because of this. So when the thirteen of us decided to stay in Enchantas forever, we also decided to close the Forbidden Cave forever. It was a big decision for us, even though we still had the power to open the doorway. We made an oath and chose not to open it again because of Destiny's plan. Again, we believed Fate brought us here for a reason. Anyway, the day we closed the doorway to Earth was also the day two more Humans came through. They were struck with amnesia and had no idea where they had come from, only that they ended up here. We invited them in and gave them a home. We taught them magic, and they remained here peacefully for a few Ages. That was until they suddenly remembered their past life and wanted to return to Earth. We, of course, denied their request to go back. We all truly believed that Destiny wanted them here. I have to say now that we were a stubborn group of humans, living strictly by this oath and ideal that Fate and Luck were the only entities controlling our destinies. We brainwashed ourselves and refused to accept any other ideas or desires. That is how those awful Crusades started. The two others seceded from our group and claimed themselves as the Witch and Warlock. They disputed and argued against the morals of Fate and Luck. They claimed Chance and Freewill were the elements of Destiny's plan and declared war on those who opposed.

"The war lasted what seemed to be forever. Many lives were lost. During this time, I was losing all hope for Enchantas and what it once had been. I was afraid it would never again be a harmonious world. That was until the day I received a message stating that soon, four humans would pass through the Forbidden Cave and bring stability back to our land, a sense of balance for Destiny. We ended up losing the Crusades, but I still truly believe in this prophecy. I believe you four are those humans."

"I still don't get how we are going to help." Ryan shook his head.

"You have already done most of it. Everything you have done since you arrived has changed our world. You have enlightened many, and they believe in the prophecy. They in turn enlighten others, which creates more and more movement toward peace."

"I don't think we started any movement toward peace," said Ryan. "It looks more like another Crusade!"

"I don't want to start a war!" Sally cried, sounding troubled.

"We do not want another war either," Brian replied. "But a lot of Enchantians believe it is the only way."

"What would you suggest?" Mel asked.

"There won't have to be a war if the Witch and Warlock know the truth."

"What truth is that?"

"Little do they know, our stubborn ideals of Fate and Luck have changed since our banishment."

Mel was skeptical. "After a war and banishment? You finally change your ideals? How have they changed?"

"As I said before, we once strongly believed that Fate and Luck were the only elements that controlled the Destiny of every creature in Enchantas. But we were half wrong. The Witch and Warlock were also right about the ideals of Freewill and Chance. You see, the synthesis of these four elements—Fate, Luck, Chance, and Freewill—worked both together and separately, simultaneously toward the same goal."

"Destiny's plan?" Sally guessed.

"Correct! It was never one or the other; it was as if Destiny was a large bubble that connected the four elements by a web of principles."

"Oh, I think I understand now," said Mel.

"So when can we go home?" John blurted, becoming a little annoyed.

"Not yet. We do have the power to send you back, but we are banished to this island until the curse has been lifted. We must be in the Valley to open it up."

"How do we lift the curse?"

"You can't. Only the Witch and Warlock can."

"Okay, I get it," Ryan chimed in. "So if we just let them know that you have changed your ideals about Destiny's plan, they may reconsider the banishment, and you can send them back to Earth just like us? So no war, just peace."

"Exactly. They are a very capricious couple, though, meaning that they may need some convincing."

"How do you expect we do that? And why haven't you told them this before?" Mel asked, still unconvinced.

"I am unable to answer the question of how to convince them. We have not seen them since the day of the banishment. We have not been anywhere other than this island. The only news we receive from the outside world is from Firp and our magical telescope. Firp was born on this island and doesn't share the same curse. Speaking of which, are the stories true about how horrible conditions have become in Enchantas?"

"Considering what you said it was like before, it's changed a lot," Ryan replied. "Poverty, greed, despair, slavery, alcoholism, loss of hope..."

"Yes, many creatures have lost hope and have turned to the bottle and gambling for pleasure and the escape from reality. Towns such as Ruphport have been tempted by greed and lust; gambling is their drug of choice. Other places, like Foxtown, have become an industry of selfishness and egocentrism. They all care for themselves and not others. Our time has gone. Our unity is gone. I often wonder: could we even bring peace back to Enchantas? Could it even be saved by the temptations it has been introduced to during the Ages we have been banished?"

"That's hypocritical," Sally pointed out. "You sound like you are losing hope yourself."

"You see, we need to unite our morals and ideals with the Witch and Warlock to stop this world from destroying itself. That was the best thing about Enchantas; it did not have the same problems as the human world. Now it seems that it does."

"So you really think it'll work by asking the Witch and Warlock to commit to peace?" Mel asked. "I think that's a little far-fetched."

"Well, it's worth a try," Sally responded.

"All right then. What about the Griffins? The Gargoyles asked us to find the Griffins to join the cause."

"That is perfect!" Brian exclaimed. "If you meet with them, they may be able to arrange a meeting with the Witch and Warlock without confrontation. If there's one thing I have learned about the Witch and Warlock, it is that they do not back down from a fight."

"So it seems that you would like us to go about this peacefully," said Ryan. "But everyone else seems to be preparing for war."

"That is why it is imperative to make peace with the Witch and Warlock first, before any type of real war begins. Our hope is that with the return of the Knights, Enchantians will truly believe in peace and harmony again. So you must go. Time, as they say, is of the essence."

"Master Brian," Firp said as he walked back inside. "Their ship has departed. What should they do?"

"Well, Firp, as I have always said, practice makes...?"

"Perfect. Yes, sir. I will try."

"What's going on?" Sally asked, worried.

"Your ship is gone, and you will have to find another way to get to Cloud Island. Firp here needs more practice with his transportation spell."

Sally raised her eyebrows. "Is he any good?"

"Just like with any pupil, everything is a learning experience." He hovered toward the other side of the room. "Now come over here by the fireplace so Firp can send you there."

"Master—" The Frog was a little uneasy. "Remember last—"

"Shush now, Firp." He chuckled. "You don't want to frighten them."

"Frighten us?" Mel asked, alarm bells going off in his head. "That's not reassuring."

Firp stared deeply into their eyes, holding his scepter aloft. As he meditated, the crystal shined red, blue, green, and yellow beams across the room, just like they were on a dance floor with a disco ball. Firp embarked on his spell:

"Into the Clouds, way up High;
Send these Prophets to the Sky!"

A bolt of green lightning zapped from the scepter and struck them. In a blast of illumination, their faces contorted in surprise, and they vanished into thin air.

"Did I do it right, Master?"

"I believe so, Firp. I just hope the four elements of Destiny are on their side."

"I do too, sir."

Chapter XVIII

The Griffins

Mel awoke alone in a cold, empty, and narrow stone hallway. Flickering torches guided his way, but the feeling of loneliness sent shivers down his spine.

"Ryan?" he yelled. "Sally? John? Anyone there?" His inquiry was met with silence. He proceeded slowly, with caution, and as he made his way through, one tunnel became two.

"Which way do I go?" he muttered to himself.

He turned left and continued to walk down the cold tunnel.

Fear grew with each step as he made his way to another crossroad. This time there were three separate hallways: right, left, and straight. An old saying came to him: when you get to the fork in the road, take it.

"Oh, brother," he muttered, choosing the right tunnel, walking faster. Shaking his head in disbelief, he continued to call to his friends. The tunnel split again.

"What is going on here?" he screamed, spit flying. "Say it, don't spray it," he muttered to himself, choosing the one on the left. Mel proceeded briskly straight through the next six crossroads.

"Okay, now I'm getting really pissed off!" Mel took flight, running as fast as he could through the labyrinth of tunnels.

Sweat dripped from his forehead, his armpits, between his shoulder blades as he made his way through the stone-walled maze. It was at least five ticks of running until he finally came to a large opening containing a large block of moldy cheese. The smell filled the room, reeking of a wretched aroma. He quickly covered his nose and yelped, "Are you serious? I ran all this way for this?"

The room offered access to three other tunnels, which he was dreadfully contemplating taking when suddenly a large brown rat with a white lab coat appeared before him.

"Hello, Mel," the rat said in a dark, scratchy voice. "How does it feel?"

"How does what feel?" he replied with his hand still covering his nose.

"I will take care of that smell for you," the rat chuckled. The chunk of cheese and its odor disappeared. "How does it feel to have mischievous pranks pulled on you? This maze is a reflection of yourself and how you treat others. Instead of you being the scientist, you are now the rat."

"That's just stupid. Who cares about my pranks? That has nothing to do with anything. Just let me out of here."

"In time. We must wait for the others."

"Others? Where are they?" Mel asked. "What did you do with them?"

"Patience, my friend. They will be here soon."

"Who are you?"

"I am Destiny."

Mel bellowed with laughter. "You have got to be kidding me. Destiny is a rat?"

A window opened above, and millions of small, colorful marbles rolled into the room, covering the entire floor around them.

"What are these?" Mel tried to step over them, but there were too many.

"Each one of these marbles is either the memories, emotions, beliefs, thoughts, desires, dreams, or ambitions of every Enchantian. Some would say I am a bit of a pack rat. Believe me, I am no rat. I am an essence of belief that has just now taken rat form."

Mel picked one up and saw a rabbit holding a sword. "Why are you showing me these?"

"You all must know your place and the reasons you have been brought here."

The rat snapped his bony old fingers, and the marbles rolled back up the walls and into the window above.

"So if you are this so-called Destiny, why are we all in Enchantas?"

"Oh my gosh, that was really annoying!" Ryan sprinted into the room, panting. "Hey, Mel. I thought I'd lost you. Where are Sally and John?"

"I don't know. I thought I was the only one here until I met this rat who claims to be Destiny."

"I am Destiny," the rat intoned sternly. "Hello, Ryan."

"Hi. So why aren't we at Cloud Island with the Griffins? What happened?"

"I brought you all here," said the rat. "I will explain everything very soon."

"What the hell was that all about?" John crashed to the floor, huffing. His body was drenched with sweat. He put a cigarette in his mouth and lit it. "I so need this!"

The rat smiled. "Hello, John."

"Hi. What's up? Nice to meet you." John lay on the cold stone floor, puffing on his cigarette, oblivious to his surroundings and the talking rodent.

Sally flounced into the room with fury. "Will someone please tell me what's going on here? I take it this rat has something to do with it."

"Sally!" Still on his back, John laughed. "Nice to see you finally have an attitude."

"My fellow humans, I am Destiny. I am an essence of belief that has just now taken the form of a rat. Please pardon my appearance."

"Your appearance is fine," Mel said impatiently. "You were about to tell us why we are here."

"Did you bring us to Enchantas?" asked Ryan.

"No, I did not open the Forbidden Cave. There has been some other magic at work here." The rat took a deep breath and continued. "However, I do believe you all have been sent here to fulfill a prophecy."

"Oh, not this again," John muttered. "Really?"

"Yes, John. Really," the rat continued. "I believe this prophecy will bring peace to this world as well as peace to yourselves. You are all from different backgrounds. You have different kinds of friends, family, and beliefs, which makes you the perfect group to fulfill this prophecy."

"How are we the perfect group?" Ryan was bewildered. "We're a mess!"

"As I was saying, your unique differences and character traits have made you great mediators of Life's challenges."

"How's that?" Ryan wondered.

"For instance, Ryan, you are a strong and mighty person but too proud to ask for help."

Ryan nodded in agreement. Any resistance or need to put up a phony front had basically been knocked out of him.

"John, you are also very stubborn and strong-willed, but trust has never been a strong point of yours. Sally, you are lonely but caring without doubt. And Mel, you are wise but ignorant of your own potential. These are all great qualities, and you have overcome your weaknesses through your travels in Enchantas. Trust, humility, pride, empathy, relying on others, and learning to befriend one another despite your obvious differences has made you all great mediators to our world, as well as your own. You were all brought here to learn about yourselves and discover what you are capable of."

"And what would that be?" John took a drag from his cigarette and stood up.

"Loving everyone else as much as yourselves. That is what truly brings peace to any world. Love is the one essential thing that balances any living being. It makes them better in all aspects. I realize the tremendous strain this journey has brought you all. I know you all miss your families, possibly more than any of us realized. However, I am hoping your thoughts have changed, and you are willing to help this world become what it used to be: peaceful. This character-building passage has been transformative for you. You have all grown into admirable individuals. You see, you must all see the good in everything. Optimism is what makes it easy for Enchantians to place their faith in Fate, Chance, Freewill, and Luck. That is how they try to find the good in everything."

"So what you're saying is that this entire experience was a test of some sort?" Mel cringed. *What was this? Bible camp?*

"Not at all," the rat replied. "Life is a test. You were brought here to teach the ways of optimism to the Enchantians and to stop the fighting."

"That sounds great and all," Mel pointed out, "but we had one goal in mind that brought us together. That was going home. What do these Enchantians have to look forward to?"

"Show them that there is more than one way to believe in Destiny. There is no wrong way; just believing that I have a plan for everyone should be enough. To follow their hearts, love one another, trust in your fellow Enchantians, and to look for the good in everything."

"So what do we do now?" Ryan asked. "Are we still going to the Griffins?"

"Yes, you are, but I am not sure if the Enchantian plan will work. So I urge you all to take the Knight's advice and not ask the Griffins to join the army, but to help mediate peace."

"Do you actually think that will work?" Sally asked.

"I am not sure. I am sorry for diverting you from your mission, but I wanted you to get answers from me."

"Thank you for that, Destiny." Ryan sighed. "We do just want to go home, though."

"And you will." Destiny paused and stepped closer. "You all must go now and use this knowledge to your advantage."

Mel put his hand in the air. "Wait a second. I have a couple more questions."

"This is all I must say for the time being, Mel." Destiny took a few steps back. "Please stand together, and I will transport you all."

"But—"

"Let's just go," John said and sauntered over to the others.

Ryan and Sally held hands as the other two flanked them.

"Good journey, my human friends." Destiny lifted his furry brown arms and snapped his long, skinny rat fingers. "I hope all goes well."

***

The sky was an intense light green up above the orange and white clouds. Griffins soared above with ease and elegance. They were beautiful creatures with wings and heads of an eagle and the claws and tail of a lion. There were hovering about fifty feet above Cloud Island, which changed appearances as much as the clouds. One could get lost easily if trapped on this island of the clouds. The four explorers suddenly appeared in the sky above the city and freaked out upon realizing that nothing was underneath them. They instantly began to plummet toward the cloud.

"Oh nooooo!" Sally cried as she grabbed Ryan's arm tightly. "We're falling!"

"Was this supposed to happen?" John flapped his arms feverishly in the false hope of staying aloft. "I *hate* heights!"

"I don't know." Mel twisted aimlessly in the air. "We shouldn't have trusted that rat!"

Suddenly the cloud extended its shape, catching them mid-air. It was soft as cotton and lighter than the air. It seemed solid, but they could punch their arms through it if they really tried. It was as if the cloud had its own thoughts and controlled what it could hold.

"That was a close one." Ryan smiled at Sally. "But you have to agree, it was sort of fun."

The others could not disagree with his comment. They all looked up. Watching the griffins glide and wheel through the sky was a wondrous sight.

"Hello, humans," a soft voice said from above. Her voice was deep but had a soothing effect. A large griffin landed in front of them, ruffling her feathers.

"I am Brista, the Princess of the Griffin tribe. Who, may I ask, are you?"

At first Ryan was intimidated by her size, but her voice was soothing. "We come in peace to seek you out."

"Who sent you?"

"The Gargoyles," John responded.

"We were also sent by the Knights—" said Ryan.

"Gargoyles?" she snarled. "What do they want?"

"They would like to declare a truce and bring peace to all Enchantians."

"Just like Dex." She shook her head. "What is he really up to?"

"What do you mean?" Sally asked.

"What did Dex tell you about how we parted?"

"He mentioned something about your betrayal, which resulted in the banishment of the Knights of Minerton," Ryan replied.

"Hogwash! That is only a partial truth!" She laughed. "I am sure Dex never mentioned we were lovers."

They looked at each other. No one recalled Dex mentioning this.

"I was too drunk to remember my conversation," admitted John.

"Figures. Males." She grimaced. "The real story was that we were all fighting to protect the Knights. They were our founders, and to this day I do not withhold my love for them. However, Dex and I were to be married at the conclusion of the Crusade. That, of course, inspired me to fight harder for our cause. But toward the end of the war, our hope of winning diminished.

"This was when Dex and the other gargoyles turned to liquor and ale for support. They started to neglect their duties while we griffins worked double duties as the protectors and troops of Fate's army. My fellow griffins came to me complaining, which of course in turn drove a wedge between Dex and me. Not long after I realized that, his love for the bottle became greater than his love for me.

"One night an enormous fight broke out. I hurt him, but in his drunken anger he hurt me worse. I was bedridden for a couple of Seasons. That is how badly I was beaten. During the time of recovery, the Witch and Warlock came to visit me. Some say I was tempted; however, I believe I was reborn to a new way of thinking and a new set of beliefs. They showed me that Fate and Luck were not controlling my destiny. Freewill was my new belief, and I embraced its essence with everything I had left. I took my fellow griffins and left the world below. Some say I am a selfish traitor, but I do not think so. I left him and his drunken self to that pitiful existence he calls life."

"Do you regret it?" Sally asked.

"Not at all. As I said, I love the Knights, but that life is over now. I have—we have *all*—moved on. Our lives in these clouds have been full of peace and serenity ever since."

"What if I were to tell you that we have recently met with the Knights, and they would like to make a deal with the Witch and Warlock?" Ryan stepped closer.

"I'd say that would be between you and them. Not us."

"We need a way to meet them. Could you help us?"

"I am not quite sure they would trust you. Rumors of your presence in Enchantas have churned all sides of Destiny's plan, the old and the new ideals. I ask, what are your views on this ordeal?"

The four looked at each other, afraid to say the wrong thing. They had only been in Enchantas a few days. They had met countless beings, and even Destiny itself was confusing. There wasn't a Human alive that could obtain a true sense of what their beliefs were, much less determine how effective they were.

Mel spoke up. "Although we have not been in Enchantas very long, we can see that the beliefs are clearly broken."

"What?" the griffin said, shocked. "Do you realize what you are saying?"

"We realize we haven't met everyone in Enchantas, but many of the residents we have met are pretty messed up. This whole ideology that was once a peaceful pursuit has now become the motive to destroy this beautiful world. I, for one, would change my entire belief system. The Knights have. They have converted their belief system to include all forms of principles."

"Interesting, and how would you go about achieving this?"

"Starting with peace and love," Sally suggested. "What better way to start than with the Griffins and Gargoyles?"

"Exactly," Ryan added. "As a wise one said, 'Loving everyone as much as yourselves brings true peace to the world.' Fate, Luck, Chance, and Freewill are all elements of the bigger picture, Destiny's plan. Love is the one essential thing that balances these out and makes everything perfect."

"Impossible!" she snarled. "I could never love anyone that hurt me as badly as those gargoyles."

"But the Gargoyles have changed their ways," Ryan pleaded. "There doesn't have to be any war in Enchantas."

"I don't care. That peace and trust was broken many ages ago, and we will never be harmonious again."

"What about helping us so we can meet the Witch and Warlock?" Mel asked. "There has got to be a way we can convince them to change."

"Look," Sally said, "I understand why you don't want to reconcile with the Gargoyles and why it's so important to you, but we really don't want to start another war. We really need to speak to the Witch and Warlock. We have to try to convince them that peace is the better way. We have spoken with the Knights, and they believe they were wrong about Destiny's plan. They want a truce, and this truce is a means for the Witch and Warlock to go back to Earth."

"You are a liar!" They all turned as the Gypsy appeared, screaming. She had been hovering unseen beneath the orange cloud just below. Her eyes gleamed with purple hate.

Persona Weapons emerged faithfully and efficiently from the bracelets. Ryan brandished his sword in front of him while John concealed his spear tightly against his side. Mel clenched his boomerang nervously. He had never used one before. A golden whip emerged from Sally's wrist. She had been wondering what her weapon would be. It fluttered in the wind. She gripped it tightly with pride, although she was unsure how to use it. She would try to figure it out.

"Lies! All lies. I can see through you. You wish my Godparents to release the curse so the Knights can retaliate and avenge the lost war all those ages ago! I will not let that happen. I will not let you ruin my life here. I am finally in their good graces, and you will not ruin that. I have just been granted authority from the Witch and Warlock to execute all of you in the name of Freewill; that is if you will not side with us."

"Side with you?" Sally cringed, feeling the whip's power thrumming up her wrist into her torso.

"Yes, Sally." She stepped up to Sally. "Your final chance to be my friend."

"Sorry, Lexis," she said, grabbing Ryan's hand. "I'm with them."

"Fine." The Gypsy ground her teeth.

"We just want peace!" Ryan exclaimed.

"You say that with weapons clutched in your hands! As I can see from this encounter with the Griffins, you will not side with us." A magical broom hovered from the cloud; Lexis mounted herself on it and floated above Brista. "Brista, take them to the fortress. I will have my troops prepare for an execution."

"Yes, Princess Gypsy."

Lexis swiftly zoomed toward the horizon as hundreds of other griffins landed, surrounding the kids. There was nowhere to flee. Once again they were captive.

"Give us your bracelets." Brista put out her paw. "I am sorry it has come to this."

The four handed over their bracelets and were then locked in separate steel cages.

"Great. We're flying again!" John huffed.

The griffins picked up the cages easily and flew toward the Witch's and Warlock's castle.

Chapter XIX
Battle for Enchantas

The sky was thick with smoke, and sulfur fumes burned their lungs as they were carried through the dark, desolate land of the Witch and Warlock. The reddened sun behind them peeked through the gray clouds. Lifeless, implacable stone mountains surrounded them; they could barely make out the giant outline of the black castle in the distance. Dead trees and thorny bushes scattered the ground beneath them. It was a somber journey for them, knowing they were headed to their own execution. As they descended slowly toward the stone courtyard of the castle, the fog began to dissipate, and they could see thousands of eager soldiers awaiting the execution. Legions of foxes, imps, skunks, badgers, weasels, cats, trolls, and gremlins snarled at the sight of the four humans. The purple-eyed Gypsy Princess already stood on a stage overlooking the Army of Freewill.

John had been hoping that their descent to flat land would ease his nerves, but the sight of the legions of monstrous troops gave him no relief.

"My legions!" the Gypsy announced. "I have hope for our cause! Our belief in Freewill will not wane, for I bring you the so-called Prophets of Destiny!"

The crowd thundered with anger as the griffins set the humans down in front of them. The sound echoed across the mountains, and avalanches of rocks were hurled in landslides to the barren floor below. The imps curled their greasy lips while the gremlins showed their evil grins, snarling and barking horrifically. The foxes' piercing yellow eyes watched while the cats hissed their loathing and waved their menacing claws at the petrified humans.

Sally shook with fear, her eyes glued to the crowd. Ryan looked at her, worried more about her than himself. "Sally," he said softly, "everything is going to be fine. Trust me."

She turned with a vacant stare, already going into shock and desperately trying to hang on to her faith. "I don't think so, Ryan." Shuddering, she turned back to the panting crowd.

An imp, gremlin, fox, and cat kicked open the doors of the cages and pulled the four outside. They were tossed to the ground and surrounded by the other troops. As they rose to their feet, they were roughly shoved forward. They saw the gruesome faces of each legion gawking at them with contempt and hate. Some had drool oozing from their mouths in anticipation of their human meal. Some from the crowd yelled, throwing screaming vegetables at them. The cries and screams were unbearably loud and frightening.

"I cannot wait to eat this one!" cried a fox from the crowd, looking at Sally. "It looks mighty tasty."

"No way. It is mine!" An imp tackled the fox from behind.

A series of scuffles broke out as the crowd argued about who was going to eat whom.

"SILENCE!" The Gypsy's unearthly shriek carried over the crowd and the troops immediately stopped quarreling. "Everyone will get a piece of them as an appetizer before our victory feast!"

"Hurray!" The crowd cheered and continued pushing the humans closer to the stage. A few started to recite a short rhyme, and then the entire army joined in chanting over and over:

"Skin 'em, shred 'em, smash 'em up;

Cook 'em, boil 'em, eat 'em up!"

"It's a madhouse here! I don't wanna die!" Sally screamed. "I especially don't want to be an appetizer!"

Mel tried to lighten he mood. "I know. We should at least be the main course."

The others did not find his comment funny. Ryan turned to Sally, trying to comfort her, but he was losing hope himself. "Sally, it's gonna be okay."

"Shut up!" yelled John, trying to wiggle his way out of a fox's grasp. "None of you are making this any better!"

"Stop trying to escape. Listen to the girl; you are all going to be dead in a matter of ticks."

"Shut up, you ugly bastard!" John landed a solid kick to the fox's midsection. The fox doubled over.

"You are going to pay for that!" the fox promised, rubbing his stomach.

They were marched through the roaring, leering crowd as the screaming vegetables continued to soar past their heads. They stopped for a moment as the troops moved aside, forming a gauntlet with a small opening for the four to walk through. At the end was a small stairway leading to the stage. The stage was a large, wooden platform surrounded by barbed wire to keep the troops from interfering with the Gypsy's grand show.

"Move it, freaks!" An imp poked Mel in his back.

"Okay, okay." Mel held his cuffed hands up. "We're moving."

They walked up the small stairway and stepped onto the wooden platform. It held four different devices: a tall, wooden post hammered into the ground, a noose hung on a wooden hook, a guillotine, and a large metal chamber.

Outside the fence, thousands of troops licked their lips, anxiously awaiting the feast.

"Welcome to the Stage of Suffering!" The Gypsy smiled, her eyes glowing with luminous victory. She set down their bracelets on a podium while continuing to address the crowd. "For the sake of Enchantas and our marvelous way of life, I am hereby granted authority by the Witch and Warlock of these lands—" She pointed up to the tallest tower, where the two dark-cloaked wizards looked down on the proceedings. The crowd turned to bow in honor. The Gypsy took a deep breath and pronounced the humans' sentence: "To make a sacrificial execution of these four false prophets!"

The crowd cheered again, jumping up and down in excitement.

"Their acts of treason and lack of allegiance to the one real ideal is a threat to our existence." She turned to the four. "Do you have anything to say for yourselves?"

"Yes, I do!" Ryan shouted, his voice ringing out clearly, calmly. "We are no threat. We have come in peace and would like to offer a treaty from the Knights of Minerton in the name of Destiny itself."

"The Knights are dead!" the Gypsy snapped. "You're treaty is worthless."

"No, it's true!" Sally insisted.

"You're wasting your breath," John said, then looked up at the Witch and Warlock. "Screw you and your stupid frickin' ideals! If war is what you want, I hope you all die!"

Mel sighed. "Well said, John, but I don't think that's gonna help us."

"I don't care." John pulled out a cigarette and lit it. "At least I can smoke one last cigarette before I die."

"Amazing." Sally gave him a slight smile. "You're actually trying to be optimistic."

"I am, aren't I?" John laughed sardonically as he took a drag. "Well, bring on the execution; I don't have all frickin' day!"

The four of them grinned. Then Gypsy pointed her thumb down. "We are ready to begin."

"That's not good," Mel observed.

The crowd buzzed louder, now chanting and humming as the bloodthirsty creatures rubbed their stomachs and licked their chops.

"I know exactly what I'm going to do with you," a gremlin said and grabbed John to pull him to the tall wooden post. He squirmed, desperate to break free, but his captor was too strong.

"Don't try to escape," the gremlin growled. It took only a moment to tie John to the stake. He was only able to move his head. His arms and legs were wrapped behind his body and tied around the large stake. There was a hole in the stage for the stake that had been hammered into the ground. Large strands of grass and hay surrounded the bottom of the stake, and the torch to light it hung a few feet away. The gremlin placed John's cigarette back in his mouth. "I hope you enjoy that smoke, because you are going to be burning pretty soon. This stake is for burning rebels." The gremlin snickered. "Don't worry. You will be alive for a little while. We'll enjoy listening to the screaming as your skin melts from your body!"

"Your turn," an imp said to Mel. He grabbed the boy and brought him to where the noose hung. "I think you will be hanged. You look like you have some good meat on you. We wouldn't want to spoil any of it, now would we?"

He stood on a small platform with his arms and legs together. The imp tossed a black hood over Mel's head and looped the noose over his head and around his neck.

Sally stood in the corner terrified as her whole life flashed before her eyes. Her eyes were wide open, and her mouth was tightly shut. Ryan frantically tried to keep his mind intact and think of something to do. He was afraid and anxious. He prayed for a miracle, because that was the only thing that could save them at this point.

A fox stepped up from the crowd and wrinkled his snout as he stared at Ryan in anger. "Are you nervous?" He walked closer to him. "Remember me?"

Ryan squinted for a moment and suddenly recognized the fox. "Trox!"

"You should have killed me when you had the chance! That is what makes you weak."

"If I had another chance, I would!"

"Don't worry; your death will be quick." The fox smiled and dragged Ryan to the Guillotine. "Off with his head!"

The crowd cheered louder while Trox tied him down to a block of wood. A large blade was connected to a rope which, when cut, would allow the blade to drop and cut off his head.

"No, no!" His fear took over, and he could not stay silent any longer. "Help! I'm too young to die!" he cried.

The crowd laughed.

"Look! The tough one is crying!"

"I'm not crying. I'm pleading for you to reconsider! You don't have to do this. You don't have to kill us!"

"That is what they all say!" the Gypsy said with a laugh. "I love the Guillotine." Then she turned to Sally and grimaced, reminded of her betrayal. "Now, my dear, it's time for you. You're a loud-mouth, aren't you? A betraying little loudmouth who is always whining about something. I had to save the best for last." She waved her arm, directing the crowd toward the metal chamber. "You'll get the Iron Maiden!"

The crowd cheered louder than ever.

272

"Wh-What's the Iron Maiden?" she screamed.

The cat clamped his paws into Sally's arms and moved her toward the large metal chamber. She struggled to free herself, but with each movement, the cat's sharp claws dug deeper into her skin. The cat opened the door to the chamber. Large metal spikes jutted out from the inside of the door. The cat hissed, screeching with laugher. "Let me get right to the point. Once we close this door, nighty-night for you!"

Sally's arms and legs were quickly tied to the posts on each corner of the chamber. The cheering crowd drowned her screams.

The Gypsy turned to the excited throng, raising her hands high into the air. The crowd applauded wildly. "Now I will ask each of these humans for their last words." She turned to Sally. "What are yours, my dear?"

The crowd fell silent; all eyes were upon her.

She couldn't see much from the inside the box, and her tears further obscured her vision. "Lexis, please. You don't need to do this!"

"Not a chance," replied the Gypsy, and a sinister smile grew on her face.

Another tear dripped down Sally's cheek before she pleaded, "HELP! HELP! SOMEONE PLEASE HELP ME!"

The crowd laughed, and the Gypsy replied sarcastically, "Now that's original!" She turned to Ryan and asked, "How about you, young sir? What've you got to say? Or are you going to start crying again?"

"Someday Fate's Army will rise again and kill you all," he said with a confident smile, squaring his shoulders. "I wish I could be there to see it!"

The crowd guffawed again, and the Gypsy shook her head. "Yeah, right. That will never happen!"

She then turned to Mel and asked, "And you? What are your last words?"

"I actually have a question for you." Mel smirked. "What do you get when you cross a lonely Gypsy and an imp?"

The Gypsy was perplexed at the question and replied, "I don't know."

"A gimpy, bipolar little girl with an identity crisis!" Mel snickered. "You are one crazy wench!"

John, Sally, and Ryan laughed heartily. The Gypsy Princess and her subjects remained silent. They didn't find Mel's riddle amusing.

"Look, lady. You really need help. How can you sit here and be proud of killing another human?"

Her eyes flashed brighter, radiating purple. She looked at Sally and thought of the friendship that could have been. The thought of another betrayal fueled her anger for the four humans. With a slight smile, she said quietly, "I'm only proud of killing you. And I can't wait to watch my fellow troops eat you."

She turned to John, who hung on the stake, trying not to cringe at the dirty and oily gremlins gawking at him. "I'm going to enjoy watching you burn!"

"I don't care," he said, spitting out his finished cigarette. "Before you light me up in flames, could you please light me up another cigarette? Because I could really use one right now."

"No, but soon you can smoke yourself to death." The Gypsy laughed shrilly, motioning to the crowd. "Now—for the moment we have all been waiting for!"

Four soldiers stood eagerly at attention, one for each prisoner, anxiously awaiting the order to kill.

"Are you ready?" she yelled to the guards.

"Yes, madam!" they chimed in unison.

She raised a hand to the crowd. "On the count of five, your fellow troops will execute the prisoners."

The foursome froze with terror in their eyes.

"Hey, guys! If you can hear me," John finally hollered, "I just wanted to say that it was nice meeting you all. I have to say, besides my sister, you three are my best friends."

"You too, John!" they called out to him.

"I know how you feel." A tear ran down Mel's cheek underneath wetting the hood that obscured his face. "I never would have thought before I went to school the other day that I would meet you guys and share this awesome adventure."

"Before I met you—" Sally stopped and sniffled from inside the chamber, but with great effort forced her voice to be strong and be heard. "My life was hopeless. Now I can at least say I'm ending it with true friends and having found the love of my life."

"Thank you all for being there for me as well." Ryan gritted his teeth. "You are the best friends a guy could ask for. And I love you Sally."

"That's enough. Shut up!" The Gypsy glared at them.

"On the count of five. Ready!"

"One!"

The troops eyes were fixed on the stage as their teeth gnashed and their mouths drooled.

"Two!"

The crowd clenched their paws, enjoying the suspense.

"Three!"

The four closed their eyes tight, hoping for a miracle.

"F—"

Suddenly, an alarm horn reverberated from the tallest tower of the black castle. One of the soldiers on the stage pointed behind the crowd. The group gradually shifted its vantage to spot an enormous army approaching, rapidly closing the distance. Leading this army was a mob of Cumberlake Valley inhabitants, including beavers, rabbits, raccoons, squirrels, and snuffballs. The first wave, the squirrels, were armed with their characteristic round shields and long spears. The second wave, the beavers, wore protective metal armor and carried large axes. Next came the rabbits with their swords and turtle-shell shields, poised for another victory. The large, round, multi-colored snuffballs bounced back and forth in tight formation, zealously anticipating successful battle. The raccoons held their arrow-laden bows high in the air, waiting for the order to shoot.

"You see?" Ryan titled his head and grinned at the Gypsy. "I told you they would rise up!"

"Shut him up, Trox!" the Gypsy commanded.

"My pleasure, madam!" Trox pulled out his sword, about to slice the rope and drop the blade, when Gusto, Peaches, and Bubbles burst upon the scene, immediately ramming Trox, knocking him into the crowd.

"Quick!" Peaches exclaimed, dropping Gusto onto the stage. "Free them!"

Peaches quickly ran to the bracelets. The Gypsy had recovered her wits and handily zapped him with a green bolt of her black magic.

"Peaches!" Sally screamed as she was freed by Gusto, who proved to be agile at untying knots with his tassels.

Peaches slowly sat up, looking at the angry Gypsy standing over him.

"You weak little rabbit. You're no match for me!"

"He might be weaker than you," John cried, tackling her to the ground. "But I'm not."

"Peaches!" Ryan pointed to the podium. "The bracelets!"

"You know"—John laughed as he pinned her to the ground—"I used to think you were hot, but now I just think you're a bi—" John couldn't finish his thought, because the Gypsy had loosened one arm and yanked it up to punch him in the face.

"General Nunu," the Gypsy cried as she wrestled with John, "prepare the troops for battle!"

A tall imp jumped high into the air and hovered. "Yes, madam. Right away."

Peaches tossed Ryan and Sally their bracelets. Ryan's sword flashed out into his hand. He quickly cut Mel free.

"Gee, thanks," said Mel. "I thought you forgot about me."

"Never!" Peaches smiled as he handed Mel his bracelet.

"Great." Mel's boomerang appeared. "Now I just have to learn to use this thing."

A horde of troops climbed the steps of the stage, charging the rebels. Bubbles shot around like a pinball, slamming six attackers into the pain-inducing barbed wire. After a few experimental flicks, Sally whipped an imp around his neck and hurled him off the platform.

"Holy crap!" She grinned excitedly and hurled another. "This is easy."

Mel looked on with amazement at Sally's fighting abilities. He turned his attention to his boomerang. *If she can figure out that whip, I can deal with this thing,* he thought. "Here goes nothing!" He threw the boomerang, aiming for the next group of predators invading the stage. Ryan had stepped forward to combat a gremlin. The boomerang deliberately dodged him and struck the loathsome creature a glancing blow to the head. Ten more of the Gypsy's soldiers plummeted to the ground before the boomerang curved back to its owner, landing in his hands with ease. "Now THAT was awesome!"

Sally waved to the faithful flying carpet she'd been so sad to leave behind. "Hi, Gusto. Come here!"

She quickly jumped onto the obliging rug, cruising over the disarranged army of gremlins, imps, and foxes. The cats hurried toward their single-masted, square-sailed ships, staging themselves for combat in the air.

"Gusto, I thought you were burned!" she exclaimed, examining each inch of nap, piling, edging, and tassels. "Oh, wow! You sewed yourself back together with yellow grass. How clever!"

Gusto nodded and zipped lower past a line of retreating gremlins, knocking them to the ground like a row of dominoes.

"Sally!" Ryan signaled to her. Gusto swooped in and hovered above the stage. "I'm surprised how well I did for never having wielded a sword before," he told Sally. "So what's next?"

"I have a plan," Sally said as they darted toward the tallest tower. "Let's fly up to the castle."

"Not if I can help it," the Gypsy muttered from the stage as she grabbed her Godmother's magical flying broom and chased after Sally. Brooms were such a cliché that she'd almost left it in the closet. Now it would be just the thing for eradicating these prophets.

Gusto flew across the stage as Sally whipped the enemy troops to clear the way.

"Sally, watch out!" John threw his spear at the Gypsy. She nimbly deflected it with a purple beam.

"Darn. What a waste," John muttered. Luckily, another spear grew from his bracelet. "Nice!" he observed, quickly stabbing an oncoming fox.

"Wow, John," Ryan said, eyes widening with amazement. "That was a nice throw. Maybe you should try out for football!"

"Yeah, right." John chuckled, aiming another spear directly into the Gypsy's mob. "That would be the day! Sorry, but I wouldn't be caught dead wearing those stupid tight pants."

An imp leaped onto the stage just as Mel threw his boomerang. Defenseless, he nearly panicked, until a long, dragon-engraved shield materialized, courtesy of the magical bracelet. Apparently the supply of weapons was unlimited. "Hey, guys! Check this out!"

John and Ryan glanced over.

"Hey! How'd you get that?" Ryan asked, admittedly a bit envious. "I could use one of those right about now!"

John nodded in agreement.

Suddenly, shields appeared in John's and Ryan's free hands. They resumed the battle, grateful for the additional protection.

Mel backed up to Ryan as Peaches covered Mel's back. Bubbles bounced all over the crowd as if he were hitting the jackpot bumpers in a pinball machine.

"John, come here please!" Peaches was holding off an aggressive fox. "If we stick together and hold the stage, we should be safe. We must work together."

The four of them fought back to back, effectively joining forces as swarms of foxes, imps, and gremlins charged the stage. Their strategy was impenetrable, and they could take on the entire army if need be.

***

Meanwhile, on the other side of the dry, desolate, rocky land, the Great Owl hovered majestically on high, addressing his troops.

"This is it, my fellow Enchantians—the battle for Enchantas. Fate has brought us here, and Fate will bring us to victory."

The army roared with enthusiasm, stomping their feet and clanging their shields as they gazed up at their leader.

Across the land, legions of opponent skunks were also massing in fervent preparation.

"Raccoons," the owl cried. "Ready?"

The raccoons yelled with passion as they lifted their flaming arrows.

"Fire!"

A cluster of the lethal missiles filled the air; within seconds, hundreds of skunks and badgers dropped to the ground. Many stood back up with arrows jutting from their limbs, rage and anger boiling over. Abruptly, General Nunu swooped down and screamed, "Charge!"

Badgers with spears and swords raced toward Fate's army, ready for a meal. Skunks armed with razor-edged shields quickly followed. The ground shook as the Great Owl and his band of rebels waited patiently for the best time to charge. A tick went by as a line of squirrels and beavers hesitated, on pins and needles as they waited for the owl to react.

"Fire!" the owl cried again. This time only a few badgers and skunks dropped to the ground. "Squirrels, beavers, charge!"

Without wasting a breath, the squirrels sprinted with their long spears in hand as the beavers followed, swinging their large axes. The rabbits stood waiting eagerly for their turn.

The two militias collided. The thundering sound of armor roared across the land. Beavers swung their axes vehemently back and forth, striking down and severing the limbs of whomever stood in their path. Arms, legs, and heads of skunks and badgers scattered through the air like gory confetti as blood squirted like drenching rain. A line of skunks stationed atop a large stone landing awaited their signal.

A group of beavers noticed their position, but it was too late; sprays of acid from the skunks gushed over them as they melted. Their fur was the first to burn away. Screams of agony bellowed from them until the melting of their skin liquefied their muscle and bones, and they were no more.

"That is what you deserve, rebels!" a skunk snarled, baring his sharp teeth. Before he could celebrate further, a pink squirrel ambushed him, stabbing him in the throat.

"I wouldn't be too cocky, pal!" the squirrel yapped, feinting to the left and spinning right to stab another skunk in its side. "Come on, troops. Follow me!"

The squirrels and beavers progressed through the turbulent battlefield toward the castle, moving with courage and ease.

"They are getting too close," General Nunu growled. "Foxes! Charge!"

The foxes leaped into battle. The discomforting blow of defeat from the previous engagement heightened their hunger for revenge. Slaughtering the dissidents was all the more appetizing.

"Rabbits!" The owl swung his left wing toward the battle-ground. "Your turn!"

Leagues of rabbits dashed with agile ferocity into the battle, clashing with the foxes, skunks, and badgers. The rabbits, united, were invincible. No one could beat them—not today.

The foxes' rage became brutally apparent as their instinctual urge to use their jagged teeth and claws rather than manufactured weapons took its toll on the intimidated squirrels and beavers. As the bodies of rebels were viscerally ripped apart, the foxes smiled, savoring the retribution. "Fresh meat!" One of them smacked his chops, as he chewed on a beaver tail.

The army of rabbits leaped to the fore to end the brutal savagery. The sight of swinging swords and raining blood covered the dark land. Those who had lost their swords, spears, shields, and axes used bloody limbs of animals and Mythics as weapons. The horrific battle for the liberation of Enchantas was not a sight for the squeamish.

The large, multi-colored snuffballs rolled swiftly into battle as more fluitenducks, armed with screaming exploding vegetables, blanketed the gray sky. Imps jumped high into the air, stabbing the birds. As they plummeted to the ground, their vegetable-filled bellies exploded, killing everyone in a thirty-foot radius. Hordes of gremlins joined the frenzy, licking any rebel in sight with their poisonous tongues.

Suddenly the desolate gray land began to quake beneath the combating armies. Warriors fell to their knees as house-sized sinkholes formed, collapsing the earth around them with startling speed, engulfing bodies that disappeared into unknown voids.

From the holes came a half-dozen bus-sized worms. Some of the colossal crawlers were the familiar blue of Slippy. Others represented accompanying shades of the spectrum, from yellow and green to red and all combinations in between. Without hesitation, they roiled and rumbled through the battle, ingesting Freewill fighters whole.

"Revenge, my fellow Nightcrawlers!" The blue worm's victory cry rang out after he sucked up and swallowed a mouthful of imps and gremlins. "We'll not let them skin us anymore!"

"Yes sir, Slippy!" five more worms grunted as they zigzagged through the crowd, sucking up only the Freewill soldiers and spitting out any accidentally ingested allies.

The colored Nightcrawlers swiveled their way through the battlefield with ease, sucking up and chewing the evil army. Soldiers threw spears, swords, and rocks at the revenging worms, but they were no help. The Nightcrawlers were too quick and strong.

"We are losing this battle," Nunu said, gripping his sword tightly. "Call out the troops for Siege Two!"

An imp nodded, leaping toward the fleet of thirty Viking ships awaiting the command to attack. The cats mewed and yowled with exhilaration as they finally received the go-ahead. They quickly lifted off, taking to the air in their flying vessels, drifting on a direct course toward the battle.

Without warning, another fleet of twenty ships were visible on the horizon, hovering in the distance over the mountains. They were not single-sailed Viking ships. They were larger, three-masted schooners, flying black dog skull & crossbone flags. They were pirate ships.

"Ramming speed, my friends!" Captain Max barked, steering his ship to the head of the fleet. "Commander Hisser and his cats won't get away this time!"

"Aye, sir!" Butch bellowed and saluted, sounding the ramming whistle.

The ships obediently picked up speed, gliding in direct pursuit of the Viking ships.

"Oh, no!" Mel gasped, looking to the sky as if he couldn't believe his eyes.

"What?" John asked, gasping for breath. "What now?"

"Those cats just launched a bunch of ships." Mel pointed, and Peaches and John watched the sky sailors pilot slowly yet inexorably toward the battleground.

"Wow, there are more ships coming from over there." Ryan squinted at the horizon. "Wait! One of them looks like the *Storm Glider!*" He laughed joyously. "I can't believe they made it!"

The Vikings had spotted the opposing armada and mustered for battle. "Load the cannons!" Commander Hisser hissed. "Sharpen your weapons. We are about to be boarded!"

The cat crews padded efficiently about the decks of each ship, hustling to load their cannons, but the felines were not quick enough. The pirate ships ravaged their hulls, destroying several vessels in one fell swoop. The ships untouched by the initial barrage quickly retaliated with their own cannon fire as leaping sword-armed cats boarded any dog vessel close enough for hand-to-hand combat.

Shards of sharp wood and nails, the shrapnel from the blood-bath overhead, poured onto the army of imps and gremlins below, wreaking havoc, despite few casualties.

A massive pirate ship hovered over the stage as a familiar voice yelped from above, "Do you humans need a lift? I believe I still owe you a ride."

"Captain!" Even though Ryan was exhausted, he found the strength to yell with enthusiasm.

"Admiral now, my boy!" Max leaned over the teak railing, laughing heartily as a rope ladder was hastily deployed.

"I am a different dog every day. Today, I am Admiral Max the Ferocious. I have earned the title!"

Ryan, Mel, John, and Peaches quickly scaled the ladder, clambering onto the deck, where they fell onto their backs, exhausted and relieved.

"Oh man." John lit up another cigarette to help him relax after the battle. He was too exhausted to care about being on the ship in flight. "I need this!"

"You smoke too much, John," Mel noted quietly. "That's why you're always worn out."

"Yeah, yeah." John took a long puff. "Whatever."

"Admiral!" Ryan looked around frantically and then pushed himself to his feet. "Sally left us during the fight on the stage. She wanted to go to the castle. She must have gone by herself. We have to go get her!"

"Sorry, my boy," the admiral sighed. "Strict orders from the owl. We must prevent the Vikings from moving to the other side of the battle."

"Ramming speed again, gentlemen!" Max shouted, lifting his sword. "You four had better hold on tight. As the saying goes, this is going to be a very bumpy ride."

***

General Nunu hovered over the battle scene as the sun started to set beyond the cold mountains, directing arrows to any rebel in sight. He kept a close eye on the air battle, where it was apparent that his Viking allies were losing ground as well. "Griffins!" he yelled. "Snap to it and help those Vikings!"

Brista and the griffins were not seriously committed to the battle. They did not entirely agree with the Gypsy, so they had remained stationary until needed. "Sure thing, General," Brista replied casually as she and the rest of the griffins girded their wings and flew toward the ships.

As the griffins reached the pirate vessels, they ripped out the sails with the barest of effort. Brista yawned with boredom.

From a distance, a gathering roar grew loud, and the sky rapidly filled with rampaging gargoyles. "Attack those treacherous traitors!" Dex's voice echoed over the air battle.

"Dex!" Brista laughed as she darted towards him. "What a pleasant surprise!"

"Brista!" Dex wrapped his arms and wings across her neck and front legs. "What are you doing here?"

"I would ask the same, but it seems that we are fighting on the opposite sides this time."

"Why are you fighting for them?" Dex held her tightly in the air, hoping she wouldn't attack. "We used to be allies."

"Keywords are *used to* Dex." She spread her wings and released herself from his grip. "I don't fight for the old ways anymore."

"I don't believe that you truly turned on our old ways, Brista," he pleaded with her.

Meanwhile the other gargoyles and griffins battled above the war below.

"I know you still love our founders and their ways," said Dex, "and you still love me as much as I love you."

"Don't flatter yourself, you conceited jerk." She rammed his chest and bit his left wing. "Since I left you, I have never been happier!"

"I do not believe your words!" Dex pushed her off of him.

"You should. I have bettered my life in the clouds, living in peace." Her hatred for him grew, but her love remained strong deep in her soul. "How about yourself? What have you done these many Ages?"

"We have also lived in peace." Dex was a little discomfited about their problem with the bottle.

"Really?" She laughed. "That's not what I have heard. I heard you and the boys have a nice party every night."

"Not anymore," he said as he threw her onto the side of a mountain. "We are sober."

"Oh, really?" She charged him again. "For how long? A couple of tocks?"

"No, a couple of days."

"Oh wow," she said, unimpressed. "Good for you! So what has changed?"

"I have hope now, Brista. What happened to us in the past was a mistake on my part. I apologize for that. I truly wish you would forgive me."

Brista stopped for a moment to search for sincerity in his stony gray eyes. To her surprise, she found it, but it did not stop her anger for what he had done to her all that time ago. "No matter what you say, Dex, my hatred for you will never change. What you did to me is unforgivable!"

"Brista," he sighed as he blocked one of her paw swipes. "We have all changed. I am truly sorry for what I have done to hurt you. Please forgive me."

"Why do you even try?" She swiped her claws and scarred his face.

"Because I have hope! Hope for us and a better future for Enchantas. I do care for you, and our love is still here. I can feel it."

Her eyes seemed to boil with rage. *Why didn't he apologize Ages ago?* she wondered, and then snarled, "You should have thought about that before."

"I know, Brista! I was too stubborn."

As her patience with his testimony grew thin, she charged him one last time, clipping off one of his wings. "It's too late, Dex."

286

Dex spiraled to the ground, gaining speed, and plummeted into a group of imps. The imps feverishly pounced on him like a pack of wolves, stabbing him repeatedly with their spears.

A surge of relief from the resentment she harbored rushed through Brista's veins; but an overwhelming feeling of regret came over her as she watched Dex being annihilated by the army of imps. Her hatred for him dissipated with each blow. The gargoyle who professed to care about her was now suffering. She felt remorse for what she'd done and knew she needed to stop this savagery. If she stayed on this path of hate and destruction, she would not be any better than Dex had been that fateful night Ages ago.

"Dex!" she screamed as she swooped down to the beaten gargoyle. Her large lioness paws swatted imps left and right, flicking them away as if they were flies feasting on rotten food. "Get out of here, you wretched beasts!"

"Brista?" Dex called out to her. His eyes were nearly swollen shut, encased by bruised flesh. His wings, arms, and legs were shattered. "Brista, I am truly sorry for this. I have never stopped loving you. Please forgive me. Please."

A tear ran down her beak; she was too late to save him. "Dex, I forgive you. And I do love you! Please don't leave me. I will never leave you again!"

A faint whisper came from his mouth, and a tear dribbled from his eye. She bent closer to his beaten mouth to hear his last words and held him until he turned back into stone. His stone body broke in her arms, crumbling to bits of rubble strewn on the desolate ground. Brista's tears became a flood of repressed emotions. She took his bracelet of Hope and closed her eyes tight, totally devastated. "What I have done?" she asked aloud. The only one that she had ever truly loved was now gone. In her mind, she had always thought that he'd be there forever. Someday they might have come back together with true forgiveness. Her love for him had never truly disappeared. She may have pushed him away when he was vulnerable all those Cycles ago, but her feelings had remained the same. Now there was no moving forward, no redemption, only a pile of stone fragments and a broken heart. She took a deep breath, inhaling as she looked up to the sky. Dex was gone from her life, but their love was and always would remain eternal.

Chapter XX
The Witch and Warlock

The sky was thick with smoke as Gusto and Sally wove through the air, trying to escape the more battle-experienced Gypsy. The Gypsy, in hot pursuit, narrowed her eyes and shot purple beams at them.

"Gusto!" Sally cried, desperately hanging on to his heavy nap. "Hurry!"

Sally employed her whip, but the fanatic Gypsy dodged each lash. Gusto abruptly altered course again, making the most of the element of surprise as he drew closer to the fleet of battling ships.

"Sally!" Ryan called out from *Storm Glider*. "What are you doing?"

"Trying to get rid of HER! Can you help?"

"Sure." John threw his spear as hard as he could. "Take that!"

The Gypsy turned to block John's spear. She succeeded, but she didn't see Sally's whip. She was squarely knocked off her broom. As she hurtled toward the ground, scurrying troops of imps and gremlins frantically reached out their arms to save her.

"Sally, what are you doing?" Ryan asked again.

"I am going to talk to the Witch and Warlock! We need to stop this war, Ryan! This is crazy!"

"No, Sally! That's not a good idea. Wait for us!"

"Ryan, don't worry." Sally smiled. "I'll be all right."

"Sally!"

Gusto poured on the power, quickly leveling off and zooming to the tallest tower. Perfectly positioned, he hovered adroitly over the balcony, clearing the rails before gently settling on the floor. As she stepped off and looked into the dark castle, Sally trembled with nerves. In the heat of the moment, perhaps she'd miscalculated. She was tired, alone, and not sure she made the right decision. Much of the zeal that had carried her this far had evaporated. She turned back to leave but was dismayed to see that Gusto had returned to the battle. She was on her own.

The room in the castle was unlit. She could see little in the dark interior. It smelled like a book of matches mixed with stale wine.

"You should not be here, child," a deep feminine voice emanated from the shadows. The woman's glowing red eyes were the only noticeable light in the pitch-black chamber. "Leave now with your army, and no one else will have to die."

"I have come here to offer peace." Sally's voice trembled. She couldn't see anything but the Witch's eyes. She quivered in fear but continued, "We have met one of the Knights, and they offer peace and a way to let you go home. Remember our world? Remember Earth?"

"That dream has already died!" the Warlock boomed, his eyes gleaming from a corner to the left of the Witch. "We don't wish to return! Our life is here now."

"You must agree to this treaty. Do you really want all of these Enchantians to die?"

"For our cause, sacrifices must be made to ensure that our ideals of Freewill and Chance live throughout these lands. No one else must be harmed by the standards of Fate and its plan."

"But the Knights have changed their ideals on Destiny's plan! They have included Freewill and Chance."

"Lies!" The Warlocks eyes lit with anger as all of the candles in the room lit simultaneously. The dark, cloaked couple inched closer to Sally. Completely creeped out, she backed toward the balcony. "We do not believe your deceitful little lies."

"Why would I lie?"

The Witch levitated closer to Sally. Her searching eyes turned from searing red to a brilliant crystalline blue. A startling awareness had come over her. "Richard!" she said softly, turning to the Warlock. "Oh my God, Richard. This little girl is Sally."

The Warlock's eyes were turquoise prisms as he drew closer to the Witch. "Sally? Our daughter Sally? It cannot be—" His voice broke.

The Witch removed her hood. Her shiny, curly brown hair fell softly to her shoulders. Her lower lip quivered. "Richard, yes. This is our daughter Sally."

The Warlock took off his hood and placed his glasses on his nose. He squinted for a moment, and tears sprang to his eyes. "Sally? Is that really you?"

"Mom?" Sally was stunned. Shock paralyzed her body. Her eyes watered as she studied their faces intently, flooded with recognition. "Dad? Is this really you, or is this a trick?"

"We should be asking the same thing," the Warlock replied, unconvinced. "You came here asking about a peace treaty. What if this is some trick, luring us into a trap? Nothing here is as it seems."

"I'm here. I am Sally," she stuttered. "And you both died four years ago! I went to your funeral."

"Died?" asked the Witch, incredulous. "We never died!"

An uncomfortable silence filled the room.

Then the Warlock smiled. "Before we came here, we used to spend our summer weekends in a small town a few miles from our home. Our Sally loved to go to the races."

"I remember that."

"If you are our real daughter," the Warlock surmised, "Then you could tell me what kind of races. Sally—if indeed you are Sally—what kind of races?"

"Horses, of course. My favorite was Sunflower."

"Oh, Richard!" The Witch ran to Sally, grabbing her up and hugging her. "It *is* Sally! I knew it."

The Warlock quickly followed his wife, and the trio clasped each other wholeheartedly, overwhelmed with joy. Multitudes of happy tears poured onto the stone floor.

"Mom, Dad, what happened?" Sally wiped off her wet cheeks. "I mean, I've had nightmares about your death. I have missed you so much."

"We've missed you too, honey!" The Witch kissed her forehead.

"Tell me what happened," Sally requested.

The Warlock sat down at a large table. "It started when your mother and I were on our way back home from my company Christmas party. We slid on a bridge, skidded, and crashed."

"And when we fell into the river rapids," her mother continued, "we lost consciousness. We ended up in a cave."

"That's when we lost our memories." He grabbed his wife's hand. "I even forgot who your mother was."

She stroked his cheek lovingly. "We walked through a dark cave and ended up here in Enchantas."

"My friends and I also happened here by accident," Sally said, nodding. "Not by car. We fell down a well. And we didn't turn into witches or warlocks, either. Why did you? What happened?" Sally withdrew from the group embrace, very confused. She pointed to the battle outside. "You used to be good people." She gestured derisively at their ridiculously Gothic cloaks. "Now look at you."

"Oh, Sally." Her mother moved in for another hug. "You must understand that we have done some awful things, but it was borne of the frustration of being trapped in this world and wanting always to come home to you."

"Your mother is right." The Warlock sighed, feeling a nearly unbearable amount of remorse. "When we finally regained our memories, we realized that we had also forgotten all about you. When the Knights forbade us to leave Enchantas, we became enraged and fought with them."

"Yes," the Witch affirmed. "And when that didn't work, we realized we were stuck here forever. It made us bitter. It also made us hard and strong."

"We took over the land in spite of the Knights' ideals."

"Sally, dear, you have to understand that we have tried everything to get home. Nothing would work. The Knights' magic was simply too strong."

"We even went as far as casting a spell to bring you here," her father added. "We couldn't leave this place, but we could abduct people from Earth. That's how Lexis arrived."

"Lexis?" Sally asked. "You brought her here?"

"Yes, she was our fault." Her mother reluctantly spat out the confession.

"We were trying to bring you here," her father explained. "We missed you so much, Sally! Our spells backfired and brought her here instead. It was an accident of Chance."

"Why didn't you try again?" Sally argued. "I missed you more than you know. I would have loved to be here with you. Grandma does what she can, but my life has been hell since you died."

"We are so sorry, Sally," her mother pleaded. "The spell was too dangerous and unpredictable. We might have abducted some other stranger who would have been stuck here like us. Our consciences would not allow that."

"Exactly. We kept the truth from Lexis," her father added. "After Lexis discovered that she could never go home, she was so distraught that we promised each other to never conjure that spell again. Transporting people here and compelling them to stay forever was no better than what the Knights had done to us. We had to face our responsibilities to Lexis. So we adopted her as our own child and raised her as your sister."

"Sister?" The irony of her potential friendship with Lexis had thrown Sally into a loop of confusion.

"Yes, you have a step-sister now, Sally," her mother answered.

"But she is so"—Sally cringed—"evil. And she is definitely mentally unbalanced if not outright crazy."

"Yes, we know," her father said matter-of-factly. "The problem was that we became very overprotective. We didn't want her to be influenced by the old ways."

"Also," her mother added, "it didn't take us long to question her emotional stability. We believe she is a little passive-aggressive bipolar."

"So there is magic that could have brought us here? Did you bring us here?"

"No, Sally. We have not used that spell in a very long time."

"I brought you here!" the battered Gypsy Princess said as she stumbled into the room.

"Lexis!" The Witch swiftly ran to the miscreant's side.

"I found your spell in the other room," the overwrought young woman hissed. "After I read it, I realized how I got here. Your overprotective ways backfired because the more isolated I was in this castle, the more I wanted friends and companions."

"Lexis, do you realize what you have done? You started another War!"

"I know. Isn't it amazing?"

"No, Lexis, it isn't. That was why we banished the Knights. We wanted to end the war, not start another one."

"Whatever." She laughed. "You should have thought about that before you lied to me." She moved closer to Sally, checking her out from head to toe. "So this is my stepsister, huh?" She sneered nastily. "So that's why I felt so compelled to befriend her. We must have a lot in common. That's the only reason you adopted me."

"Yes," the Witch said, terrified that Lexis might hurt Sally. She certainly had the power to do so. Channeling that energy was taking every bit of her Godmother's strength and wisdom. She focused on the positive, on her adopted daughter's desperate hunger for affection. "This is so wonderful, Lexis! Now we can be a happy family."

"No!" the Gypsy howled at the top of her lungs. "I had a family. I had an uncle and a good job in our world, but you stole it from me. You stole my life. Now I am going to take away yours."

She grabbed Sally's throat and squeezed hard. "I should have killed you when we first met."

"Lexis, no!" The Witch drew out her scepter with the agility of a sharpshooter, zapping a bolt of green lightning at her wayward Gypsy daughter.

The impact catapulted Lexis across the room, and she bounced hard off the wall. "Fine. If you won't let me kill her, I'll be satisfied to know that you'll all be stuck in this world with me!" Undaunted, she got up and brushed off her dress.

"Wait, that's not true. We can go back home!" Sally faced her parents, rubbing her bruised neck. "Let me get back to the Knights. What you have come to believe about them isn't true. The reason I came up here is to urge you to accept a peace treaty. Stop the war and bring peace. If you free the Knights from banishment, they'll send all of us back home."

"And you believe them, Sally?" her mother asked.

"Yes, I do."

"What about the movement we have started here?" Richard looked at his wife. "We have many followers. We cannot abandon them."

"Mom, Dad..." She took a deep breath. "The Knights have been enlightened with a new belief. They believe Fate, Luck, Chance, and Freewill all work together to fulfill Destiny's plan. So you aren't abandoning anyone. Only compromising."

Richard and Susie stared at each other, contemplating the options. They glanced outside, where thousands of Enchantians were slaughtering each other.

"What choice do we have?" Richard took a deep breath. "We need to stop this fighting."

"You're right." Susie walked to the ledge of the balcony and turned back. "We need to stop this war, Richard. We need to go home."

"No!" Lexis yelled. "I will not let you stop this war. You are both hypocritical traitors." As she threw a ball of lightning at them, Ryan, John, and Mel jumped onto the balcony, deflecting it with their shields.

"Sally!" Ryan gave her a huge hug. "I'm so happy you're all right! What possessed you to come on your own? Don't ever do that again!"

"Lexis. Stop." Richard stepped close to his adopted daughter. "This war needs to stop. You can come home with us. Back to our world. Back to your family."

"I don't want that. You ruined my chances for that life. Now, when I've finally become something here, you want to take it away. You always find a way to ruin my life!"

"Lexis," Susie disagreed, "that is not true."

"Of course it is!" Lexis clenched her teeth and glared at Sally, stomping a high-heeled foot. "Now that your *real* daughter is here, everything will change. You never loved me. You never cared! You're Godparents. You were never real parents."

"Of course we loved you!" cried the Witch.

"Real daughter?" Ryan's eyes widened as he glanced back and forth from Sally to the Witch and Warlock. He simply couldn't think of them as Susie and Richard.

"No, you didn't! You never loved me." She grabbed the battle-worn broom. "I'm staying here, and you can't stop me."

"Lexis!" The Witch returned to the edge of the balcony. "Wait!"

It was too late. The distraught Gypsy had already flown away. Susie and Richard watched as their Goddaughter vanished into the horizon. There was nothing they could do. She was a troubled young lady with her mind set. The Gypsy was well on her way to become the new evil Witch of Enchantas.

"Real daughter?" Ryan asked again. He couldn't help staring from mother to father to daughter. "Seriously?"

"I'll explain everything in detail later." Sally kissed Ryan on the cheek and grinned. "Thank you for coming to save me."

Sally moved to stand with her mother and father at the balcony's edge. They gazed down at the still-raging battle and then looked up at the ships returning fire high in the sky. The formerly beautiful and enchanting world was once again destroying itself over ideals and beliefs that had never been theirs in the first place.

"We must stop this battle now," Sally softly intoned, worried for both sides.

"Consider it finished." Her father smiled at her and produced a large horn. "Cover your ears, everyone!"

Richard the Warlock blew into it resoundingly, producing the loudest noise anyone had ever heard. The mountains surrounding them rumbled and echoed with the force of the tone. The ground below shook. Everyone fighting below abruptly stopped and covered their ears.

"Now, please cover your eyes," Sally's mother instructed. Together the Witch and Warlock bellowed their spell:
"Enchanted curse from our mighty hands,
Bring lost life back to the lands!"
The couple brandished their scepters, clinking them together to create a blinding yellow light. Trees and plant life below grew instantaneously as all the creatures great and small abandoned the fracas, jumping and hopping away in all directions.

Sally's parents looked at each other and chanted:
"Thirteen Knights were exiled and banished;
Transport them back, from whence they vanished!"
Another light emanated from the scepters, and immediately thirteen long-robed humans materialized on the crowded balcony. They all carried scepters and dragon-engraved shields. Their beards fell to their stomachs. Firp stood next to Mel, giving him a large frog grin.

"Knights, we would like peace in Enchantas," announced Richard, cutting to the chase. In his mind, too much time and too many lives had already been sacrificed.

"And forgiveness for the banishment," added Susie. The Witch and Warlock fell to their knees, repenting for their past evil deeds.

Brian stepped forward, bowing graciously. "It is we who should be asking for forgiveness. We have forgotten about family and love because we have been here so long. We should have allowed you both to go home Ages ago." He looked at Sally. "Will you forgive us also?"

Sally could only nod and cry as she looked up at her mother and father. Then she gathered herself.

"Everything happens for a reason, Brian," Sally explained in her soft, gentle voice. "It was hard to go through this journey, but I've learned a lot and wouldn't trade it for anything. I'm more optimistic now, and the lessons I have learned have made me who I am today. I hope I can say this for all of us. I'm glad that all of this has happened." She glanced at Ryan and smiled before turning back to the Knights. "With that said, I forgive you, too."

"Magnificent," Brian said, smiling. "I promised you all a way home. But first, we must stop this battle."

While the Warlock's horn had put a damper on the melee, terrible violence was being perpetrated, Enchantians slaughtering Enchantians.

The Knights levitated in formation, wafting with superior control to dead center in the middle of the battlefield. Carcasses and bloodstains covered the ground; even the new plant life could not disguise the carnage. With a flick of each Knight's wrists, the dead disappeared and the wounded became healed.

"Fellow Enchantians," Brian's voice echoed majestically over the battlefield. It carried to other cities and towns throughout Enchantas, including Gnome Village, Foxtown, Rabbit City, and Ruphport. "Peace has been offered. For far too long we have been divided among ourselves, divided by morals and beliefs that should not have been separated. Come now, my fellow Enchantians! The war is over. The fighting is over. Let us now go home, leave the past behind and gather our thoughts and hopes for our future. We were once a noble and peaceful world. Let us bring it back and love again!"

The battle-weary Enchantians looked up at the Knights with sheer awe. Many were amazed to see them alive. Many listened with intense focus and concentration to the wise and healing words. Without argument, both sides dropped their weapons and shook hands. They quietly made amends. The beginning of a new era was upon them. Peace was restored.

Chapter XXI
The Journey Home

The white morning sun radiated over the purple and blue-tinted valley. To the plants, it was just another day, but for the six humans, it was a farewell to a wondrous adventure in a very strange land.

Ryan held Sally's hand tightly, very happy that he'd had this opportunity to get to know her and discover what a wonderful young woman she really was. He was excited to go home and see his brother, but he would not be surprised if his parents weren't there.

Sally was elated, delighted beyond belief to be returning with her parents. She couldn't wait to see what her grandmother would say. She wondered how they would explain it to her. As she took a calming breath, she felt the compass rub against her chest.

"Owl!" Sally ran to the Enchantian leader. "I should return your compass."

"Why thank you, Sally," the owl said. "I am glad that you found it in the Forbidden Cave."

"Me too. It helped a lot. And I'm sure you'll have some use for it during these times of change."

"Yes, we will." The owl's voice grew louder. "And I am sure that you and your friends will not neglect to return those magical bracelets."

"Oh, yeah. Of course." Ryan promptly removed his and gathered the others. "We almost forgot. I don't think we'd want our Persona Weapons to go off in school."

John chuckled. "Speak for yourself."

Ryan handed the owl all the bracelets. He grasped the tip of the owl's wing, bowing, and shook his feathers in an impromptu handshake. "We will miss you all."

"Thank you, Ryan. Goodbye, humans," the Great Owl said as he joined the thirteen Knights. "We will miss you."

"Speak for yourself, Ryan." John lit up a cigarette and crinkled the pack with his fist. "I'm just glad to get home so I can get another pack of smokes." He had felt a sense of loneliness come over him, as though he'd grown to revere Enchantas. He also had a feeling he'd miss this place, but his stubbornness made him too proud to admit it.

Behind them, small groups of other Enchantians came to greet them farewell. The fairies, a few snuffballs, Peaches, Gusto, Max and his crew, Cupid, and Slippy lying behind—they were all there to say goodbye.

Dyad fluttered up to John, her sisters were directly behind her. Her black hair blew in the wind. John paused for a moment and swallowed. "Dyad, I really wish I'd gotten the chance to you know better. There is something about you that—"

"Shhh..." She fluttered up and pulled the cigarette from his mouth. John was too love struck to argue. "I feel it too." She hovered next to his cheek and kissed it. "But now is not the time to embrace our feelings. Thank you for saving Enchantas, John. I will never forget you."

John wanted to stay with Dyad, but he knew that for now his feeling for her needed to remain private. His primary goal was to go home, protect his sister, and take care of his father.

"John," Brista said, strutting up to him, her bravado tempered by the fact that she'd obviously been crying. "Before Dex died, he asked me to give you this."

When he saw the bracelet in her paw, he gasped. "The Bracelet of Hope? I can't take this!"

"You must. His last words to me were to make sure you received this. He said you would know what to do with it."

As she dropped it into his hand, he suddenly realized it was the perfect gift for someone in desperate need: his father. "Oh, thank you so much. And please don't worry; this is in very good hands."

As Mel watched the goodbyes and well-wishes, he felt conflicted. Why go home? If he stayed there, he could do his own thing, live his own life. "Lixy Fruit beats mother's home cooking any day," he muttered under his breath.

"Hey, you know what?" Mel piped up. "I think I'm going to stay."

"What?" Sally said in surprise.

"Mel?" asked Ryan. "That's nuts. Are you sure?"

"Don't leave me, man," John said, punching him lightly on the arm. "Come on. I was just starting to like you. Besides, you can't let me be stuck with these two."

"John." Sally was insulted.

"I'm just kidding."

Mel looked around, smiling. "You know, I am starting to believe I'm destined for great things. Only"—he paused, gazing at the group of Enchantians—"only not in our world. There I can learn chemistry, engineering, and magician tricks. Here, I can actually make a difference. I can actually learn some real magic. Besides, I hate my mom's cooking."

They all laughed and shrugged as they hugged him. John, of course, fended off a hug. He shook Mel's hand with real disappointment.

"Are you all ready?" asked Brian.

The five departing Humans nodded as they stood in the middle of a purplish-blue-grassed hill.

"I'm ready," said John. "I can hardly imagine how my sister is feeling right now. I've been gone for five days."

"John," said the owl, "you will not need to worry."

"Why's that? You don't know my father."

"Time works differently from our world to yours."

"The owl is right," Brian added. "Twenty-tocks, or one day, in Enchantas is only about fifteen minutes in your world."

"Oh, great!" John, enormously relieved, wondered if he would still describe moments in time as tocks when he returned to their world.

"So we have only been gone for like an hour?" Ryan was enthralled. "Now I won't miss football practice!"

"Can I come watch?" Sally asked and kissed him on the cheek.

"Oh, come on, you two." John stepped in front of them. "You two are gonna make me sick. So how do you turn this thing on? I mean open the Forbidden Cave?"

Without further notice, Brian recited the spell:

"The Fate of Destiny
Had a plan,
To bring long lost peace
To the land.
If these prophets held the key,
Take them away,
And set them free."

Suddenly the sky turned indigo, and firefly-sized pale blue lights flicked on the hillside. The lights illuminated the darkened valley, pulsating with a beautiful ballet of unpredictable dancing and bouncing shimmers. The design resembled the reflection of a ceiling above a lighted indoor pool.

The light vanished and the sunlight emerged, daylight in the sky once again. A familiar cave appeared, framed by a wood-and-stone entrance.

"Hey, guys!" Mel yelled. "Let's make an oath that no matter what, we will always be friends. I'm really glad to have met you all. Good luck!"

"We will," said Ryan. "You take care of yourself here."

"Deal," said John. He ran back to shake Mel's hand again. "Now don't be a stranger, and come visit once in a while."

"Goodbye, Mel!" Sally and Ryan walked hand-in-hand toward the stone entrance.

"Oh, and by the way"—Richard looked at the kids—"we're having a homecoming party at our house. You're all invited."

"Dad?" Sally said, a little uneasy. "What is Grandma going to say?"

"Oh, don't worry dear." Her mother smiled with a little wink. "We have some magic left to use on her."

They all stood in front of the cave, waiting for someone to take the initiative and step in. John glanced at Ryan and laughed, "So are you going to wimp out again?"

"Wimp out?" Ryan looked at John, bewildered. "What are you talking about?"

"Oh, don't deny it. I heard you back there when we were about to be executed."

"I have no idea what you're talking about."

"And I quote, 'Help! I'm too young to die!' I heard you loud and clear." He pointed to Sally. "And so did she."

305

"Well, I guess I was just taking Destiny's advice and asking for help for once."

"Oh, yeah right." John chuckled. "Nice comeback."

"Oh, shut up." Ryan shoved him a little. "You're just stalling because you're afraid to go in there." Ryan let go of Sally's hand and long-jumped into the Forbidden Cave.

"What? That's not fair. I was supposed to go first." John followed Ryan into the darkness.

"Great," Sally muttered to herself as she grabbed her parents' hands. "I guess I'm going to have to get used to those two anyway, right?"

The three of them slowly stepped in as they were whisked back to reality...back home.

EPILOGUE

Unexpected Visitor

Two Months Later...

The sound of screaming fans rumbled through the parking lot. A beautiful brown-haired girl leaned up against a blue convertible Corvette. She wore a bluish-green dress, which brought out the gorgeous shine of her eyes, and long-laced high-heeled shoes. Her lucky diamond earrings glittered from her earlobes, casting sparkles as the lights of the football field gleamed over the trees. Students cheered loudly as cars squealed by, honking their horns.

"Go Panthers!" students cheered all around her. The homecoming football game was over, and Willington High was once again victorious.

She smiled, waiting patiently as the parking lot emptied. Out of the shadows came two figures: tall, strong boys. They shoved each other, jesting as they approached the girl.

"My best game yet." John tossed a football into the air as Ryan caught it.

"Yeah, you did an awesome job!" Ryan tossed it back to him. "That was a phenomenal fifty-yard throw that I tossed to you for the winning touchdown."

Sally shook her head and opened the car door. "You boys should get over yourselves."

"I think Ryan should get over himself," John said. "He's afraid I'm gonna take away all of his glory."

"Hey!" Ryan shook his head, disagreeing. "Not at all. I'm really glad you decided to join the team."

"Well, I wouldn't have if I didn't quit smoking."

"Johnny!" a pleasurable voice cried. An excited young girl ran up to him and gave him a hug.

"Hey, sis!" John was stunned, and pleasantly so. "I didn't know you were here."

"Yeah! You were great out there."

"Hey, John, we gotta get going." Ryan kissed Sally as she moved to the passenger side. "You two want a ride?"

"Sure," John replied. "C'mon, Becky!"

Out of nowhere, a fluttering blue light floated up to them, calling out, "Humans! We need your help!"

The light dimmed enough to reveal a distinct profile within, revealing Dyad the fairy.

"Dyad!" John was over the top. "What are you doing here?"

"John?" Becky shivered, grasping his bicep tightly. "What in the heck is that?"

"It's a fairy."

"A fair–" she began, but she was interrupted by the frantic Dyad.

"Professor Mel is in trouble." She fluttered hysterically around them like a moth drawn to flame. "Enchantas needs your help."

"Professor Mel?" John asked.

"Yes," Dyad said urgently. "It has been many Cycles since your departure from Enchantas. Much has changed. Mel is the professor of Advanced Potions at the Enchantian Institute of Magic."

"Wow, much has changed."

"Let's hurry," Dyad said, growing brighter. "Time is of the essence. Remember that time is different here than Enchantas."

"Let's go!" Sally urged. "We can't let anything happen to Mel."

"Enchantas?" Becky asked, puzzled. "What's going on here?"

"Becky, there's a lot I need to tell you, but it looks like I have to go." John put his hand on her shoulder. "There's something I need to do."

"John," she said, looking into his eyes, "I'm coming with you!"

John thought for a moment and contemplated the alternative: their father, who still had not received the Bracelet of Hope. John worried about leaving his sister behind and alone.

"She can come, John." Dyad floated over to both of them. "But we must hurry. Every tick counts."

"All right." John glanced at the other two and back at his sister. "You can come with us."

"Where is it we're going?"

"I'll explain everything when we get there. Just close your eyes."

The four closed their eyes to block the blindness of Dyad's magic.

"Ready?" Dyad lifted her arms and intoned:

"Fairy games, playful fun,

To Enchantas, here we come!"

The bright blue light consumed them as they instantaneously disappeared from their world and back to the incredible world of Enchantas.

ABOUT THE AUTHOR

Corey M. LaBissoniere is a resident of Houghton, Michigan in the northwest part of Michigan's Upper Peninsula. He is a graduate of Houghton High School, Gogebic Community College and Michigan Technological University. When he is not writing, he works as an Adoption Specialist at a local Agency, enjoys a good game of billiards with his father, delights in extreme sports, likes outdoor activities, loves to travel and appreciates a good story.

www. coreylabissoniere .com